Savage Ice

Ice Breaker Cold Case Romance

Cynthia Eden

He's been protecting her since he was sixteen years old...

Beau LeBlanc has a killer grin, a voice that can seduce a saint, and a serious reputation for being mad, wickedly bad, and exceedingly dangerous to know. Growing up, everyone always thought he was trouble with a capital T...until one night the bad boy became a hero. He rushed into a burning house and saved *her*—Avalon Trahan. He still bears the scars from the flames on his body, but it was Avalon who marked his soul. For her, he wanted to be more than just the most dangerous guy in town.

They grew up. He kept watching her.

Beau knows that he's obsessed. He also knows that someone has to look after Avalon because the fire wasn't the last time that her life was in danger. Over the years, he's had to step in when she needs help...not that she knew he was there. He stayed in the shadows. Watching. Waiting. And eliminating the threats that came her way. You didn't screw with what belonged to him.

She's been his fantasy for years. He's been her dark hero.

He never expected Avalon to walk into his bar. To come straight to him. But when she does, she's a temptation he can't resist. Beautiful, bold, and smart, she's everything he has ever wanted. Desire explodes between them. A need he has fought for so long is suddenly a blazing inferno that he can't control.

But Avalon needs Beau now more than ever before. A killer has her in his sights—a man who loves to see the world burn. And this predator won't stop until he finishes what he started years ago...The fire is going to come for Avalon again. And this time, he'll make sure no one is there to save her.

Author's note: The Ice Breakers are back once again! A serial arsonist is ready to set the world ablaze. To stop him, Beau and Avalon will have to trace a trail of murders back to the killer. Avalon is a true-crime author with ties to the Ice Breakers, and she will need their backup to unravel the mystery of her past. She's also going to need some serious protection. Good thing Beau is more than willing to get up close and personal with her. Prepare for smoking-hot pages, danger that will chill your heart, and a hero who is too well acquainted with the dark side of love...and obsession.

Prologue

Excitement hummed through his blood.

Five...

Four...

Three...

Two...

The engine purred to life before Beau LeBlanc could even finish counting down to one. A sleek, beautiful purr of power from the Jag—a ride that had to be worth an easy one hundred grand. If you were gonna buy something so expensive, then you really should protect your possession a whole lot better. And not say, let a teenager swipe it in less than five seconds.

A wide grin curved Beau's lips as he prepared to get the hell out of—

Smoke.

He stilled right before pulling the driver's side door closed. The night was still. Damn quiet. Nothing was happening in the Garden District. Sure, he knew folks would be partying it up hardcore on Bourbon Street, but this was the tamer part of the Big Easy. The sophisticated, rich-as-hell part. Gated homes. Security cameras. Fancy rides that just begged and sweetly pleaded to be stolen by an enterprising person such as himself.

But...

The scent of smoke grew stronger.

He should ignore the scent. He had a job to do. People who would be waiting on this car. *Drive away.* Yep, that was exactly what he should do.

Except...

Had he just heard the faintest crackle of flames?

Beau found himself sliding out of the Jag. He didn't turn off the engine. He was just going to take a quick peek and come right back. Satisfy his curiosity. He hurried around the edge of the tall bushes. Turned the corner on the street and staggered to a stop.

Holy shit.

The house was en-freaking-gulfed. Flames were bursting from the mansion. Red, orange, and gold, the fire seemed to be eating the lower level of the massive structure. As he watched, one window erupted and sent chunks of glass spraying into the night. A soundless whistle escaped him because he'd never seen a fire like this. Maybe in a movie once. Not in real life. Not up close. Not so wild and hot and so—

"Help me!"

His gaze whipped up to the second floor. Then up higher. *Third damn floor.* Because the house—mansion— was huge. A window was partially open on that level, and he saw a small arm waving in the night.

Someone was trapped in that house.

The rest of the rich-as-hell street was dead quiet and dark. No one was rushing to the rescue.

"Help!"

So he...did.

Beau hurtled from the darkness and straight toward the flames. He didn't slow down when he reached the front door. Instead, he just barreled into it as hard as he could. It flew open. He'd thought it would be locked and that he'd have to ram his way in, but it gave him no resistance. Smoke filled his lungs and he coughed and choked as he raced for the stairs. He felt the fire grab his shoulder. A white-hot, burning touch that pierced him straight to his soul, but Beau didn't stop.

He rushed up the stairs. The smoke followed him. Seemed to choke him. His eyes watered and his chest heaved and somehow, he actually made it to the third-floor landing. But then he froze because the smoke was so thick, and he didn't know where the hell the victim was and...

He was no damn hero.

Why was he in the house?

Criminal. Piece of trash. Should lock his ass up. Gang thug.

Whispers filled his mind as he hesitated. Beau knew exactly what he was.

His shoulder throbbed and ached. He needed to get out of there.

"Help!"

The scream came from the right. Spinning in that direction, he yanked up his shirt in an effort to cover his mouth. With one hand, he held the shirt, and with the other, he reached in front of him as he searched for the door. The acrid scent of smoke—and was that gasoline?—surrounded him.

It was freaking pitch black up there. His hands touched something. Big. Sturdy. Wooden?

He'd thought to find a door, but, hell, this felt like some kind of shelf or cabinet or—

"*Help!*"

The scream was coming from behind whatever the fuck this was. Beau heaved and shoved, and he heard wood grate as the damn thing gave way and flew to the side. Then he stumbled into a room and—

"Thank you!" A body collided with his. Much smaller. Softer. Feminine. She coughed and shuddered against him. "Someone—someone put the bookcase in front of my door —" Coughs interrupted her. "I-I couldn't get out!"

He grabbed her hand. "We're getting out. *Now*." He felt dizzy and sick, and her hand was way too fragile in his grip. He had to get her out of that nightmare.

They turned, hurried back to the stairs...and saw hell waiting.

The flames were eating their way up the stairs. Smoke was so thick.

His lungs seemed to clog.

She trembled against him. He hauled her back into her bedroom. Kicked the door shut. Grabbed a cover from her bed and shoved it beneath the door.

"We're going..." Coughs broke through her words. "To die..."

The hell he was. No way was he dying as some dumb teen. He had plans. He was gonna be feared. Respected. He would have his own bar. Have his own crew. Have his own damn Jag that wasn't *stolen*.

He was going to have *everything* he wanted.

She threw her arms around him. "I don't want to die." Her hand scraped over his right shoulder. Pain blasted through him and almost brought Beau to his knees.

She had some kind of nightlight glowing in her room.

Small. Square. The only illumination in the place. But her window was open. Open a few precious inches, anyway. The window she'd been using before when she called for help.

He pried away from her and grabbed the pillow from her bed. Beau ripped the pillowcase in two. "Put it over your mouth." One part for her. One for him. Like the scrap would do much good, but it was better than nothing. Then Beau rushed for the window.

"Jammed," she muttered. "I-I couldn't get it...h-higher..."

Yeah, it was jammed. Screw it. He drove his fist through the glass. The glass shattered. He started bleeding, and he just punched harder. He punched until the windowpane was gone, and he could gulp in air. Except that air just tasted of smoke, too.

If they didn't get out of that room, they were dead.

He looked back at her.

Small. Long hair that tumbled over her shoulders. Oversized pajamas. Hunched shoulders. Shudders shook her body again and again.

What was she? Like, a hundred pounds? He could handle that. Maybe. His idea was a real shit one, but it was the only idea he had. "Get on my back."

She didn't move.

"I'm—" He almost hit his knees as dizziness flooded through him, and Beau threw out a hand to grip the window frame. His blood smeared over the edge. "I-I think I can crawl down." There was some kind of gutter or drain or some shit that extended down the length of the house. He'd spied it a moment ago. Or at least, Beau thought he had. With all the smoke, it was hard to be sure of anything.

Fuck. Maybe he should just jump. It was the third story.

He could survive a jump from that height, couldn't he? Sure, maybe he'd wind up with some broken bones, but getting his bones smashed would be better than burning alive.

She hopped onto his back and held on tightly. A death grip.

He might survive the jump, but Beau didn't want to risk her. He needed to make sure she got down without any broken bones. Or burns. Or...

Hell, I don't even want her scratched.

Slowly, carefully, he climbed out of the window. Grabbed his lifeline—because, yeah, that was how he thought of what was some kind of long drain—and started to descend. Her legs were curled around his waist. Her arms locked around his neck. His right shoulder pulsed with pain, but he ignored it. Down, they went and—

And he felt the fucking lifeline give way. Heard the screech over the crackle of the flames and knew in that stunned instant that they were both going to fall. He twisted his body, moving so that he'd be beneath her and the ground rushed up to him as—

Oomph.

He hit. They'd made it halfway down before the fall. The impact shuddered through him because he'd taken the worst of it. She was on top of him, and as he fought to suck in a gulp of air, she rose above him.

"Be okay!" A choked plea from her right before her fingers ran over his face. "Please, please, don't be broken!"

Too late. He'd been broken for a long time. Ask anyone. His would-be foster parents. The social workers. The mom who'd ditched him long ago when she left him sleeping in a church pew and never looked back. The asshole dad who'd never cared a bit about him. He was no good to anyone. Worthless. Trash. He was—

"My hero," she breathed.

He blinked and stared up at the angel above him.

"You're my hero."

Sirens wailed in the distance. And, beyond his angel, he saw the flames shoot from the third story window.

***

SOMEONE WAS STROKING HIS HAND. A soft, gentle touch.

Beau slowly opened his eyes. At first, he wondered where the hell he was. A white room. Antiseptic smell. Bright light trickled through the shades to his left. But then he saw her.

A pretty teen with long, reddish blond hair. She perched in the chair near his...hospital bed? She held his hand, and she sent him the sunniest smile he'd ever seen in his life. Dimples winked in her cheeks.

"You saved my life."

The hell he had.

Wait...

Oh, yeah, he had.

"You're a hero."

Nah. He was a jackass. A car thief. A gang—

"You're the most amazing person I've ever met."

His chest began to ache. Beau lifted his right hand to rub it and—shit, his shoulder hurt.

She clutched his left hand all the tighter. "You got burned on that shoulder, but you're going to heal. You ah..." Her eyes —a truly incredible shade of deep, dark green—drifted down his body. "I'm afraid you broke a lot of bones when we fell.

When I..." A rush of her breath. "When *I* fell on top of you. You've got some cracked ribs, too. But I swear, you are going to heal. The doctors say that you will be fine in a few weeks."

He didn't look down at his body.

He looked at her hand, holding his.

"My name is Avalon," she said. "And...what's your name?"

Avalon. He swallowed. Could have sworn he tasted ash. But Beau made his gaze lift to her face. She looked close to his age. Maybe a little younger. Innocent. Beautiful.

And she...she was staring at him like he was some kind of superhero.

"Beau," he heard himself mutter.

Her smile came again. A smile that flashed her dimples once more.

His heart beat faster. Beau knew trouble when he saw it. And he was staring straight at some serious, serious trouble. Only that trouble was disguised as a cute teen girl.

"You're my hero," she told him.

He'd never been that before. And he knew he never would be again. He was on a different path. One full of destruction and pain. But...

But for just a moment, with her, he became something else.

Something—someone—who wasn't so disturbed. Who wasn't chased by demons and pain. Someone who could touch something good and not destroy it.

He became Avalon's hero.

And she...

She became his hope.

Chapter One

Avalon Trahan sat across the table from an ice-cold serial killer. His bright blue eyes showed no emotion. No curiosity. She wasn't sure that Everett Thomas actually felt emotions. At least, not the way most people did. Normal people.

Though, over the years, Avalon had come to understand that "normal" was really a very relative term.

Two guards were in the small room at the prison with her. Everett was cuffed—ankles and wrists all connected together and secured to the floor. She shouldn't be afraid of him. There was no way he could hurt her in this environment.

But staring into his soulless eyes, Avalon felt her stomach drop.

This was the man who had brutally murdered four women before finally being apprehended and found guilty. Georgia had the death penalty, and Everett was in line to get a needle shoved into his arm. Death would be coming for the man who'd so cruelly tortured others.

"Pretty lady, what do you want with me?" Everett asked softly. His gaze never left hers.

"My name is Avalon. I'm a writer."

He didn't change expressions.

"I'm curious about your story."

Now, for the first time, his eyes did seem to lighten with emotion. An almost feverish intensity. "You want to hear about what I did to them?"

Them. The women he'd hurt. Viciously abused with his knife.

Avalon kept her hands beneath the table. This wasn't her first time to speak with a sadistic killer. Actually, her job involved talking to the worst of the monsters out there. Plenty of people thought that she was crazy to do this particular job, but it had called to her over the years. Darkness always called to her. Or at least, it had since the night her life had changed when fire swept into her world.

Her chin lifted. "I want to hear about the night the police caught you."

His eyes narrowed.

"They found you handcuffed and unconscious in that barn."

He leaned forward.

The guard on the right tensed.

Avalon didn't alter her pose. "You seemed to be in the process of fleeing. You had a bag found in the trunk of your car." The bag had contained clothing.

As well as several knives. Duct tape. Photos of his vics.

Everett grunted.

"But someone...stopped...you from running." A mystery that had been in the news ever since Everett's arrest. "I would like to know what happened."

"You and the fucking world," Everett rasped.

"Yes." She nodded. "The fucking world would like to know. That's why I'm here. I write about people like you. Your motivations. Your crimes. Your punishments."

His breath came a little faster. He leaned forward just a small bit more.

"Who caught you?" she asked. Because this was something that had captured her attention. Everett would have gotten away from the cops. His car had been gassed up and ready to go.

But someone had gotten to *him* first.

Given him a concussion. Knocked him out. Left him for the cops with an honest-to-God red bow tied around his neck.

"If I knew..." A low rumble from Everett. "I would have found the bastard, ripped out his intestines, and tied that shit into a bow."

What a lovely visual. "So you have no clue."

His jaw hardened.

Everett was a handsome man. Technically speaking. Chiseled jaw. High cheekbones. It was his physical appeal that she believed had disarmed his victims. People tended to go through life expecting, well, expecting monsters to *look* like monsters. And not like handsome movie stars. Or male models.

They want the bad guys to look as dark and twisted on the outside as they are on the inside. Sadly, that wasn't the case. In her experience, the worst monsters tended to have perfect exteriors. The better to lure in their prey.

Her breath whispered out. "My goal is to find the person who left you in that barn."

His head cocked to the left.

"I solve mysteries." She rolled one shoulder in a calculated shrug. "You are the second killer to have been left—bound and unconscious—for the police in the last two years."

"I never confessed to being a killer."

No, he hadn't. But the evidence was clear. His DNA had been found on three of the four vics.

"Since I never confessed, I prefer that you don't use the term with me."

She swallowed. "You are a convicted killer. A jury found you guilty. Don't blame me if you don't like the label you were given by the court system." A deliberate attempt to antagonize him. "In fact, you should blame the person who left you in the barn."

"I do fucking blame him."

Heat. It lanced beneath the words. Her head dipped. "Then perhaps you can assist me in finding him."

He scoffed at her.

Right. Like it was the first time that had happened to her, either. Over the years, most of the criminals and killers she met tended to underestimate her. Their mistake. Her secret skill.

"How the hell would you find him? The cops couldn't find him."

She didn't know how hard the cops had looked. They'd been more excited to just have Everett Thomas in custody. Everyone had been glad when the Slasher was off the streets. "I'm not law enforcement. I can work around the system."

The guards glared at her. She flashed them her dimpled smile. It tended to disarm people.

They just glared more.

Oh, well. Back to her target.

She lost the dimples and focused on Everett. "You're set to die. I would think that—before you get that swift trip to hell that is waiting courtesy of a lethal injection—you'd like to know who helped send you on your way."

He didn't blink.

"Walk me back through your life," she invited, keeping her voice calm with an extreme effort of will. "The last few days, before you planned to make your big escape from town, tell me about what you did. Who you saw. What you—"

Laughter cut through her words. "I was celebrating those last few days." His grin held no dimples, and the wicked pleasure in it sent ice sliding through her veins. She knew why he'd been celebrating.

Victim number four—Holly McRae—had been stabbed twenty-two times just days before he'd been locked away.

"I went out on the town," he said, and she could feel the memories around him. "Drinking and dancing. Found some new bars that I sure liked one hell of a lot."

"Which bars?"

"Can't remember."

Yes, he could. She stared into his eyes. "You were in Savannah, Georgia. The area was your hunting ground. The bars were where you picked your prey."

"Were they?" He glanced at the nearest guard. "I'm bored. Thought she'd have some pics to show me. I do enjoy it when reporters bring back old pics for me to see."

So he could relieve his sadistic crimes. Yes, Avalon would imagine that he would enjoy that particular activity. "I'm not a reporter."

The guard shuffled forward. He pulled a set of keys from his pocket. They jangled as they bounced in his hand.

"Thought you said you were a writer." Everett's lips twisted.

"I write true crime books."

"So you should have seen all the photos." He widened his eyes. "Hey, maybe we can team up and you can prove that I'm innocent."

"Impossible." The guilty couldn't be proven innocent.

The guard released the lock that had bound the ankle and wrist cuffs to the floor. Then the guard curled one beefy hand around Everett's shoulder and hauled him to his feet.

"Why is it impossible?" Everett demanded.

"Because we both know you killed those women."

The guard stepped back. "Time to go."

This talk had certainly not gone the way she intended.

Everett slammed his fisted hands—and the attached cuffs—onto the table in front of her. The table bounced, the cuffs rattled with a screech, and it took every single bit of Avalon's self-control not to flinch.

"What the hell?" A snarl from the guard.

Everett stared into her eyes. A little furrow appeared between his brows. "I don't scare you?"

"It takes a lot to scare me."

Both guards had grabbed him now. They were hauling him away.

She kept her hands fisted in her lap. Kept her arms close to her sides. Kept her breathing calm and kept her gaze dead set on him.

Everett smiled at her. "Four bars. Moonshine. Whiskey Sour. Midnight Rave. And LeBlanc's."

The guards almost had him through the doorway.

"If you find that sonofabitch...cut out his intestines and tie them in a bow!"

The guards yanked him out of the room. The door slammed shut with a clang. Avalon released a long, slow breath. She didn't get out of the chair. If she'd tried to rise immediately, she was afraid that her knees might have turned to jelly, and she'd just fall in a puddle on the floor. Considering that there were currently eyes on her—eyes that had been watching that little chat the entire time—she didn't want to screw up her confident facade by taking a header onto the floor. So unprofessional.

Another slow breath, and Avalon turned toward the one-way mirror that waited to the left. The warden would be behind that mirror. So would the DA. After all, it wasn't as if she could have gotten an audience with a notorious killer without their help. "Did you know about the bars?" she asked. Her head tilted, and her hair slid over her shoulder.

Then she waited. Patiently. Still in her chair because she knew her weak knees. A few moments later, the door opened. DA Douglas Baptiste strolled in. "Got to be honest, I didn't think he'd tell you jackshit."

"I look like his preferred victim. And I knew how to dangle the bait." She reached for the briefcase at her feet. She made sure not to lift her arms too much as she arranged the briefcase in her lap. Not like she wanted the DA to see the giant sweat stains under her arms. Because, oh, yes, she'd been sweating bullets during her standoff with a serial killer.

"The DA's office is very interested in determining the identity of the individual who secured Everett Thomas for us." His dark eyes never left her face. She knew all about Douglas Baptiste. The child of Haitian immigrants who had come to this country and worked hard to create a better life—a new life. Douglas Baptiste had graduated valedictorian from his high school class. He'd gone on to edit the law review at Emory where he'd earned his JD. Douglas ran a tight ship at his office. He made sure the streets were safe.

And he did not like the idea that some random vigilante might be out there, doling out his own form of justice.

Even if he stopped the bad guy when the cops hadn't been able to do the job.

"Did you know about the bars?" Avalon repeated her question patiently.

"I'll have some officers check them out."

Which she decided to translate as DA speak for...*No, I didn't know. Thanks so much for your help. You are incredible.* Or at least, that was how she interpreted things. "I can check them out." And that was her way of saying...*I will be going to these bars. Talking with the staff. Looking for leads.* Because in her experience, certain people didn't share well with cops. Share well. Play well. Same thing.

"We'll handle things from here on out. But thanks for trying."

And that was very bluntly a...*Get your ass out. We are done.*

"I see." Avalon stood. The chair legs groaned as they slid over the hard floor. "I guess that means our partnership is at an end?"

He stared politely back at her. "I'll have a guard escort you out."

Don't let the door hit you in the ass.

She nodded, clutched her briefcase, and headed for the door. But she stopped and had to ask, "Are you worried that he'll strike again?"

"Everett Thomas is in a maximum-security prison. The man spends most of his time in solitary confinement because we have to protect him from the other inmates. They want to rip him apart. The guy is a trophy to them." A long exhale. "Everett won't be claiming any other victims."

Avalon looked over her shoulder. "I'm talking about the

person who cuffed Everett and left him with a bow for you. That is the *second* time your mystery vigilante has caught a bad guy in the Savannah area. Think he'll go for time number three?"

"I think..." Douglas cleared his throat. "I think someone is hunting very dangerous individuals. And if that person is not very, very careful, it would be extremely easy to wind up as a victim. Or to just wind up dead."

"I'll take that as a yes answer."

"Goodbye, Avalon."

Get your ass out. Now. She winked. "As always, it's been an absolute pleasure, Douglas."

Avalon kept a serene expression on her face as a guard did, in fact, escort her back through the facility. Past all the bars and locked doors and inmates who screamed and catcalled at her. Avalon's pace remained steady, and her gaze focused straight ahead. When she finally got to the last door, it took all of her self-control not to break and run for the car.

The door creaked open. Fresh air hit her. Sunlight. She thanked the guard and the warden—because he'd been waiting just beyond that door. Avalon slowly made her way to her vehicle, and with each step, she was far too conscious of the crunch of her high heels on the graveled parking lot.

She slipped into her car. Shut the door. When her hands lifted to grip the steering wheel, she saw the shaking of her fingers. "Sonofabitch." Her breath shuddered out. She closed her eyes. And saw Everett Thomas lunging for the table as he slammed his hands down on its surface.

Monsters scared her. They absolutely terrified her to the depths of her soul.

She just worked extra hard so they couldn't learn that truth.

* * *

A GHOST from his past had just walked straight into his bar.

Beau LeBlanc shook his head. He even closed his eyes. But when he opened them, the vision before him did not alter. The woman with the strawberry blond hair and killer body remained standing just inside the entrance of his place.

Sonofabitch.

His hands flattened on the bar top. He stood behind the counter and tension poured through every muscle in his body. She hadn't looked his way yet. Instead, her head was angled away as she seemed to slowly take in every single inch of LeBlanc's.

Turn around. Walk back out. He hardly dared to breathe.

She didn't walk out. She did turn toward him. Even across the busy bar, he could have sworn he felt the impact of her stare like a touch upon his skin. His breath heaved in when she began to walk toward him.

"Uh, boss? Why are you behind the bar?" A nervous question from the new bartender. The one he'd been determined to check on moments before.

Now, however, he just bluntly told the new hire, "Fuck off," because he had other priorities. Priority one was currently dodging her way through the crowd and coming right toward him.

And he was not moving.

Avalon Trahan. In the freaking delectable flesh. All grown up—very grown up. With curves that could—and probably had—made plenty of men drool. She wore a simple black dress. One that fell to her knees. One that curved around her throat and shoulders. Not like the damn thing plunged daringly between her breasts or flashed the tops of her silken thighs. *If only.* But it did fit her like a second skin. Sleek and sexy. And when she approached the bar—gazing at him with a faintly curious expression—he wondered exactly how he was staring back at her.

With stark hunger? Dark obsession? Both?

And she probably has no fucking idea who I am. Because as far as Avalon knew, it had been well over fifteen years since their paths had last crossed.

As far as she knew.

"Uh, hello." Her voice rolled over him. Soft and husky and fucking hot.

He growled.

Her eyebrows shot up.

The new bartender edged closer. Hadn't he told Shaun to fuck off? Beau was pretty sure he'd been damn clear about that. Just in case, Beau's head turned toward the bartender. "I've got her." *Always.*

Shaun's head bobbed in a quick nod before he did an about-face and hurried toward the other end of the bar.

Beau looked back at her. She'd reached for one of the drink menus that had been left on the top of the bar's counter. For a moment, his gaze got caught on her delicate fingers. Then his stare trickled up. Lingered on the tattoo that circled her right wrist. At first glance, some might mistake it for a bracelet because the dark ink was so intricately and perfectly designed. But, no, that wasn't some bangle circling her wrist. It was beautiful ink.

"So, what's good in this place?" Avalon asked as her attention seemed to focus on the drink menu.

"There is nothing good here." Could he sound less growly? Not at the moment. Totally beyond his capabilities.

"You should get the hell out." There. Done. He'd warned her away.

She lowered the menu. Tilted her head to the side. And stared at him with curiosity clear in her eyes. Not fear. Not anger. Curiosity. Oh, hell.

One of the many things he knew about Avalon? Curiosity was killer for her.

"Why would I want to leave? I just got here." Her smile bloomed. Double freaking dimples. Cute on her when she'd been a teen. Sexy as fuck now. "Besides," Avalon continued as she winked at him, "maybe I could go for a bit of bad."

The loud drumming of his heartbeat filled Beau's ears.

"Will I find that here?"

His hands were still flattened on the bar's counter. He found himself leaning forward. His nostrils flared as he caught her scent. Light. Floral. Not jasmine. Was it... lavender?

"You seem familiar to me." Her gaze sharpened on him.

The fuck, no. The last thing he needed was for her to recognize him. *Fifteen years.* Surely, she would not know him. He wasn't some scrawny-ass kid any longer.

She pulled in her lower lip. Nibbled it lightly.

Sonofa—

"Have we met before?" Avalon asked him.

He stared straight back at her. "I have no clue who you are, lady." What? Like he couldn't lie? He excelled at lying. Stealing. Ass kicking. Oh, he certainly had lots of useful skills. Typically, the bad kind. Ask anyone. There was a reason the cops in Savannah, Georgia, tended to skulk around him. They were always trying to lock him up for some crime or another.

Too bad for them, they had trouble making charges stick.

"No clue, huh?" Her delicate jaw seemed to tighten for a moment. "How unfortunate."

"Not really." Time to move away from the bar. Let Shaun do his job before the poor asshole passed out over there. Beau could feel the guy's nervous looks. If Avalon wasn't going to leave the bar, then he would get the hell away from her before he did something that he would regret. Something like, oh, say...

Haul her across the counter. Kiss her with all the need he'd held pent up for *years*.

A real-life fantasy should not walk into your bar. That shit shouldn't happen. It was just way too much temptation for a man to handle.

"Let's change that situation." She flashed that killer smile again as she extended her hand across the counter. "Hi, I'm Avalon."

I know. He'd never been able to forget her, while, apparently, he didn't even rate in her mind. Call a guy a hero once, change his life forever, then forget him. Typical.

But then, it had been years. And she hadn't seen him since he'd been a beaten and burned kid. While he...

Ah, yeah, he'd seen her plenty since that fateful night.

Stalker.

Her fingers wiggled as they dangled in the air. "Are you going to leave a woman hanging?"

Beau realized that he couldn't hear anything else in the bar. The other conversations and the music that the band played had all become muted. Her voice rolled over him like a warm wave, and he found himself lifting his hand. Curling his fingers around hers.

Fuck me. A jolt of electricity surged through him when he touched her. Absolute awareness that came with a charge that could not be ignored.

"Wow." Her eyes widened. He knew she'd felt the charge, too. "It's, uh, nice to meet you."

We've met before.

"Do I get a name?" she asked.

He should speak. Not just stare into her eyes like a besotted idiot. How had her eyes gotten even deeper, even greener? She had some dark shadow on her eyelids. A little liner to accentuate them. Maybe the makeup was making her eyes look greener. Her lips were soft pink. Full. Dangle earrings swayed lightly from her ears.

Her hand was soft and warm in his grip. He should let her go.

"I could just call you Mr. Mystery Bartender."

"I'm not the bartender."

"No?" She made no move to pull back her hand. She did lean forward a bit more, as if imparting a secret. "Don't know if you've realized it, but you are standing behind the bar."

"Yes." Just that. Nothing more.

Her eyes seemed to dance. "You get where I have some confusion."

He got that he needed to let her go. So with a serious effort, he did. His hand immediately lowered behind the bar where it fisted. He could damn well still feel her. Such soft skin.

She'd always been softness. He'd been calluses and rough ridges.

Why in the world was she in his bar?

"Uh, boss?" Shaun was back.

Why was Shaun back?

"Boss." Shaun cleared his throat. "There are some cops here. They want to talk with you."

Typical. His breath blew out. Must be a day that ended with Y.

"What should I tell them?"

Beau hauled his gaze off Avalon and took in the very obvious detectives and their bad suits as they lingered near the entrance of LeBlanc's. "Tell them to fuck off."

"That sounds like a bad plan." A loud whisper from Shaun. "I don't think they're gonna like that."

Beau shrugged. His bartender scurried away. No doubt, Shaun was off to deliver the message.

And Avalon kept studying Beau. "I agree with your nervous bartender." She nodded. "Sounds like a bad plan to me. In my personal experience, cops do not enjoy being told to fuck off." Her lips pursed. "Tried to warn Douglas about this very thing, but did he listen to me? Oh, no."

He barely caught that last mutter because he was watching the cops as they closed in. They'd stepped around Shaun and were currently heading in Beau's direction.

Really? Did he look like he had time for this shit?

"So you're the boss. Not the bartender. Got it." From Avalon. "LeBlanc's." She cleared her throat. "That would make you Beau LeBlanc." She seemed to taste his name. Savor it. "I don't suppose that you happen to remember—"

"Beau LeBlanc!" The man in the stale beige suit flashed a badge. "Detective Jeremy Abbott. This is my partner, Glenn Mayo. We need to ask you some questions."

"Um, do you?" Absolute boredom from Beau. "Tell me, who did I kill this time?"

Jeremy's eyes nearly bulged out of his head.

Beau laughed softly. "A joke, gentleman. A joke." One they clearly had not appreciated. Too bad for them.

Avalon's short nails tapped on the bar. "Pro tip, cops

don't like it when you joke about murder. Any murder talk tends to make them twitchy."

His attention shifted back to her. "Too bad. I enjoy joking about it."

Her lips parted.

"Are you familiar with Everett Thomas?" The question came from the cop identified as Glenn. Slightly balding. Nervous hands. A gaze that flickered a bit too much toward the wall of liquor behind Beau. Sweat dotted Glenn's brow.

How long you been sober, Glenn? Instead of asking that question, Beau rolled back his shoulders. "I think I saw him on the news." He let his eyes widen. "Isn't he the man who killed all those poor women? Such a damn shame."

Glenn nodded. "We...we're doing some background work. Got a few questions. You ever remember him coming to your bar?"

Beau gestured toward the packed bar. "Detectives, take a look around. It's like this every night." He smiled. "I have zero idea who comes in and out."

"You got security equipment?" Jeremy pushed. "Cameras?"

"I'm afraid my cameras have been out of order for a while. I do keep meaning to fix things." Bullshit. Some of his clientele just preferred extreme privacy. So did he.

But I do have cameras now. You just can't see my footage.

Glenn darted a glance toward the cash register. "You keep a record of all your transactions?"

"Do I look like the IRS?" Beau crossed his arms over his chest. "Credit card receipts. Sure, we got those records. If someone paid in cash—as lots of the people here do—then I am not going to be able to help you much. But feel free to talk to my staff."

The detectives exchanged a long glance. Nodded. Then they ambled off to talk to some of the waitresses. Who wouldn't prefer talking to the gorgeous waitresses? And not the growly, always-annoyed bar owner.

He watched them for a moment. Slowly dropped his arms back to his sides. Then turned his head and—

Avalon's eyes were on him. "They didn't try very hard, did they?" A soft sigh slipped from her. "I knew they'd do a piss-poor job. That's why I had to come in myself."

The drumming of his heartbeat was even louder in his ears. "I don't follow."

"It's interesting that two detectives come into your bar, they drop the name of the most notorious—and brutal—serial killer to make the headlines in the past five years, and you don't so much as blink."

"Was I supposed to blink?" Deliberately, he blinked. "Like that?"

Her nails tapped again. "Aren't you curious about why they're asking about him?"

"I'm not curious about many things." Not a full lie. He was only curious about certain things. Like...her. Beau had always been very, very curious about her.

"Oh, well, I'm curious about everything."

He knew that already.

She rolled right on by saying, "I'm curious about cops. I'm curious about big, broody, not-bartenders who glare at me with seriously intense, brown eyes." She held up her hand as she continued ticking off her points. "I'm curious about the fact that you don't even blink when a notorious serial killer is mentioned, even though that killer told *me*, not even twenty-four hours ago, that he'd visited your bar shortly before his arrest."

Sonofabitch. "You spend lots of time hanging out with serial killers? Is that your hobby?" It was more than a hobby.

"Ah, see, now you're curious."

His jaw locked. Her choice of profession had always caused him alarm. He'd needed to take extra steps to ensure her protection. *You just had to enjoy hanging with killers, didn't you?*

"You're curious about me and my questions." Her face became very, very somber. "I can satisfy your curiosity."

Baby, I bet you could satisfy all sorts of things. "I believe I told you before that you should leave." If he hadn't told her, he should have. Never in a million years should she be in his bar. She shouldn't be so close to him. She shouldn't be talking to him.

How am I supposed to hold on to my control now?

"I can tell you exactly why the cops are here." She wet her lips. Nearly had him growling. But then she continued, "And when I do that, you can tell me why you're pretending that you don't know exactly who I am."

He almost forgot to breathe. And he didn't do that shit. He wasn't some dumb punk. "You told me you were Avalon—"

She surged over the bar counter and grabbed his shirtfront in her hand. Fisted it. "Listen, Mr. Big, Bad, and Dangerous."

He looked down at her hand.

"I remember you." Low. Even huskier. "It's pretty hard to forget the man who saved my life, even if he has grown up to have insane muscles, a jaw that looks like granite couldn't chip it, and eyes that have me feeling like you've stripped me naked a dozen times since we first started talking."

Shit. He'd been trying not to look too hungry. But in his

mind, hell, yes, he'd stripped her naked more than a dozen times already.

"I remember you," she repeated, even softer. "Hard for a girl to forget her hero."

His eyes slowly lifted until they locked on hers. "You are making a mistake." She should understand that fact right now. "I'm no one's hero."

"You are mine." She jerked him forward and planted her lips on his.

Chapter Two

BAD MISTAKE. SUPER BAD. HORRIBLE, TRAGIC, HUGE mistake.

But when a hero walked straight out of a woman's memories—dreams and fantasies—you had to be ready to seize the moment. Or, in this particular instance, be ready to seize the hero. And she had.

Avalon had practically crawled across the bar counter. She'd nearly torn his white t-shirt as she hauled Beau closer. And her mouth was currently planted hard to his. And he was...

Doing nothing.

Standing there. Still as a statue. And just as hard as one, too.

She should retreat. Pull back. She'd made a serious tactical mistake. But she just hadn't expected to walk into this warehouse-turned-bar and find her hero waiting with those sexy-as-sin eyes. Dark and deep eyes that Avalon swore could see straight into her soul. *Eyes like his know every secret I possess.*

And he wasn't moving.

"Uh, boss?"

It was the guy she suspected to be the real bartender.

Beau still wasn't kissing her in return. She should retreat and try to pull up her tattered pride. Clearly, Beau was not even mildly interested in her, and she needed to calm the hell down. It was definitely not appropriate behavior to jump your hero when you saw him. Her bad.

But before she could pull up her pride and make her embarrassing retreat, his big, powerful hands flew out and locked around her waist. One swift move had her completely over the bar top before she could even gasp. Her lips did part, and in that instant, his tongue plunged inside as he took over the kiss. Beau's strength was incredible, super sexy beyond belief, and she found herself curling her arms around his neck and holding on tightly as she enjoyed what was quickly becoming the absolute hottest kiss of her life.

He didn't kiss gently. No subtle seduction. He tasted her like someone who'd been starving for years. Stroked and thrust and his wicked, wicked tongue had her moaning and arching closer.

What are you doing? Slow down, slow down! Her internal warning to herself. She should slow down. Not rub against him so much. Not moan so eagerly into his mouth. So what if this was the man who had saved her from the fire? The man she'd spent her teen years and adult life longing for? The man her therapist had once told her could never, ever possibly live up to the image she'd created of him?

Screw all that.

This. Is. Beau. Her Beau.

"Uh, boss?" A throat cleared.

Beau's mouth reluctantly lifted from hers. Her breath

heaved in and out, and her rapid heartbeat had her chest nearly shaking. Or, heck, maybe it *was* shaking. Her entire body shook.

Her feet weren't even touching the floor. He still held her up. If possible, his gaze had gone even darker. Avalon knew desire when she saw it, and it was sure as sin raging back at her from the depths of Beau's dark and deep gaze. In that instant, he looked at her as if he could eat her alive.

Go right ahead.

"You, ah, have that meeting coming up soon, remember?"

She should look over at the man speaking. And she would. Eventually. At the moment, her gaze was too busy being stuck to Beau. "You remember me." Her hand slid down and over his right shoulder. Just to be sure. And...

Yes.

She could feel the faint ridges of his scars beneath the thin t-shirt.

"It would be better for you if I'd been able to forget." Rumbled. Beau lowered her until her feet hit the floor.

Avalon sucked in a breath. Then another one, deeper this time. Did Beau understand just how sexy his voice was? Deep and dark. It was the kind of voice a woman could imagine coming from the hottest part of the night...

As the man thrust deep and hard into her and sent them both racing to oblivion. The kind of voice made to say naughty, wicked things.

Her tongue swiped over her lips, and she swore she could still taste him.

"Do you always go around kissing every man you meet?" Beau asked her.

Was that anger in his voice? Her brows rose.

"Considering I met a serial killer yesterday and chose *not* to kiss him—"

Beau's eyes narrowed.

"Because he was absolutely terrifying and as close to a demon on earth as I think you can get," she continued determinedly, "then, no, I can say with utter certainty that I do not, in fact, go around kissing every man I meet." A pause. "You're special." Incredibly so. Special to her. "But I believe you already know that. Or are you going to pretend that you don't recognize me?" Her hand slid over the scars beneath his white t-shirt. A careful caress. "Because these scars say you do."

He backed away, fast.

Her hand was left hanging in the air, and her body suddenly felt very, very cold.

The nearby bartender cleared his throat. He seemed to do that quite a bit.

"The meeting is delayed," Beau snapped. "Tell Saint that we will catch up again soon. The past decided to step up and explode in my face tonight."

Was that what she'd done? Explode? When she'd kissed him, desire had certainly exploded within her. But Avalon didn't exactly like the way Beau had worded things. She hadn't exploded in the man's face.

His fingers curled around her wrist. Right over her tattoo, and he had to feel the sudden leap of her pulse. "Come with me." A curt order.

Her free hand flew back and grabbed the bag she'd dropped on the bar before she'd, ah, gone over it. In a fit of passion and all that.

This is not me.

But, sometimes, she didn't know exactly who she was.

Beau was tugging on her, the young bartender was

gaping, and she couldn't very well turn and run away. Not when she'd come in the bar in order to get answers. *And I found my hero waiting for me.* She sent Beau a bright smile. "Since you asked so nicely..."

He growled.

Growls weren't sexy. She'd certainly never found them to be. Until now. Dammit.

Beau stalked back toward a narrow hallway. Then turned into an office. His hold on her never wavered. With quick steps, she crossed the threshold. He slammed the door shut and used his grip to immediately haul her against the wall.

Where he proceeded to cage her with his muscled body.

Oh, boy.

Her breath heaved. Her hands rose to press lightly to his chest. Yep, lots of muscles. Incredible power. And the way he was glaring? She *might* have been afraid were it not for two important points.

Point one. She spent her days and nights talking to the most sadistic serial killers out there. As far as she knew, Beau was no killer. He was a bar owner.

Point two? He'd saved her life when she'd been a teen. People who saved you didn't typically turn around and hurt you. At least, she certainly hoped they didn't.

"What the hell kind of game are you playing?" Beau gritted out.

Her brow furrowed. "What makes you think I'm playing?" The kiss had been dead serious. Way better than her teenage fantasies. Should she mention those fantasies? Tell him how many times she'd thought of him over the years?

One day, he'd been recovering in the hospital.

The next...

He'd been gone. And no one had any clue how he'd vanished. She'd been left standing there, holding a bouquet of silly flowers that she'd bought for him, and Beau had been nowhere to be found.

"You waltz into *my* bar..."

Right, his bar. Which did bring her back to the serial killer problem she faced.

"And you come straight to me. You kiss *me*." He glared. As if she'd committed some horribly vile offense.

She waited and restrained herself from pointing out that he had kissed her back. After a tense moment or two.

A muscle flexed along his jaw. What a jaw. Square and covered with a light layer of stubble.

"Avalon."

The way he said her name sent a shiver over her. She realized that she was supposed to respond. She wasn't normally one to stay in silence. Fast retorts were her specialty. But never in a million years had she expected to find her hero that night. "Ah, that was...an incredible recap," she finally told him. "Top notch."

His eyes narrowed even more. "I don't play games with bored debutantes."

"Oh. That hurts." It actually kind of did. Sure, he didn't know her, but...still. "First, I'm not bored. I don't get bored. I find ways to amuse myself. I've always thought life is too short to waste being bored."

"So what am I? Your latest amusement?"

Not at all. "You're the man I've been searching for since I was a teenager."

Yep, that shut him up. He looked down, seemed to realize he was, in fact, caging her tightly. Hotly.

"So..." Her voice came out rather like an invitation. Whoops. Oh, well. "Either kiss me again or give me some space. It's a little hard to think clearly when your past comes racing back at you," Avalon told him. She meant those words. He had completely thrown her off. Because when she'd known him before, LeBlanc had *not* been the last name he'd given at the hospital. So she'd walked into the bar, expecting to gear up for a question-slash-grilling session with the owner and staff. But when she'd spotted him through the crowd, her world had turned upside down.

Of all the bars, what are the odds that I find him? Now?

"You don't want me to kiss you again." His eyes were on her mouth.

"What makes you so sure?" Her right hand rose and pressed to the stubble along his jaw. "I was the one who kissed first a few minutes ago. You were the one all stiff and cold. Took a bit to thaw you out. But I finally managed to get the job done."

Lightning fast, one of his hands rose and curled around her wrist. "This is the last warning I'll give you. Don't play with me."

His hold was tight, but not at all painful. As if he had complete control of his strength. Good to know.

Then he let her go. Backed away. Paced to stand behind the desk. He didn't look at her but focused instead on the small window that looked out over the water. The bar had a prime location right next to the river. And the interior of the warehouse had been beautifully revamped into a trendy bar. Every tourist in a hundred-mile radius would want to visit. Correction, they *did* visit. There had been a line stretching outside full of people eager to get in LeBlanc's. She'd had to bribe a bouncer in order to slip inside. LeBlanc's was currently *the* place to be.

But she wasn't there for the atmosphere or the great booze. "I have questions."

His shoulders stiffened. "I was at the right place at the wrong time. I went into the fire. We both came out. End of story."

"It was actually the right time for me," she corrected. "Just so we're clear. If you'd been a little later, I would have been dead." That window had not been opening fully. Would she have broken the glass the way he had? Crawled out and grabbed that old drain?

Fallen and broken so many bones…

He looked back at her. For the life of Avalon, she could not read the expression on his face. So she kept talking. "My parents were at a charity ball that night. I was alone. Someone *moved* that bookshelf in front of my door. I couldn't get out because it was too heavy for me. I shoved and shoved, but it wouldn't move." Did he have any idea what it was like to know that you were trapped and would be dying? "The window was jammed. I couldn't get it higher than a few inches—"

"Nailed. Not jammed." Groused.

Her shoulders lifted. Fell. She took a step toward him, then caught herself. "You remember me."

"Hard to fucking forget." His hand rose and rubbed along the back of his right shoulder. "Got a permanent reminder that I see every single day."

She flinched.

His hand dropped. "That's not what I—dammit, you should not be near me. You should not be in my bar." His brow furrowed. "Why the hell are you in my bar?"

They'd get to that, later. First, "Where did you go? You left the hospital. You only stayed a few days. You weren't healed. You were still wearing a cast, you had so many broken bones, and your shoulder was covered in burns. You needed medical treatment."

"I got treatment. Just someplace else."

"I looked for you." Her quiet confession. "I couldn't find you."

He slowly turned to face her fully. "You were better off without me."

Not something she would ever believe. "They never caught the arsonist."

His lips thinned. "But your parents got guards for you. You never went anywhere without a bodyguard until the day you graduated high school."

"H-how do you know that?" The faint stutter showed her surprise.

His gaze cut from her. "I know a lot of things about you."

She took a slow, gliding step toward him. "Then you have me at a disadvantage, Beau *LeBlanc*. Because I know next to nothing about you."

"It's my real last name."

"And the one you gave me before wasn't? The one you gave at the hospital wasn't? Why would you lie about it?"

He didn't blink. "Why are you here?"

Fine. "I'm here because someone left Everett Thomas handcuffed and unconscious and put a bow on him so that he could be a present for local cops. I'm currently trying to find that someone." And, important question, was she staring directly at that someone?

He laughed. "Why would I give a shit who did that? From the stories I read, Everett was making a run for it. Cops were too slow. If he hadn't been stopped, another woman would probably be dead. Several women."

Yes, quite possibly. "This wasn't the first time a dangerous killer was detained in such a manner."

"Do tell."

His mocking tone had her jaw hardening. "The cops have kept the other details from the press. Not like they want everyone knowing a vigilante is targeting killers."

"I'm still not seeing a problem." He scraped his hand over his jaw. "And I'm not seeing why this involves me. Now, our walk down memory lane was certainly hot and entertaining, but I do have places to be. Got people to intimidate. Lives to ruin. You know, the usual."

"Are you trying to be funny?" She couldn't quite get a handle on him.

"No, I'm being dead serious."

And he looked like he was. "I talked to Everett yesterday."

"Why the fuck would you want to do that?" Before she could respond, he shook his head. "Don't understand why you want to be around any of those bastards."

"You..." She cleared her throat. "You know what I do for a living?" If he knew, that meant he'd been keeping tabs on her, didn't it?

His grin flashed. It was the first time he'd smiled at her. And, as someone who had what she thought of as a pretty good smile—one that worked well at disarming people—his grin absolutely floored her. Mostly because there was only one way to describe his smile.

Killer.

Slow, sensual, the grin spread across his face and had her heart rate kicking up. It was the kind of grin that would, oh, make a woman want to drop her panties. Yeah, she'd just gone there. His smile counted as being sexy as sin. Twice as hot. And she found herself lifting a hand and fanning herself.

Mid-fan, she stopped. Fisted her hand. *What is happening here?* So, yes, she had an, um, crush. A very long-standing crush. But she did not need to be overreacting to a handsome man's smile for goodness' sake.

He slowly eliminated the space between them. And even though she'd faced off against more twisted killers than she wanted to count, Avalon found herself almost retreating from the man who'd saved her life.

His hand lifted. His fingers curled under her jaw. "Why do you like playing with killers?"

"I'm not playing with them. I'm getting answers."

His grin slowly faded. "Liar."

Chapter Three

THIS WHOLE SITUATION WAS WAY, WAY OUT OF control. She tried to get back on track. Hard to do, when his touch was making her whole body ache. "Everett named four bars that he visited before he was caught by surprise and left handcuffed. Moonshine. Whiskey Sour. Midnight Rose. And LeBlanc's."

A nod. "And that's why you're here tonight. And why the cops stopped by. Good to know. For a minute there, I thought you'd tracked me down because you'd just never been able to forget me, and you were dying of unrequited love for yours truly."

Her mouth opened. Remained open. What could have been a squeak emerged. What. The. Hell?

"It was the kiss that made me suspicious. When a strange woman kisses you like her very life depends on it..." His head lowered. His mouth hovered over hers. "It does give a guy ideas."

"I'm..." *Staring at his mouth.* "I'm not strange."

"Sweetheart..."

The endearment rumbled from him and made her toes curl.

"You play with killers for a job. If that doesn't qualify as strange, I'm not sure what does."

Again, she wasn't playing. "I get their stories in order to help people. When you can understand their motivations, when you can see how they hunted, why they selected certain victims, you can learn to stop them. You can be on guard. You can—"

"You want to know why he hunted you, don't you?" Low. Deep.

She licked her lips.

"Never caught. Still out there. The arsonist—the fire killer who got away. Why'd he pick you? Why were you a victim? Did you spend all these years playing with monsters because you're trying to figure out what made you a victim?"

Okay, so, she'd been with him five minutes, and the man was psychoanalyzing her. Very effectively psychoanalyzing her. Why not just rip her skin away and peer straight into her soul?

His thumb brushed over her lower lip.

"Instead of being scared and hiding from the world," he murmured, "you went straight for the monsters. Takes one hell of a lot of guts to do something like that." There was no missing his admiration. "Of course, it's also dangerous as fuck." He let her go. Stepped away. Put his hands behind his back. "But you do you, sweetheart."

The second time he'd called her sweetheart in that deep, dark voice of his.

"Thanks. I usually do." She lifted a slightly trembling hand and shoved back her hair. Big problem. Normally, she could sit across from a convicted killer and maintain her pose of fake calm. But with Beau, she was ragged at the edges after only a few moments of conversation.

At her response, his mouth kicked into a half-grin.

"Did you do it?" Avalon blurted.

"It? Sorry. You'll need to clarify. Turns out, I do lots of things."

"Happy to clarify." A quick exhale. "Did you slam a two-by-four into the back of Everett's head?" Because one had been found at the scene. One that had included hair and tissue from Everett. "Then did you cuff him and put a bow on the guy?"

"Doesn't really seem like something I'd do," Beau mused. His gaze darted down her body. Slowly. Then came back to her face. "I tend to spend my nights busy with other activities."

"Great to know." Her nostrils flared. "That wasn't actually a hard no, by the way."

"It wasn't?"

"No."

"*That* was a hard no."

She stared at him. It had been.

He...winked at her. "This walk down memory lane was far more amusing than I anticipated. Tell you what, feel free to stop by my bar again anytime. Drinks will be on me." He headed for the door. Hauled it open. Then just stood there, holding open the door. Clearly waiting for her to leave.

She'd gotten zero helpful answers. One hot kiss, yes. But zero real answers. Exhaling—rather huffily, she knew—Avalon squared her shoulders and marched for the door. She didn't exit, though. She stopped on the threshold and turned to look at him. "Yes or no."

"Another game?"

"Yes or no," she repeated, "did you attack Everett Thomas?"

"I remember the fellow coming in the bar. He was rather a...nuisance to one of my waitresses. Got handsy. Didn't understand when to back off, so I may have escorted him out."

Her heart surged in her chest. "That's a very specific memory."

"My mind works like that. Very *specific* things get burned into my head."

She knew his wording had been intentional. "Burned, huh?"

"Um."

"Yes or no, did you attack Everett?"

"Gonna believe me if I say no?"

The question caught her off guard. "Why would you lie to me?"

"Freaking adorable, that is what you are. Sexy and adorable. A very tempting combination." His grip seemed to tighten on the door.

"You didn't answer me."

"No."

She blinked.

"Happy?"

"No." She was not.

"Ah, so we both can say the word. Good for us. Goodbye, Avalon."

That goodbye sounded final. She turned her head away from him. Stared straight ahead and— "Dammit!" Avalon whirled and caught him staring at her with blatant longing.

What?

But in a flash, an unreadable mask was back in place on his face, and she thought that maybe she'd imagined the longing. Or projected what she was feeling. Because... "I thought about you for years! And when we're finally face to face again, you barely have time to talk to me? Seriously? Haven't you ever been curious about me? Didn't you ever wonder what became of me? I would have died without you!"

He shrugged. *Shrugged.* "You're in the news a lot. I think I've read one or two of your books. I knew what became of you."

Well, fantastic for him. "*I* didn't know what happened to *you!*"

"Here I am."

Yes, indeed. Here he was. Living in the exact same town she lived in. He'd been so close, and she hadn't known. Soon, though, she'd know everything.

By this time tomorrow, she intended to absolutely rip into his life and discover every detail that she possibly could.

"I wouldn't."

"Excuse me?" What was he talking about? What had she missed?

"You're curious about me. You want to know more. You're going to use those research skills of yours and dig into my life." A negative shake of his head. "I don't recommend doing it. You won't like what you find. I'll become one very tarnished hero in your mind. The disappointment will consume you."

"Have skeletons in the closet, do you?" He was just making her more curious. A bad mistake.

"More like I have bodies buried under the bar."

She laughed.

He didn't.

"You're so fucking beautiful." Gruff.

And Avalon stopped laughing.

"Be careful in this world." Flat. Grim. "There are too many people who like to destroy beautiful things."

People like Everett? People who needed to be stopped?

She stepped over the threshold. Tried to think of something to say. This couldn't be how their night ended. Not how they ended. Not after all this time. Avalon spun back toward him. "I—"

He shut the door.

And she heard the flip of a lock.

"Dick move," she snapped.

Did soft laughter echo through the door?

"I will be back." A warning for him. But when she came back, she'd be armed with a whole lot more intel. "Goodbye for now, Beau LeBlanc."

* * *

"GOODBYE, AVALON TRAHAN." His hand pressed to the wood of the door. Yep, total dick move. But he'd had two options. Either shut the door and be a dick...or grab tight to Avalon and never freaking let go.

When your obsession walked straight up to you in your own bar, it tended to screw with your head. Break your control. Make you want to take and take and take the one person you wanted the most.

Avalon was here. I kissed Avalon. My Avalon.

She didn't know about the things he'd done in his life. At least, she wouldn't know yet. But the woman was truly hell on wheels when it came to investigative work, and he understood that she'd start digging at the first opportunity. She truly would not like what she discovered. No one ever did, not when it came to his past.

I kissed Avalon.

And it had been even better than in his fantasies. His damn dick was still hard.

He jerked his hand from the door. Whirled for his desk.

A knock rapped on the door. Every muscle in his body locked down. Avalon wasn't giving up. And if she was so determined to see him again, then, screw it. She'd get him and she'd find out what happened when his control absolutely shattered.

In a flash, Beau ripped open the door. "I'm sorry, I shouldn't have slammed—" He stopped.

One of his bouncers—Kai—lifted a dark brow at him. Kai had grown up in Maui, and Beau didn't really get why the guy had left paradise. But, hell, they were all running from something, weren't they? So when Kai had turned up, wearing one of the loudest Hawaiian shirts in the world and looking for work even as shadows filled his eyes, Beau had offered him a job.

That had been a year ago.

"Boss, did you just *apologize*?" Kai stared at him as if Beau had two heads.

So Beau flipped him off. He and Kai were friends, dammit, and if you couldn't tell a friend to fuck off, then who could you tell? *Oh, wait, I tend to tell everyone that.* "I wasn't apologizing to you."

"Sounded like you were. I'm the only one here."

He glowered.

Kai smirked. "You thought I was the pretty lady."

He raked a stare over Kai's six-foot-two frame and bulging biceps. "Yep, that's what I thought."

"She's gone. Recognized her, of course, from the photo I saw on your phone that time."

Sonofabitch.

"Remember when you showed it to me that night when I drank your ass under the table?"

Beau crossed his arms over his chest. "Why are you talking to me right now?"

"Because she left alone. On foot. It's close to one a.m. And I know about your...habits."

His teeth snapped together. "On foot?" Why the hell hadn't she taken a taxi or a ride share or some shit?

"Uh, huh. Walked right out on her own two feet. Want me to make sure she gets home all right? Seeing as how I know she's important to you, I thought you might want someone to be there for her—"

He shouldered past Kai. "Run things while I'm gone." He'd been training Kai as a bouncer-slash-manager. The man could handle the bar.

And I'll handle Avalon.

"On it!" An immediate reply from Kai. "You just go take care of that very, very important business. And may I say, she is even hotter in real life."

Beau stopped. Turned. Looked at Kai.

"Got it." An understanding nod. "I may not say that. Message received."

Beau growled, then he went after his prey. Not like it would be the first time that he trailed Avalon Trahan into the night.

Not the first time.

Not the fifth.

Hell, Beau had lost count of the number of times he'd followed her through the dark. Because...

I'm the woman's fucking stalker.

And she had no idea that she'd just kissed her stalker as if she'd been hungering for him her entire life.

Chapter Four

Same story, different night.

Avalon walked straight into the darkness like it was an old friend who would embrace her and keep her safe. A total lie, of course, because the darkness was never safe. The life she'd chosen wasn't safe.

And someone had to watch over her sweet ass.

It was a job that he'd been doing for years. All without her ever being aware of him.

Sometimes, when he didn't live close enough—when his work took him to other cities or hers took her away from him —he'd hired people to keep watch on her. Her parents were dead now. Killed in a devastating car wreck when she'd been a senior in college. He'd been at the funeral. Had wanted to go to Avalon as she stood alone and grieved.

But he'd watched. Just watched.

Exactly as he did now.

Her job made her a target. Her past made her a target.

And if people knew just how much of a weakness she was for him? That would make her one hell of a target, too.

But he'd learned one thing in this brutal world—you protected what mattered.

So he'd protected her.

He still protected her. You didn't fuck with what belonged to him.

He followed her through the night. Not too close. Not making any sounds that would alert her. But keeping Avalon within sight. Of course, she darted through alleys. Hurried through snaking small streets that would look quaint during the daytime but spoke of danger in the night. And when a shadow detached from a wall and began to follow her down one of her twisting paths—

His hand shoved against the chest of the shadow. "That's a mistake you don't want to make."

A knife came at him. Fast and swift. So he twisted and broke the hand that held the knife. It clattered to the ground. Beau kept walking forward. Shaking his head, he pulled out his phone. Sent a quick text. Someone would need to handle the bastard who'd just made a tragic mistake.

And still, Beau followed her. Her steps were quite certain. Very sure. No hesitations from her. When she cut through the trees that waited up ahead and veered to the right, his jaw locked. She should know better. One hell of a lot better.

A growl broke from him, and at the sound, she stilled.

Sonofabitch.

His first mistake. In all of these years...

She whirled around.

But he was part of the shadows now, and she didn't see him. Actually, she seemed to stare right through him. He drank her in. She was on the edge of the park, and the light from the crescent moon and the glittering stars let him see her shadowy form.

Avalon.

He'd like for her to make a good decision and not go into the damn park. Sure, it was a tourist hotspot during the day, but at night? A whole different ballgame.

She hesitated. Glanced at the park.

Then chose to stay on the sidewalk and skirt around the edge of the park. Sure, this route was longer, but it was one hell of a lot safer. Points for Avalon.

Her pace had picked up. Almost running now, as if Avalon had realized a predator stalked her. Good for her.

Sticking to the shadows, he kept following her.

When Avalon hurried under a streetlamp, there was a sudden shriek. She spun even as a black cat bounded from behind a garbage can. In her hand, Beau was very pleased to see that she gripped a taser.

Nice, sweetheart. But you'll need a lot more than that to protect yourself from some of the monsters in the night.

She made it home. No more incidents. No more scares. He watched from across the street as Avalon hurried into the historic home that he knew she owned. Two stories. A Victorian. Gray exterior, with white trim. Lots of interesting nooks and crannies. Even a turret on the right. He had a friend who would have loved the house. Of course, that friend would have preferred it painted black, but that was a story for later.

He waited until the front door shut. Until he saw the lights flash on inside. First, downstairs. Then, after a few moments, upstairs. In the turret that he knew was part of her bedroom. For a moment, he saw her shadow behind the white curtains of the windows. She headed toward the curtains as if she'd open them to the night.

But then a second shadow appeared.

His body tensed.

Avalon wasn't involved with anyone. Not right now. He knew that for certain. He—

The second shadow grabbed the first and yanked her back.

"*Avalon!*" His roar shook the night.

* * *

HANDS GRABBED HER FROM BEHIND. Surprise and horror blasted through Avalon, and she opened her mouth and screamed as loud and as hard as she could.

"Bitch, there's no hero this time." He threw her body onto the floor.

She hit hard, with her elbow ramming into the wood and her knee banging like a hammer into the floor. She scrambled forward, ignoring the bolt of pain in her left knee.

He grabbed her by the hair. "Do you like the fire? I've been told you do."

She couldn't see him. He was still behind her. She hadn't glimpsed his face. She reached up and clawed at his wrist.

He *laughed* and slammed her toward the hardwood once more. Her hands slapped down right before her face would have hit the floor.

"You are going to burn," he promised.

Her gaze jerked to the right. Her purse was on the chair inside of her doorway. Her taser was in the purse. If she could just get to it, she would tase his ass so hard. The floor groaned behind her. Why hadn't it groaned before? If it had, she could have gotten a little advance notice that she was not freaking alone in her home!

But with that groan, she struck back hard with her foot.

She made crushing contact with his shin, and when he bellowed, she lunged for the purse. Her fingers snagged the strap just as he grabbed her again.

"You'll be alive when you burn. You will be—"

A crash came from downstairs. A very, very loud crash. One that was immediately followed by a roar.

A roar that was her name.

* * *

HE KICKED IN THE DOOR. Had to kick it twice before the lock broke and the door flew open. Even as the door banged into the wall, Beau was shouting Avalon's name.

An alarm started beeping somewhere. He flew up the stairs three at a time. Fury and fear fueled his blood. He was absolutely terrified of what he'd find upstairs.

Avalon had to be alive. She had to be safe.

And whoever had been waiting for her? The fool was dead.

He reached the landing. Spun for the right. Saw her open bedroom door and the two figures fighting on the floor. Avalon was grabbing for her purse with one hand while her other pushed against the chest of some hulking asshole all in black. One wearing a damn ski mask.

"Get the hell away from her!" Beau thundered as he ran for the bastard.

The bastard's ski-mask-covered head whipped up. Even as his attention shot to Beau, Avalon pulled something out of her bag. She shoved it against his chest. The attacker jolted. Hard.

And Beau slammed into him. They flew through the air as the bastard's body shuddered, and they landed on the hardwood floor. Beau drove his fist into the man's face. Over and over. And, fuck that, he ripped off the ski mask as he raised his hand to—

A punk kid stared back at him. Big, muscled, yeah, but young as hell. Pimple-covered face. Scraggly beard.

"What. The. Hell?" Beau roared.

He'd busted the kid's lip. Pounded his face into a mess.

The intruder wasn't fighting back. His body kept jolting.

Beau slanted a fast glance at Avalon. She was on her feet and still holding tightly to her taser. "You okay?" he demanded.

Was that a freaking bruise forming on her cheek? A red spot now, but it would soon be...Snarling, he looked back down at his prey. His fist drew back once more.

"Don't! I-I was hired, man! Shit, don't!"

Fuck that. Beau drove his fist into the attacker's jaw even as he ordered, "Call the cops, Avalon. Now." Then he grabbed the asshole by the front of his black shirt. "Why are you here?"

Beau heard Avalon speaking fast and frantically behind him on her phone.

Blood dripped from the man's mouth. "S-scare her... paid to..."

"You don't scare her. You don't touch her. You don't even breathe in her direction from here on out. From this moment forward, you ever so much as *think* of her again, and you're dead, do you understand me?"

A swift gasp from behind him. He didn't look at Avalon. If he saw another bruise forming on her skin, he might lose his mind. "The cops, Avalon," Beau prompted her. "Call them, now." His glare remained on the SOB before him. "Who paid you?"

"D-don't know..." He heaved against Beau's hold, stupidly thinking he could get away.

Beau pounded him back against the floor. "Let's try again. Who paid you to break into her house and *scare* her?"

"Door was unlocked!"

"Oh, the hell it was!" Avalon chimed in as she scurried forward. She'd ditched her phone.

"Stop!" A blast from Beau. "Do not get close enough for him to touch you."

The punk's gaze darted to—

"I'm sure I told you not to look at her again. Look at me."

Scared brown eyes met his.

"Do you have any idea who I am?" Beau asked him.

A shake of sweaty, disheveled brown hair.

"I'm Beau LeBlanc."

The kid's eyes widened.

"You've heard of me," Beau murmured. "Good. Since you know who I am, you understand that you are fucked."

"Why is he fucked?" Avalon wanted to know. "Oh, no, are you like...are you a crime boss, Beau? Because I'm getting some serious vibes from you right now. How can a hero be a crime boss? *How?*"

"Who hired you?" Beau snarled.

"Don't know! I swear—*don't know!* My brother was supposed to have the job, but he got fucking sick. I-I took the gig from him. Ask my brother! Jesus, don't kill me! *Don't!*"

A substitute attacker? Was this BS for real?

"I got paid cash. Money was w-waiting for me. Was told what to say through a text. I swear...I was only scaring her!"

Such a lie. Did he look like a man who believed lies? "I don't think there's a brother. I think you're bullshitting me.

That's your second fatal mistake of the night. Your first was hurting *her*. And you did hurt her. You bruised her. Your hands were on her when I came inside. So screw the story about you just *scaring* her. We both know it's bull. You were here to hurt her, and I want to know who hired you to—"

Whoosh.

He heard it. Like a wave surging through the air. An odd sound. One that made the small hairs rise on the nape of his neck. His head whipped toward Avalon.

She stared back at him with wide eyes. Then her delicate nostrils flared.

She turned for the door. The sound had come from downstairs.

I left the front door open. I raced inside so quickly. Didn't search downstairs. Just ran up to her.

Had a second attacker been in the house? Or had someone followed Beau inside her home?

"Is that..." Avalon's voice trembled. "Is that smoke I smell?"

He could hear crackling. Instantly, Beau let go of the asshole attacker and surged to his feet. He reached for Avalon.

The punk shoved a shoulder into Beau's side and barreled for the door. "Not catching me!" A high-pitched yell. Then he was rushing from the bedroom. Charging into the hallway.

Beau gave chase and saw the kid stop at the top of the stairs.

Because smoke was rising from the bottom of those steps.

But the attacker paused for only a moment before he raced down to the first level. Beau didn't give chase. He looked back and saw Avalon, seemingly frozen. "We have to go, sweetheart, *now*."

She jerked. Hard. Then ran—not for him but for the laptop that perched on an oversized chair near one of her windows. After grabbing it, Avalon clutched the laptop to her chest then looked around frantically. She darted toward the closet.

Hell, no.

"We save you," he growled as his hands locked around her waist and hauled her back against him. "But we're not wasting time saving useless shit."

"It's important shit! Not useless!"

If the house hadn't been on fire and the bad guy hadn't been getting away, he might have smiled. But it was the wrong damn time for a smile and the right time for an immediate exit. "I'm not going through a window again. Really not in the mood to have my body broken." Recovery had taken long enough the first time. He hauled her toward the bed. She kept clutching the laptop like it was made of gold. He grabbed a cover from her bed and tossed it around her.

"What—"

He lifted her and slung Avalon and the cover over his shoulder. He felt the laptop bang into his back, but he wasn't going to pry the damn thing out of her hands. If she wanted it so badly, then she could keep it. All he cared about getting out of that house? Her. *Avalon.* He rushed down the stairs with her slung over his shoulder. The flames were crackling and dancing, but they weren't eating up the stairs yet. Smoke was getting heavy, seeming to scald his throat and nostrils. When he reached the ground floor landing, he saw that the fire was mainly in her den. The flames ate at the carpeting and the bookshelves and the piano, and the flames twisted and heaved as they spread.

Yeah, screw that crap. Not staying to see the full show this time.

The front door still gaped open. Had to, since he'd kicked the thing in and shattered the lock. An alarm still beeped from somewhere in the house, and he ignored the beeping as he hurtled toward the exit. The dark night waited, and smoke blew from the house even as he erupted with his precious cargo still over his shoulder. Straight ahead, he could see the young punk running at the edge of her property. "Stop!" Beau shouted.

Of course, he didn't stop.

Beau lunged forward. Still holding Avalon, he lunged after his prey.

And the punk ran straight into the street.

A roar filled the night right before a terrible, wrenching scream echoed. Beau was staring straight at the fleeing attacker, so he saw the hit. A black car took shape in the darkness. One that shot right toward the punk. One that hit him with a powerful crunch. Or maybe that sickening crunch was all of the kid's bones breaking. Because the attacker flew into the air. His body twisted and turned in a flash that somehow seemed to last forever. Then he hit the cement. When he landed, he didn't move.

"What's happening?" Avalon squirmed in Beau's grip. "Let me down! *What. Is. Happening?*"

His hold tightened on her.

The black vehicle raced away. No taillights ever flashed. The driver never braked. The engine roared louder as it fired off down the street.

And the man in the road still wasn't moving.

Somewhere in the distance, a siren began to scream.

The cops that Avalon had called, finally coming to the rescue?

Slowly, carefully, he lowered her to the ground. The cover he'd grabbed in the hopes of protecting her from any flames fell around her feet. She looked at him, then back toward the road. "Beau...?"

"Stay here." He ran for the figure in the road.

He heard her footsteps thudding behind him.

Dammit! Beau whirled. "The driver could come back. *Don't go into the street!*"

"You're going into the street!"

Yeah, he was. "Someone has to see if he's dead or alive." But Beau already had a feeling in his gut about that answer. He'd caught sight of the unnatural angle of the man's neck. Seen the blood pooling around his head.

Beau rushed toward the prone figure in the road. His teeth clenched even as he wrenched out his phone and used the light to better check the man. *Broken doll.* Yeah, that was how he looked. So many broken bones. And a whole lot of blood. Beau knelt next to the kid. Put his hand on the guy's throat and wasn't a bit surprised not to find a pulse.

The siren—now sirens—grew louder. He heard voices and knew some of her neighbors were coming out. People always liked to gape at a tragedy.

Beau began to pat down the dead man.

"What are you doing?" Avalon's low whisper.

He cut his gaze back to her. She was on the very edge of her property. On the grass. Not the road. Points for her. Beau didn't answer. He did pull out the man's wallet and snap a pic of the ID. Right before the first patrol car roared to the scene, he shoved the wallet back into place and rose to his feet.

"He's dead?" Avalon asked.

"Better him than you."

She flinched. Right. That had been brutal and cold. But that was who Beau was. Brutal and cold to his very core. But inside the cold wall of ice that surrounded him, a fire raged. One hotter than the flames burning in her home.

Someone sent that bastard after Avalon. Then that same *someone* had been waiting outside. The second SOB had set the fire. Had killed the kid before he could talk to Beau.

Beau stalked to Avalon. The lights from the police cruisers lit up the scene. A fire truck came racing down the road. He didn't even know who'd called the firefighters. Maybe a neighbor? But their response time was fucking fantastic.

"Anyone else inside?" A bark that came from either a cop or a firefighter. He didn't look away from Avalon in order to see who had fired out the question. In that instance, with her face lit with the swirling lights, with her eyes so stark and afraid, he couldn't look away from her.

"No one!" Avalon's answer. "No one else is inside!" One hand clutched the laptop against her chest, but her other hand flew out and pressed to Beau's chest. Voice lower, she told him, "You saved my life."

"There's a dead man in the road!" Beau called out. But he was sure the cops had already noticed the body. If he could have looked away from Avalon, maybe he would have even seen them checking the vic.

Attacker turned vic.

"How were you even here?" Avalon shook her head. "How did you know what was happening?"

Yeah. Two very interesting, pertinent questions. Questions that the cops would probably ask, too. No one would buy that he'd just been out for a random stroll in her neighborhood. And him saying that he'd followed her home from the bar probably wouldn't go over so well.

His history with the cops wasn't so grand.

Beau leaned toward her. His lips brushed over her ear. "You told me to meet you here." His mouth skimmed the shell of her ear.

She shivered.

Over her shoulder, he saw the firefighters racing inside her home. He hoped like hell that they could put out the flames and save the place. For her.

"I-I didn't tell you…"

"You told me," he repeated, and maybe he did deliberately skim her ear with his mouth that time. It took all of his self-control not to grab her, toss her over his shoulder again, and get them the hell away from that scene.

She's not safe. Avalon is being hunted. And every single protective instinct he possessed—and his protective instincts were always in overdrive when it came to her—screamed a stark warning at him.

Danger chased her again.

"You told me to come here," Beau rasped. "And that's what you tell the cops. I was walking up the sidewalk when I saw the shadows upstairs. I realized someone was in the house with you."

Her hand fisted on his shirtfront. "You followed me."

Was that a thread of fear in her voice?

She was right to be afraid of him. Most people were. He eased back and stared into her eyes. "I would never hurt you."

She stared at him.

The blue lights swirled around them. Firefighters shouted orders. Neighbors kept right on gaping.

"I want to protect you." Always had, always would. The

years hadn't changed that. She didn't get it. She was his one good thing. The person he'd saved. The person who looked at him and didn't see a monster or criminal or—hell, evil. She saw *more*.

"You followed me," she repeated.

Sweetheart, I've been following you for years. Not the time for that particular confession. From the corner of his eye, he saw that uniformed cops were closing in on him. "You're in danger. I can protect you."

"How?"

It's what I do. "Let's get rid of the cops, and you'll find out."

She still had his shirtfront fisted in her hand.

He waited, barely breathing and...

She nodded.

Fuck, yes.

Then she shot onto her toes. Her hand released his shirt but only so she could wrap her fingers around the nape of his neck and tug him toward her. Then, against his ear, she whispered, "I don't trust you, Beau LeBlanc."

Surprisingly, the words hurt. But he ignored the ache in his chest. She was right not to trust him. "Good for you."

She sucked in a swift breath and eased back.

Staring into her eyes, he felt it was only fair to warn her, "Trusting me can prove to be a fatal mistake."

Chapter Five

Even for someone who spent her days interviewing killers and studying crime scenes, the day had been...a bit much.

More like a waking nightmare.

Avalon swiped her keycard over the lock at the hotel suite—the presidential suite because Beau had insisted that she be put in that particular suite at the ritzy hotel—and when the light flashed green, she shoved open the door.

Weary beyond belief, Avalon walked over the threshold. She was far too conscious of Beau trailing in behind her. "You didn't have to pay for the room." Completely unnecessary. She had plenty of her own money.

"Your house is currently soaked, ash covered, and it reeks of smoke. Not like you could have stayed there. It's also a crime scene."

Yes, it was. Because a man had been murdered there. Or, technically, right in front of her home. Beau had seen the attack. Blessedly, she hadn't because she'd been tossed over his shoulder at the moment of impact. But she'd still heard the gut-wrenching sounds. The pain-filled scream that had choked off. The crunch of bones.

What she hadn't heard? The sound of a car screeching to a stop as the driver tried to brake. According to Beau, the driver had never braked. Instead, the driver had been lying in wait and he'd deliberately plowed down her attacker.

He looked barely eighteen.

She put her precious laptop on the table near the couch. The suite had a sitting area, a small kitchen, a freaking grand piano—the piano caught her attention and she frowned at it for a moment—then she ignored the suite and turned to confront Beau. "I meant you didn't have to actually *pay* for the suite. I have my own money. I could have taken care of the bill." Thanks to her parents and her own career, she had quite a bit of money. One of the firefighters had managed to get her purse and her phone out of the house for her.

Beau crossed his arms over his chest and stared back at her. "I wanted to help."

"You've saved my life—twice now—so I think that counts as you helping me plenty. Way more than should be expected." Part of her wanted to throw her arms around him and hug him tightly as she thanked him again and again. When he'd come bursting into her bedroom, the relief she'd felt had made her nearly light-headed. And, weirdly enough, she'd...known he would come.

She'd actually looked up and thought...

Running a little late, are you? But, of course, that was ridiculous.

Wasn't it?

Not like the man spent his days and nights playing guardian angel for her. Until that very night, their paths hadn't crossed in years. So why was she reacting this way to him? What was wrong with her?

Maybe it's the adrenaline. Or the fear. Or the crazy attachment I've always felt to him.

"You're pissed at me." Beau winced. "You're glaring, so it's pretty obvious."

Actually, yes, she was angry. Add that to her mix of emotions. "You asked me to lie to the cops. I don't like lying to police officers." It was not her standard mode of operation. "Call me crazy, but it feels criminal. Considering I was the victim, lying didn't make sense."

He nodded. "I can see that point of view."

He could? How wonderful. "Talk."

"I thought we were." A little furrow—a damn, oddly cute furrow—appeared between his brows.

"Beau."

"Yes, Avalon?"

She huffed out her breath and strained to keep the little bit of patience that she had left. "How the hell were you at my house?"

"Simple." A nod. "Try not to get angrier, though, would you?"

"I make no promises. Spit it out."

"I followed you."

Goose bumps rose onto her arms. "Say that again." Wait. Did she want him to say it again? Maybe she wanted to have misunderstood.

"I. Followed. You." Very clear. No way to misunderstand. His hands fell to his sides. He took a step toward her.

Instinctively, she took a step back.

"Easy." Soft. As if he were speaking to some sort of frightened animal.

Her eyes narrowed at that particular word. "I don't see anything *easy* about this situation. Quite the opposite, in fact. I've just been told that you *followed* me to my home. Why in the world would you do that?" And, P.S., she never liked anyone telling her to be easy or to settle down or any of that shit. Phrases like that tended to be the equivalent of waving a red flag right in front of her face.

"One of my bouncers informed me that you had left the bar alone. While the city is certainly gorgeous, danger still waits in the dark. I wanted to be sure that you made it to your destination safely."

"Isn't that going a bit above and beyond for a woman you barely know?"

He shrugged. "It was a slow night until you arrived. Not like I had anything better to do."

He was straight-up lying to her. "There wasn't any danger waiting."

A burst of laughter escaped him.

The laughter was oddly warm and deep, and she wanted to hear it again. "Fine," Avalon bit out. "There wasn't any danger waiting until I actually got home." Then there had been plenty of danger.

But he was shaking his head. "You barely escaped a mugging on McGregor."

Her brows shot up. "What?"

"Don't worry. I convinced the gentleman of the error he'd nearly made. He shouldn't be troubling anyone for a while."

"Not troubling anyone for a while..." Avalon licked lips that felt suddenly parched. "Want to translate that for me?" She was suddenly very conscious of each hard beat of her heart. Impossible not to be when the pounding seemed to echo in her ears.

"Not particularly. He didn't hurt you. He won't hurt anyone else. That a good enough translation?"

Her hand pressed to her chest. Her heart raced so fast and hard she just had to make sure it wasn't about to lunge out. "You stopped me from being attacked near McGregor." *That* was what he was telling her?

"Um."

She took that as a yes. Even though it came out as an "um" from him. "So that means you've saved me three times?"

A smile stretched his lips. A secretive one. As if he knew something she did not.

The last bit of her patience snapped. "Beau."

"Yes?" He stared expectantly at her.

"How many times have you saved me?"

"You just said three," he reminded her.

But she had the feeling there were more instances. Impossible. Right?

"Perhaps you should just be grateful I decided to play the role of gentleman and go for a stroll tonight. If I hadn't gone out, if I hadn't stopped in just the right spot, if I hadn't looked up and seen the shadows in the turret window, our story could have ended differently."

"I had a taser. I used it." She hadn't been helpless.

"Yes, I do remember his shudders. Excellent job, by the way. Most impressive."

His shudders. The dead man's shudders. Her goose bumps got worse. "I...was going to run outside. Go to a neighbor's house and get help."

"It's possible that when you ran out, the second attacker would have been waiting for you. Maybe that was the plan."

"No, he said I was going to burn."

His eyes seemed to go even darker. But Beau knew this

already. He'd been at her side as she repeated the story to the cops.

"He told me I'd be alive when I burned." Like that wouldn't give her new nightmares. "And then my house got set on fire."

"I heard the firefighters saying they think an accelerant was tossed around your den. The second attacker started the flames and that was the whoosh of sound we heard."

"You think the—the second attacker was the man who drove the black car." The killer.

"Don't you?"

Yes. "The cops didn't seem so sure."

"Those were the uniforms. Not the lead detectives. You got a break-in, an arson, a hit-and-run…and murder. The big guns will be taking over the investigation. Honestly, I'm surprised the uniforms didn't hold us at the scene longer. But I'm sure we'll be called to the station in the morning."

She was sure of that, too. "I have friends at the police station. And at the DA's office." People who could help them.

"How lovely for you. My friends tend to run in different circles."

Avalon shook her head.

"Hardly surprising that you're friends with the cops," Beau added. "I'd expect nothing less from you."

Avalon rocked forward onto the balls of her feet. "I keep getting the feeling that you know way more about me than I know about you."

"Because you haven't dug into my life yet. You will. You and that trusty laptop of yours."

Yes, she would dig. With her trusty laptop.

His expression hardened. "Your friends at the police station are going to tell you to stay away from me."

He was so close that she could reach out and touch him. She wanted to touch him. In order to stop what she was sure had to be a bad impulse, Avalon fisted her hands at her sides. Her nails dug into her palms. "Why would they say that?"

"Because you should stay away." He didn't even hesitate with his response.

"Why." Not a question.

"Because they'll tell you that I'm dangerous. Trouble. Unpredictable and uncontrollable."

"And are you those things?"

"Oh, sweetheart." That killer grin of his flashed again. "I am all of those things and more."

"You're trying to scare me."

"You mean you aren't the kind of woman who falls for the bad guy? With your obsession for killers, I am shocked."

Was he mocking her? Avalon's eyes narrowed. "I don't have an obsession with killers."

He stared straight into her eyes. Seemed to stare straight into her soul. "We all have our obsessions."

"Oh, really? What's your obsession?"

"You."

The room seemed to shrink. Or maybe he just got bigger. It also got hotter. "That's...a joke."

"But you don't know me well enough to determine when I'm joking."

"I know you well enough to say that you're not obsessed with me!"

"I'm obsessed with keeping you safe."

And he sounded as if he meant that. Beau looked as if he did, too. The hard features of his face appeared dead serious. "Why?"

"You ask that a lot."

"Side effect of my job. I always want to understand motivations. You understand motivations, and you might be able to stop the crimes. The killers." Wasn't that the whole reason she did what she did? Not like she enjoyed sitting across the table from sadistic killers who made her stomach twist and her fingers tremble. But the more you knew about monsters, the better you could control them. Stop them.

Maybe even change them?

"I like your optimism." He swung away.

Before she could stop herself, her right hand flew out and curled around his upper arm.

Heat. It lanced up her fingers, chased across her arm, and drove straight to her core. People talked about electric attractions, but this was different. It was more of a primitive heat that flared between them. No denying. No pretending. When he looked at her and his pupils flared, she knew he felt the awareness, too. "Where are you going, Beau?"

"I do have a home." His head tilted. "Unless you're inviting me to stay with you?"

"Of course, not!"

"Well, that was certainly a fast no. Don't worry about hurting my pride. I'm a big boy."

Yes, she could see that. "We...I...I don't have sex with strangers."

How could dark eyes heat so much? "But I'm not a stranger."

In that instant, facing off against him was more intimidating—in a way different manner—than sitting across the table from Everett Thomas had been.

"Don't worry." Soft. "I wasn't asking for sex. When I do, you'll know."

Her hands went to her hips. "Then what did you mean?"

"I meant the sofa converts into a bed. If you're scared, I'm happy to play guard and protect you until morning comes."

Oh. Her hands fell. "That is kind of you."

"Right. Kind. Goodness and light. I am all that is upright and upstanding in the world."

She heard the mockery. Didn't like it. "You just told me you were dangerous. Trouble."

A shrug. "Can't a guy be all those things? I'm different, with different people."

She had the feeling that he might just be serious.

"For example, someone who wants to hurt you? I'm the most dangerous asshole that fool will ever face. No one hurts you on my watch."

"Why would you care so much about me?" They'd gotten back in each other's lives hours before. For all intents and purposes, she was a stranger to him.

A stranger he seemed to know far, far too well.

"You ever have one good thing?" Beau asked her.

She had no clue what he meant.

His laughter came again. Low. Sexy. "Of course, you have lots of good things. You do your charity runs. Raise money for sick kids. You volunteer to build houses for disabled veterans. You have all kinds of *good* things in your life. You *do* good things."

"How do you know that stuff?" Way too much about her. Butterflies fluttered in her stomach.

Instead of answering, Beau told her, "I don't do a lot of good things. Don't get me wrong, I'm no Everett Thomas. Not like I do the worst shit imaginable. But until the night I met you, let's just say that *good* wasn't a vocabulary word I knew." He rolled back his shoulders. "You are my good thing. I look at you, and I know that I'm more than the world thinks I am. You matter. You are my good thing. And I'm not going to let some prick terrorize you."

You matter. "So, what, I should consider myself under your protection or something like that?" Avalon laughed.

He did not. "You've been under my protection for quite some time. Consider it seriously amped up until I find out who the hell was driving that car tonight—and I destroy him. I *will* destroy him. That's a promise."

She could not move.

His hand rose and his knuckles brushed over her cheek. "This hotel has the best security in town. This suite has the best security *in* the hotel. No one will get up here. I know the security guards on staff, too. I'll make sure they are keeping a very close watch on the cameras for this floor. You will be safe here."

And that explained why he'd insisted on the presidential suite.

"Want me to stay?"

She opened her mouth. Almost said yes. But there was too much work for her to do. Too many alarms ringing in her head. "No."

"Too bad. I would have very much enjoyed spending the night with you, Avalon. Fantasy fulfilled."

He had not said—

He was heading for the door once more. She rushed to follow him. Her fingers grabbed the doorframe and held tightly to it as he walked over the threshold. He didn't look back as he strode down the hallway and headed for the elevator.

He'd been right. The floor was very secure. Only the presidential suite was on this level. A big, massive suite.

With the equally massive grand piano. "You know I play the piano."

He didn't stop.

"You know I play the piano just like you know where I volunteer."

"Lots of people play the piano as a way to unwind. You had a tough night. You might want to de-stress."

Sex is great for de-stressing. Her lips clamped together so she would not share that fun fact.

He was almost at the elevator. To access this floor, you had to have a special keycard. She had one of those keycards.

He had the other.

Beau's hand rose, and he pressed the button for the elevator.

"Should I be afraid of you?" The question spilled from her.

Beau stiffened. Then turned slowly to peer back at her. "Maybe."

Boom. Boom. Boom. Her heartbeat was way too fast. "Do you want to hurt me?"

"Never." Immediate. "I would *never* do anything to hurt you. I want to keep you safe." His expression turned savage. "It's the driver of that car who will be hurt. The killer."

She didn't leave the safety of her room. Not fully. "Then why should I be afraid of you?"

The elevator dinged. "I said that *maybe* you should be afraid."

"Why?"

"Your favorite question." The elevator doors opened. He stepped inside. But turned to look back at her. "The answer is...because I want you."

Boom. Boom.

"I want you very badly, Avalon. But I would never, ever do anything you didn't want. You're the one who came to me. Probably would have been so much better if you'd stayed away. But you didn't. You walked into my bar. Walked up to me. You're the one who kissed *me*."

Yep. Guilty as hell.

"Now you're in my head. Before you were a memory. A dream. Now you're real. I can still taste you. And I want more."

The doors closed.

I want more, too.

But first...

She slammed her suite door shut. Flipped the locks. Even dragged a big chair in front of the door because a woman could never be too careful, and she'd had one hell of a scare that night. Then she grabbed her laptop. Booted up. And got to work.

Beau LeBlanc knew far too much about her. It was time for her to learn all about her hero. And to find out just why the cops thought he was so dark and dangerous.

* * *

THE ELEVATOR DOORS OPENED. Beau stepped out. He was still on the top floor. Avalon's floor. A sweeping glance assured him that the door to the presidential suite was shut. Then, smiling and satisfied, he slid back into the elevator. He'd just taken a short ride moments before. He'd had no intention of actually leaving the building until he was certain that Avalon was safe for what remained of the night.

He rode down to the lobby in silence. He toyed with sending out a text. There were people he wanted working this case, but it was cutting close to four a.m. They'd give him hell if he woke them up now.

He'd let them sleep for two more hours.

Whistling, he left the elevator when it reached the lobby, but he still didn't exit the building. Not yet. The night manager was waiting for him.

Percy rubbed his hands together. "Everything to your liking?"

Beau grunted. The presidential suite would work, but, no, there was very little about this pisser of a night he liked.

Except for kissing Avalon.

Beau forced his back teeth to unclench. "Her security is priority, understand?"

Percy stopped rubbing his hands. He nodded. Three times.

"She's VIP. The only VIP in this hotel as far as you're concerned."

Percy nodded a fourth time. "Absolutely."

Percy owed him—a lot. Plenty of people did. Beau tended to work in favors, among other things. "I want to know the minute the cops arrive. I'm thinking they'll be here around seven, maybe eight." Which didn't give Avalon long to sleep.

"The cops?" Percy's dark brows shot up.

"Yeah, they'll be coming. Got a little matter of a murder to handle." He looked at his watch. Damn late. But there was still work to be done. "Avalon really needs her sleep." Though he doubted she'd be hopping straight into bed. More likely, the woman would be booting up her laptop and working to uncover all of his dirty little secrets.

He had so many secrets.

"I can stall the cops until eight," Percy offered. "I'll stay after my shift to make certain things are handled appropriately for you."

Beau lifted his head and smiled at the night manager. "Percy, I've always liked you." Actually, he had. From the minute he'd found the kid digging in his dumpster behind LeBlanc's. Too scrawny, too dirty, and with one hell of a chip on his shoulder.

Percy had reminded Beau of himself.

Except...Percy didn't need to go down the same path. That path led to hell.

So he'd sent the kid in a different direction.

"Her safety is priority." Beau wanted to make sure there was no doubt on that point.

Percy nodded. A fifth and final time.

Beau headed into the night. He didn't like the scene that had gone down at her house. *An attacker waiting inside? One who told her that she'd burn?*

The flames tonight had reminded Beau too much of another time.

Another place.

The scars on his right shoulder seemed to ache.

Avalon had now escaped two fires. How many more times could she escape death?

* * *

IT ALWAYS AMUSED him when monsters pretended to be normal.

From his position in the shadows, he watched Beau LeBlanc stride out of the ritzy hotel. The man took his time. Acted like he owned the place. He'd put Avalon in that hotel. Behind the doormen. The security guards. Locked the princess away.

He glanced up.

He'd bet for all the world he'd locked her in the tower. The safest place, right at the very top.

He knew Beau LeBlanc. After all, it was important to

know your enemies. Beau was a very dangerous man. Only he liked to pretend sometimes that he wasn't.

Liar, liar. I know what you keep locked inside.

Beau was heading away from the hotel.

Away from Avalon.

He pulled out his lighter. It had belonged to his father. The only thing of the bastard's that he had. Gold on the outside. Smooth. Cold. A flick of his wrist, and the top swung open. His thumb moved of its own accord. A habit, second nature, and the flame flared to life.

Beau glanced back. Too late.

He'd already killed the flame.

But he smiled from the darkness. Because he had prey. The fire was going to burn again soon. In a blaze bright enough to consume the past.

The past...

Avalon Trahan.

Beau would not be able to save her again. After all, the dead couldn't save anyone. And if Beau didn't get the hell out of his way, the bastard would be a dead man.

* * *

THE FIRST THING she found was the murder charge.

Avalon's breath shuddered out even as her body leaned toward the computer. Beau had been locked away because...a patron of his bar had been found beaten to death. Witnesses reported the dead man had become rough with one of the waitresses in LeBlanc's. Beau interceded. The two men fought and, the next day...

Dead.

Her fingers tapped on the keyboard as she fought to

learn more, but even as she explored and pushed deeper into Beau's life, his voice whispered through her mind.

You've been under my protection for quite some time. Consider it seriously amped up until I find out who the hell was driving that car tonight—and I destroy him. I will destroy him. That's a promise.

Chapter Six

"How long have you known Beau LeBlanc?" The detective tapped a pencil on the edge of the desk.

The cops—detectives this time, not uniforms—had arrived at Avalon's hotel room shortly after eight a.m. They'd seemed a bit annoyed with the very friendly hotel manager who'd been with them. Avalon had no idea what had set off the detectives, but when they'd asked her to go down to the station with them in order to answer questions, she'd willingly obliged. Not like she had things to hide from the cops. And she *did* want her case solved. She'd picked up some new clothes from the shop in the hotel, changed quickly so she didn't have to wear the dress that still smelled of smoke, and they'd been on their way.

Now, they wanted to know about Beau. How long had she known him? Well...

"Years," she answered with a roll of one shoulder.

The detective to the right—a woman with short, red hair and sharp eyes—stopped tapping her pencil. "When did you first make his acquaintance?" she asked.

Detective Lynn Baker. Avalon had chatted with her a

few times before. She'd chatted with most of the detectives at the station since she'd moved to Savannah. Tenacious. That was how Avalon would describe the other woman. Lynn never gave up on her cases. "June twelfth." Two days after her birthday. Her parents had thrown a big party for her at the country club. All of her friends had been there.

And then, on the night of June twelfth, no one had been there.

She'd been alone and terrified.

Beau came.

Lynn's brows climbed.

"It was a very hot night in New Orleans. One made even hotter by the fire that swept through my house and almost killed me. But Beau was there. A much younger Beau." Her hands remained in her lap, hidden below the table. "He got me out of the house."

Lynn turned and glanced at her partner. Now the partner? Campbell Cunningham? Avalon was not as much of a fan when it came to him. He tended to be a prick who made up his mind way too quickly about suspects. And he liked to maintain his high case-closure rate at all costs.

Lynn's stare darted back to Avalon. "The arsonist who burned your home in the Garden District was never apprehended."

She wasn't surprised the detectives knew that bit about her past. Not like it would be hard to access the info. And, considering that last night—

"Now two fires have been set in your homes. One when you were a teen, and one last night." Campbell blinked his hazel eyes at her. Charming eyes. No, disarming eyes. Only they neither charmed nor disarmed her. "Two incidents and one common denominator."

Yes. She'd figured this was coming. She glanced toward

the clock on the wall. Almost nine thirty. And, just as she'd had the crazy thought last night as she fought with her attacker, she wondered...

What is taking you so long to arrive—

Just as the door to the small interrogation room flew open. "I can't believe you all had a party and didn't invite me." Beau filled the doorway. Seriously, filled it with his wide shoulders that brushed against the wood. He exhaled heavily. "I mean, come on. I was at the fire last night. If we're going to get witness statements, shouldn't I be invited to participate? Don't you care at all about getting my story?"

Campbell's chair legs screeched as he leapt to his feet. "What in the hell are you doing here?"

"Joining the party. Told you that already. Thought I was pretty clear and loudly vocal." Beau didn't even glance his way as he kicked the door shut and strolled for Avalon. His features darkened as he studied her face. "Sweetheart, you have shadows under your eyes." He stopped near the table. "Didn't sleep at all, did you?" His hand reached out, as if he'd touch her cheek.

The chair legs screeched again. She flinched.

Beau's hand froze. "Busy doing research, were you? Too busy to sleep?" He leaned toward her. "Found out anything interesting?"

"Mr. LeBlanc!" Lynn's sharp voice. "How did you even get access to this room?"

Avalon looked over at the female detective. The second bit of screeching had been Lynn's chair shoving back as she leapt to her feet. Both detectives were clearly not pleased to have Beau present. Meanwhile, the tightness had finally eased from Avalon's chest.

Knew he would come.

"Seriously?" Beau shook his head. "How did I get

access? I opened the door and walked inside. It was easy." Beau's hand fell to his side. "I do know my way around this station pretty damn well."

Because he'd been arrested again, not too long ago, on a different murder charge and booked in this exact station. But he'd been released fairly quickly that time. Cleared.

He is always cleared. Beau has never been convicted of any murder. Though he'd been suspected more than a few times.

He winked at her. "Stop looking like you've seen a ghost, sweetheart."

Ghost wasn't quite the right word she'd use for him.

"Walk back out the door! Get out of this room!" Campbell snapped. "We were in the middle of questioning a crime victim!"

Beau crossed his arms over his chest. "You need more sleep." Words aimed at Avalon, just as his decisive nod was directed at her. "You can't run on empty. And did you even have time for breakfast this morning?"

"I grabbed a croissant."

"Chocolate?"

"Uh, yes, the nice manager, Percy, had them waiting for me."

"Bonus for Percy."

"Stop this! *Out!*" Campbell barked. "He needs to get out of here, now!"

Beau shook his head. "You just can't make people happy in this world. Half the time, the cops are yelling at me for not cooperating." His gaze slid carefully over Avalon's face. Appeared to note every detail. "But the one time I come in, trying to help out and do my civic duty, they are eager to toss me out on the street. Seems wrong, doesn't it?"

"We're not tossing you anywhere!" Lynn declared. Her

tone was far more controlled than her partner's. "We simply want you to wait in another interrogation room until we are finished with Avalon."

"Why?" Beau grabbed the chair that Campbell had discarded. The legs didn't screech because he lifted the chair up and then put it down again right next to Avalon. When he sat in the chair, his shoulder brushed hers. "Talk to us together and you can get this question-and-answer session done in half the time. Way more efficient. Then Avalon can go back to her hotel and get some much needed rest."

He was obsessing over her rest. "I'm fine." Low.

"Bullshit." Not low. Definitely annoyed.

"Avalon," Campbell began. "We will take him to a holding area—"

"*I want him here.*" Her words held hard determination. "Don't take Beau anywhere."

Beau sent her a wide smile. The one that made him look extra sexy. And dangerous. "So happy to be wanted," he murmured. "Especially by you."

Campbell's face had turned an unnatural red.

"Breathe," Beau advised as he glanced the other man's way. "Because it looks like you might be in danger of passing out, my friend."

"I am not your friend!" Campbell slapped his hands down on the table. "You're trying to kill her!"

Beau's head turned toward Avalon. "Is that what you believe? That I want to kill you?"

"The arsonist who set the fires long ago in New Orleans was never caught. Three people *died* in those fires." Angry, brittle words from Campbell. "You lived in New Orleans at the time of those fires, didn't you, Beau?"

Beau kept staring at Avalon. "I should have arrived sooner."

Yes.

"I do apologize for the delay."

"It's okay," she whispered. Her gaze had been caught by his.

"I was at your house this morning. Wanted to see the damage."

"*You were at a crime scene?*" Campbell sounded close to choking.

Beau didn't respond to him. His focus remained on Avalon. "The damage was restricted to the first floor. I know some contractors who can get to work as soon as the cops and the arson investigator give the all clear. The place *will* be perfect again. But I need to warn you that there is one helluva lot of smoke and water damage."

"Fucking crime scene. You don't waltz into a crime scene!" Campbell was, once again, choking out the words.

"Never said I waltzed in." An easy statement from Beau. "Lots of things can be seen from the outside." His lips pulled down, then he told Avalon, "Your clothes will probably smell of smoke. I know you needed fresh things, so I had an associate pick up items in your size. Got them all ready for you. *Everything* in that house can be replaced, and it will be replaced, I promise you. By the time I'm done, it will be even better than it was before."

Why? Why was he doing all of this for her?

"Avalon..." Softer. More controlled. Because the prompt came from Lynn, not her partner.

Avalon forced herself to look away from Beau and meet the detective's watchful gaze.

Lynn sent her a reassuring smile. Nothing at all like the

cocky, dead-sexy grin that Beau tended to flash. "Avalon, you told us that you've known Beau for years."

The female detective had clearly decided to barrel on with her questions. Since Avalon had said she wanted Beau in the room with her—and Avalon wasn't being charged with any crime, she was the victim, after all—the cops didn't have much choice. Avalon inclined her head in response to the question.

"Have you been in *communication* with him for years?" Lynn prompted. A deliberate clarification.

Avalon's hands remained beneath the table. She pressed her palms to the front of her new jeans. *Beau knows so much about me.*

And, now, she knew details about him, too. "I talked with him for the first time last night. The first time since I was a teenager, that is." *He'd vanished on me. Left me behind with the ashes.*

"Last night?" Lynn wet her lips. "As in, right before your home was torched?"

"Yes. I went into LeBlanc's, and I recognized him as soon as I saw him. I approached him. We started talking." She didn't think it was relevant to mention their kiss.

"You sick sonofabitch." From Campbell. "You recognized her, too, didn't you? The one who got away. So you saw her and all those old urges came rushing back. You knew you had to finish what you started and take her out!"

"I saved her." Beau's voice was mild. Total opposite of Campbell's intensity. "Both times. I understand, though, detectives, that you see me as the villain, so I will break things down for you." He rolled back his right shoulder.

The shoulder that got burned so long ago.

He turned to look at the detectives. "I was in the house with

Avalon last night. The bastard who'd been waiting upstairs? He got out. Ran into the street. He was run over by a black, four-door vehicle, and the driver fled the scene." He rattled off a make and model. "I was with Avalon during that whole fleeing-the-scene bit. I was also with her when the fire was set downstairs in her home. I was in her bedroom. We heard the flames ignite, and I knew I had to get her out of there."

"He carried me out," Avalon added.

"Like I would have ever left without you, sweetheart."

Her stomach twisted.

"Again, detectives, I was upstairs when the fire ignited. Avalon verified that. I am a man of many talents, but it's not like I can be in two places at once."

"But you can have help." A muscle flexed along Campbell's jaw. "A man like you has plenty of flunkies ready to jump and do your bidding when you snap your fingers, right? Poor bastards like Slater Wade."

"Flunkies. Did you really just use that word? With a straight face?" Beau questioned. "Who even are you?"

"*Do you admit to knowing Slater Wade?*"

Beau ran a hand over his jaw. The five o'clock shadow scraped against his fingers. "Is he playing the bad cop?" Beau asked Lynn with a grimace. "Or is he really just this shitty at his job?"

Campbell lunged—

Lynn put a hand on his chest. "He's antagonizing you, Cam."

Beau shrugged. "Is that what I'm doing? And here I thought I was asking an extremely important question. One that has not yet been answered."

"You should have been in jail by now," Campbell fired at him. "We all know that you are guilty as hell. But you keep walking. Nothing sticks to you, does it? You think you can make the cops into jokes."

"I'm not making you into anything. But from where I am sitting, you are doing an excellent job of making yourself into an ass."

Avalon's attention swung between them, and a dull ache began to grow behind her left eye. She definitely should have snagged the cup of coffee that Percy had offered to her before leaving the hotel.

"You going to pretend you did not know Slater Wade?" Campbell scoffed. "Because we're looking into his life now. We'll trace him back to you. Lying is useless."

"Slater Wade." Beau tasted the name. "That the dead man who was left in the street?"

A nod from Lynn.

"Can't say the name rings a bell," Beau retorted. "But good luck with that tracing. I will be very curious to see what you discover."

Campbell growled.

Beau smiled.

And... "Enough!" Flat. Avalon was actually surprised the word came out so calm because calm was the last thing she felt. It was her training that kept the calm veneer in place. She'd dealt with too many killers to break apart when she was just facing cops. Cops and one annoyingly sexy blast from her past.

"But I was having fun," Beau protested.

Yes, she knew he had been. "You were also being a deliberate dick." She glanced over at a glowering Campbell. "So were you. Stop the BS and let's get down to business. Beau didn't start the fire at my place last night. For the record, he didn't start the fire years ago, either."

"And how the hell do you know he didn't?" Dots of

spittle came from Campbell's mouth as he bit out the question.

"Because I saw his broken body when Beau got me out of the flames. He would have died to keep me safe." He almost had. "He didn't even know me back then. I was some random kid who was about to burn to death, and he ran into the fire to save me." Her hero. That was what he'd been to her over the years. And despite what she'd learned about him...*he still is.* "Maybe you've got a hard-on to toss him into jail, but you aren't getting him for the arsons, Detective Cunningham. I believe in Beau's innocence, one hundred percent."

From the corner of her eye, she saw Beau stiffen. But she didn't look his way again, not yet. He needed to see that the cops could help them. She understood that cops had been his enemies for most of his life, but not every cop was out to get him.

Or, at least, not right now, they didn't have to be.

She cleared her throat. "Slater Wade." The name made her chest ache because she could see him in her mind. Could feel him as he gripped her, and the terror slid through her veins once again. "I don't recognize the name. I'm assuming you're searching his home."

"Got uniforms there now." Lynn tilted her head to the side. "Guy has a rap sheet a mile long. Started when he was thirteen. Boosting cars and petty theft." One eyebrow quirked. "But unlike others with a similar start, this appears to have been Slater's first brush with the big time."

"The big time," Beau repeated, and he did not sound amused. "You think telling a woman that she is going to burn, breaking into her home and assaulting her...you think that's *big time?*" Anger rumbled in each word. But it was a carefully contained rage.

That was the way she kept feeling about Beau. Like he was contained. Holding something back.

"He'd never had a murder charge on him and from what we can tell, Slater never was linked to any arsons."

"Flunky," Beau said. He pointed at Campbell. "Your word, but clearly, that's what Slater was. Only he wasn't working for me. My money is on the bastard who ran him down and made sure Slater couldn't talk to any cops. Or to me. Because I am quite effective at getting reluctant witnesses to talk in the right situations."

Lynn's lips tightened. "I'm sure you are."

Campbell grunted.

"By any chance..." Avalon licked her lower lip. "Did Slater have a brother?"

"He has no living family at all," Lynn told her. "So, that story you said the attacker fed you about covering for his brother? Total BS."

Good to know.

"Oh, come on. We all knew the prick was lying about that detail. Even the uniforms on scene last night thought it was crap." Beau waved his hand vaguely in the air. "It's sort of strange trying to see things from your perspective, detectives. Got to tell you, I am not impressed with your interview style. Here, how about I help things along, so we are not just stuck in this crappy room all day?" He angled closer to Avalon and lasered his focus on her. "Who are your enemies?"

"I don't have enemies."

"Bullshit. We all have enemies. Hell, I've got a list that stretches for two states. At least. So, let's try again."

Her shoulders tensed.

"Who have you pissed off most recently? Everyone in

this room knows you get off on chatting it up with the most dangerous criminals out there."

"Case in point," Campbell muttered. "The prick sitting right next to you."

"He's still pushing me..." Beau didn't glance Campbell's way. "Here I am, trying to play nicely, while he is still being the douche cop—sorry, the bad cop." The words were mocking, but his gaze was dead serious.

He wanted to know her enemies.

Don't you already know? She had the feeling he knew everything about her. Even her bra size. Because he had just casually announced moments before that he'd picked up new clothes in her size for her. Avalon had caught that slip. But she didn't question him about the clothes—that would come later. Instead, she said, "Everett Thomas." He could count as a potential enemy. "I was interviewing him recently. When I left, he wasn't...pleased with me." Understatement.

"Why?" Beau's eyes gleamed. "Oh, look, I just asked your favorite question."

She was aware of the cops watching them, but her attention centered completely on Beau. Every breath she took seemed to pull her a little closer to him. His heat reached out and curled around her. "He wanted me to prove his innocence. I told him that wasn't possible."

"Why not?" Beau waited.

"Because I happen to think he's guilty as hell. I wasn't in that prison to help him. I wanted to figure out who'd left him practically gift wrapped for the cops." *Am I looking at that person?*

Beau's lips started to curl.

"Everett tried to scare me."

Beau's smile froze.

"He slammed his fists onto the table. Thought he'd make me flinch. It takes a lot more than that to rattle me." Campbell had pulled a similar move. Some people liked to intimidate with their size.

Some used other means.

Beau nodded. "He wanted you scared, but you told Everett to fuck off. You weren't helping him."

"And he told me to find the sonofabitch who'd taken him down. Then..." She watched Beau carefully. "Then he suggested I cut out his intestines and tie them in a bow."

Silence.

Beau had leaned toward her even more.

She'd leaned toward him.

His expression hadn't changed. His eyes, though, they seemed darker. Deeper. She wanted to read the emotions in his gaze. Normally, she was so good at reading emotions, but this time, she just couldn't gauge what he was feeling.

"Ahem."

Beau and Avalon turned their heads toward Lynn.

"Is this some weird foreplay for them?" Campbell asked as he scratched his chin.

"I have no idea." Lynn shook her head. "But I'd like to get back to my *murder* investigation. Seeing as how Everett Thomas is locked in a maximum-security prison, I don't really think he's the man we're after, so how about we focus on other enemies that you may have, all right, Avalon?"

But Beau laughed. The deep, rough sound held no humor. "Like prison can stop you from getting what you want." He rose. And when he did, his hand slid out. His knuckles trailed over Avalon's cheek. "You say the right word—or the wrong word—to certain individuals. And you can get plenty of people on the outside to do your dirty work for you."

"Speaking from experience, are you?" Campbell's forehead scrunched with obvious suspicion.

"Oh, come on. You know I'm right. That's why you need to pay Everett a visit. Or why *we* do." His hand lingered against her skin. "You can get a meeting with him, can't you, Avalon?"

Yes, she could. With a few phone calls, she could make it happen.

"Take me with you, and I'll find out if Everett put a hit on you."

She sucked in a breath. "He...he wouldn't have been able to put out a hit so quickly." She'd just talked with him.

Beau's expression said, yes, he would have. "He sent you out to search bars. Gave you such a helpful list of places to visit. We all know the best time to search bars is at night."

Yes.

"While you were out searching at night, Everett knew your place would be empty. So he could've had Slater lying in wait for you. A guy like Everett loves to play with his prey. He tortured his victims. I saw all that shit in the news. He liked to become their nightmares before he killed them." His hand slowly lowered. "We both know what your nightmare is, sweetheart."

Fire.

"Ahem." From Lynn again. "Can't help but notice, that's the second time you have called her sweetheart. But here I thought the two of you just encountered each other again last night."

"Wrong," Beau replied.

"Oh?" And Campbell sprang for the attack. "So you admit that you did encounter each other before—"

"I called her sweetheart four times, not two. You should both pay better attention. Don't get details wrong.

Details matter. They can be the devil, but they matter." He swung for the door. "Let's speed things along, shall we? Avalon isn't currently dating anyone. There's no angry ex who would want to hurt her. She doesn't usually tell her exes about her past. Fire makes for terrible after-sex talk."

Avalon rose.

"She has a very small circle of friends. They're super protective of her. She doesn't trust easily, so it is very hard to gain access to that coveted inner circle." He was almost at the door. "Her enemies are the killers she talks to in jail. Killers who get off on having a beautiful woman so close as they tell her every sick piece of their crimes. Those are the ones we need to focus on. Those bastards, and, of course, *him*." Beau was right in front of the door.

Is he leaving me?

"Him?" Lynn asked.

Beau glanced over his shoulder. But his eyes didn't go to the detective. Instead, his dark gaze went unerringly to Avalon. "You've been hunting him, haven't you?"

She couldn't pull in a deep enough breath.

"Oh, sweetheart..." Now his eyes did flicker—only briefly—toward Lynn. "Time number five," he murmured. Then his eyes were back on Avalon. "Digging up the past can cause it to bite you—or burn you, in this case—right in the ass. But you knew that, didn't you? And you still took the risk."

"*Him?*" Campbell demanded. "Wait, you are not seriously suggesting that—that what? That the man who burned her house when she was a teenager set the fire again last night? That's—that's—"

"One option, yes." Beau opened the door. "I'll be sure and investigate that option. Don't you worry. And I have plenty of flunkies, uh, I mean friends, who can help me out." He stepped over the threshold.

He's leaving me.

Was she just going to let him walk away? "Beau!"

His broad back tensed. "I have a limo waiting outside for you. You'll find your fresh clothes and plenty of toiletry items in a new suitcase in that limo. When you're done here, the limo will take you wherever you want to go. The driver is also a fully trained bodyguard, so you will be protected."

"I..." Avalon stopped. *I want to go with you.* But she couldn't do that. She couldn't just leave the cops.

Could she?

He walked out.

And all the light in the room seemed to get a little dimmer. Avalon realized that she was staring after him. She whipped her head toward the detectives.

Campbell was still glaring at the doorway. But Lynn was watching Avalon.

Lynn nodded. "You invited him home with you last night."

"I..." *Didn't. He followed me.*

"Wasn't sure I believed the story when I first read the report from the uniforms, but after seeing the two of you together, now I do." Lynn dipped her head toward Avalon. "A word of advice?"

She had locked her feet to the floor so she didn't run after Beau. What in the hell was that about?

"The dangerous ones often have a certain appeal. But you have to remember, we call them *dangerous* for a reason."

Avalon lifted her chin. "I know how to handle dangerous individuals. I've been doing it my whole adult life."

"Sure, but, remember that anyone can be caught off-guard. Maybe it's by a dangerous individual who waits in a darkened bedroom for you."

Like Slater had done.

"Or maybe it's by a dangerous individual who slips past your guard because he might just have the sexiest smile you've ever seen."

Campbell coughed.

Lynn rolled her eyes. "Whatever. I'm a cop, not dead."

Anger hummed in Avalon's blood. "Beau isn't a threat to me." And was she actually feeling a lick of jealousy? Because Lynn had noticed Beau's smile? *I definitely should have gotten coffee this morning.*

"Not a threat? Ha! Keep telling yourself that," Campbell muttered.

He isn't. But he is a threat to whoever set that fire last night. Her gaze darted to the clock on the left wall. "Let's finish up these questions. I have a limo waiting and places to be." And a hero to go track down.

Because Beau was not going to leave her with the cops while he conducted the hunt on his own. Oh, hell, no.

And she'd been able to tell by the look in his eyes that he absolutely, one hundred percent planned to hunt. Beau was going after the arsonist. She intended to be with him every step of the way.

* * *

AVALON BURST out of the police station as if the fires of hell were chasing her. The detectives had questioned her again and again, and most of their questions had focused on Beau. Dammit, if they wanted to know so much about him, why not just *interrogate* Beau? But, oh, no, they'd just let him waltz right out of the place.

She'd lost too much time.

She bounded down the steps and went straight for the promised limo. A big, tall, muscled male in a gray shirt and holey jeans lounged near the side of the long, black ride. When he saw her coming, he just casually reached out and opened the door.

"Took you long enough," he announced with a sigh. "I was starting to get damn bored. Not like I love just hanging out in front of police stations."

"Well, hello to you, too," she returned without missing a beat. "Look, I really need to speak with Beau, immediately." She stopped in front of him. Looked up. He was nearly as tall as Beau. "I'm betting you know exactly where your boss is right now."

"Oh, I have a few ideas." His hair was a darker, dirtier blond than Beau's. But that faint drawl was very, very similar. "Hop in."

She hesitated.

His soft laughter drifted to her. "Do you *see* any other limos waiting out here? Because I don't. I am your ride. Beau told you I'd be here. He told you to get inside when you were done chatting it up with the cops. He said you could trust me."

Nope. "He never said I could trust you."

"Well, that shit is just hurtful." One hand went fleetingly to his heart. "When it comes to you, I've been doing bodyguard duty for ages, and he should be more grateful...and trusting." A long sigh. "Whatever. We gonna keep standing here all day or are you getting in the limo?"

She looked back at the police station.

"Surprise, surprise," the driver-slash-bodyguard softly exclaimed. "They followed you. Bet they wanted to see me."

She looked back at him in time to catch him waving to the watching detectives. "Love the new haircut, Lynn. Looks freakishly hot on you."

"Who are you?" Avalon breathed.

"Consider me your hero's brother from another mother. Now, I'm starting to sweat. In or out?"

She glanced at the open door. "In." Avalon dove inside.

And she pretty much landed right in Beau's lap.

"Took you long enough," he said.

The door closed behind her.

Chapter Seven

She'd fallen onto him. A delicious sprawl. One hand was on his chest. And the other was temptingly close to his eager dick.

Alas, to Beau's extreme disappointment, she snatched her hand away from his dick. She also straightened up and jumped to the seat that was a good foot away. But she panted and her gaze darted to his crotch—to the dick that saluted her through the rough fabric of his jeans.

"Sorry about that. When a gorgeous woman jumps in my lap, it happens. Damn thing has a mind of its own." And when the woman in question was Avalon—well, his dick couldn't help but surge to instant attention.

"I didn't *jump*. I didn't even realize you were waiting inside the car!"

The limo started moving. "Have a nice chat with the cops?" Beau glanced at his watch. Not that he needed to check it again. He'd been glaring at the thing while he waited on her. "Took you long enough to finish up."

"They had a million questions."

"About me."

"Yes. And about us."

He waited. He also enjoyed the sight of her. There was just something about Avalon that always made him feel... better. Yes, she was beautiful. Undeniably. To him, the most beautiful woman he'd ever seen. But there was *more*. A hard-to-define more that had the tension easing from his shoulders and the twists disappearing from his gut.

Avalon.

She tucked a lock of hair behind her ear. The graceful movement of her hand had his stare shifting to her wrist. And to the tattoo that circled her skin. A dark band, but he'd noticed the fleur-de-lis designs hidden in the darkness.

You could take the girl out of New Orleans...

But New Orleans would always linger on the woman.

"Is he your brother?" Avalon waved toward the front of the limo.

Ah. He'd figured she'd pounce on this particular topic. "I did hear him say those words."

"So he *is* your brother?"

"I believe he told you something about a brother relationship."

She heaved out a rather cute, frustrated grunt. "*He* didn't tell me his name."

"*He* can be an ass like that." True story. He could actually be an ass in many ways.

"*You* haven't told me his name, either."

Fine. "He goes by Royal most days."

"Goes by? As in...that's not his real name? Is it like a stage name? Are you about to tell me that guy is the lead singer in a band or something? Bodyguard and driver by day, rock star at night?"

Hardly, but, God, she made him want to smile. So he did. A real smile for her.

Her eyes fell to his smile. "Dammit, she was right. That smile is trouble."

He was looking at trouble. But, back to her question about the name. "Not a rock star." Royal would be horrified by the mere suggestion, so Beau made a mental note to repeat this conversation to him later. "Usually, he's a royal pain in my ass. So I figure it's a close enough name." That was all he'd say on the matter. Royal's secrets were his own. Beau had already been more than careful enough with his responses.

Her hands twisted in her lap.

He wanted to reach out and put his fingers over hers. For now, he controlled the impulse. "You keep letting those nails of yours bite into your palms, and you'll make yourself bleed."

They stopped twisting.

"It's one of your few tells." Did she realize it? "When you get scared, you sink your nails into your palms." Truly curious, he asked, "What makes you feel better? Making those fists and hiding them from everyone? Or do you like the little bite of pain?" Beau watched her for a response. He wasn't judging. Just asking. Because there had been something he didn't know about Avalon.

You learn a lot from a distance. You learn so much more being up close and personal.

"I'm not into pain." Instant.

"Too bad. With the right person, it can be just like pleasure."

"Stop." Her eyes flared.

"I'm not doing anything." Yes, he was. They both knew it.

"You're screwing with my head."

Guilty. Only seemed fair, though, since she'd been screwing with his from day one.

"I've got to ask, do you always bust into police stations like that?"

"No." Another true story. "Often, I bust out of them."

Her breath heaved. "Can you be serious with me?"

"Oh, sweetheart, I am dead serious with you."

She peered through the window. "Where are we even going?"

"Back to the hotel. You spent all your time digging up my secrets, and you didn't get any rest. You can't function on zero sleep. Not if we're going to catch the bastard out there." A pause. "That *is* why you came rushing after me, isn't it? Because you want to team up with my awesome self to catch the bad guy? And not because, oh, you realize that you were desperate for me and wanted to fuck me here and now?"

"Beau."

He settled more comfortably against the lush seat. His legs spread in front of him. His dick kept right on saluting her. "Yes?"

"I asked you to be serious. If this...this partnership is going to work—"

"I am serious. I'm taking you back to the hotel. And we'll catch the bad guy. We'll get right to work on that *after* you've had some rest."

Her lips pressed together. Her gaze swept over him.

Beau refused to tense even though he knew...*Here it comes.* When he'd first entered the interrogation room and gone to her, she'd flinched when he reached out to touch her. Fear had flickered in her gaze. Beau was definitely not a fan of fear in her eyes. In the interrogation room, she hadn't stared at him like he was her hero.

Too bad.

She'd stared at him as if she'd realized he was something very, very different.

"How do I know I'm not looking straight at the bad guy?" Avalon did not pull the punch. The question was soft and husky and her gaze held his as—this time—she waited to see if he had a tell.

Once more, he smiled at her. "I am a bad guy. Don't forget that. I am an absolute bastard to a whole lot of people in this world." His smile slowly died away. "But not to you."

"Because I'm your *good* thing?"

Yes.

"Bad guys stalk people."

"Good guys protect people."

She shot toward him. He didn't expect that move. Was totally unprepared when she suddenly bolted at him. His hands flew out and curled around her hips. She jabbed a finger into his chest. Meanwhile, Royal was an asshat up front and hit some pothole—hard—and she tumbled to the side. They wound up tangled and half-lounging on one of the seats. She was on top. One leg between his. He was...

I want her so much.

Her gaze dropped to his mouth. Lingered. But then she gave a hard, negative shake of her head.

One of his hands tightened on her.

"Why would I need protecting?" Avalon asked.

Why would she—he threw back his head and laughed. The laughter seemed to echo in the limo. It was deep and heavy, and she stopped poking him in the chest.

"That's not funny."

"It's fucking hilarious," he managed to say. But she was pulling back, again, and that was just annoying. He sat up, mostly, and so did she. Only he kept one hand on the curve of her hip, and she remained in the seat right next to him. Her leg brushed his. Her tempting scent wrapped around him. He inhaled. Deeply. "Is that lavender?" He hadn't quite been sure of the scent before.

"You tell me. You're the one who seems to know every single detail of my life."

"Not every detail." He'd put his cards on the table. In his own way. "How about we play a game?"

She turned to look through the window. "I'm not in the mood for a game. I want answers."

"And you'll get them." He'd give them in his own way. "I'll tell you one thing I know about you. You tell me one thing you discovered about me while you were busy doing your research on that precious, precious laptop. If what you say about me is true, I'll admit it. If what you say is false... then I'll kiss you."

"*What?*"

"Same rules apply to you, of course. If I say something that is true, you will admit it. If I say something false, then you kiss me."

"I...why would I play this crazy game?"

Why, indeed? "Because you want me." Did she realize that counted as the first true thing he knew about her? "And I want you." He'd just thrown in a bonus—a true thing about himself. "There's a basic, primitive attraction between us." Not so true. The attraction went far beyond anything basic. Primitive, though? Hell, yes. "When we kissed last night, I got more turned on from the touch of your mouth against mine than I have seeing the most expensive strip shows in Vegas."

Her brows shot up. Then immediately beetled down over her gorgeous green eyes. "You spend a lot of time at strip shows?"

He actually owned a few places in Vegas, but not the point. Avalon hadn't asked about his diversified businesses. "I'm not interested in watching random women strip, but if you feel the urge to ever put on a show, know that you will have my complete attention."

She swallowed.

"I want you more than I've wanted any other woman." Truth. Bold. Flat. Done.

Her lips parted. She didn't speak.

"The game has started, by the way." A prompt because she was just staring at him. "I'm not lying about the desire I feel for you, so there will be no kiss yet."

"I do not understand your game."

Yeah, well, it was a bullshit game so...fair enough. "Tell me what you think you know about me. If it's a true statement, I'll own up to it. If it's not, I'll kiss you." She'd been nervous. Sinking her nails into her palms. Watching him with faint traces of fear that he hated. The game was BS. Total spur of the moment. A way to distract her.

But also...a way to let her know that some of the crazy shit she'd discovered about him wasn't true. *I'm not a monster.*

And, bonus, he might get to kiss her a few times. Win, win.

Avalon pulled in a deep breath. He knew she was about to step into the deep end. "You have been the suspect in multiple murders."

He didn't move. "That was certainly easy enough intel to discover. What did it take? One whole five-second search on the internet?" He clicked his tongue. "Disappointed, that is what I am. I expected questions more hard-hitting from the hotshot crime writer."

"You have never been found guilty of a murder charge."

"I believe it was Detective Cuntingham—sorry, my bad, Detective *Cunningham* who pointed out that it is hard to make some things stick."

"*Have you killed before?*"

"No."

Her gaze fell to his mouth.

"Have you?" he asked her.

"Of course, not!"

"That's adorable. Such a fast and emphatic denial. But you of all people should know that we can be pushed to take drastic actions. In the wrong circumstances, we can all be killers."

Her long lashes flickered.

The limo slowed. He didn't bother glancing out of the window. They weren't at their destination, not yet.

Her breath shuddered out. She licked her lips and said, "You were the man who left Everett Thomas for the cops to find."

His expression didn't alter. *Well, well. Jumped right to that, did you?* He wondered if her first question had been designed to throw him off so she could go in for the kill. So to speak.

"You were the one who knocked him out *and* cuffed him." Her hands pressed to the front of her jeans. Then her fingers curled into little fists.

Her tell.

"And you put the red bow on him when you left him as a gift for the cops," Avalon finished.

Silence.

The limo picked up speed again.

His right hand rose. Moved slowly toward her. When his fingers curved under her jaw, she didn't flinch away. Not this time. He leaned in so his mouth was just inches from hers. When she exhaled, he pulled in her breath. Beau wanted to devour her. "You said something that wasn't true about me." They'd gone over the rules. At least twice. "Now you have to pay for that with a kiss." He was going to—

Her head shot forward those last few, precious inches. Her mouth crashed onto his. His lips were open, so were hers, and Beau didn't hold back on the leash of his control. His tongue thrust into her mouth, he took every bit of her sweetness, and he damn well wanted more. *I want everything.*

He'd watched over her for years. Carefully staying away. Always remaining in the shadows. Never touching what he wanted most. At first, he'd started watching her when she'd been a teen. Just to make sure she was safe. That the fucking arsonist didn't come back. *Because he wasn't caught. He was still hunting. He couldn't be allowed to hurt Avalon.*

Her family had brought in protection for her. The best guards money could buy. With them at her side, he'd been sure she was safe.

So he'd...

Left.

Leaving her felt fucking wrong. He'd tried to move the hell on.

His hands curled around her hips. He pulled her onto his lap. She straddled him. Rocked against the aching dick that shoved so hungrily toward her.

When her parents had died, he'd gone back to her. Pulled, helplessly. He'd watched from a distance at the funeral. He'd felt her pain like a physical blow. She'd stayed at the cemetery long after everyone else left. The rain had begun to fall on her.

He'd remained. Made sure she got home safely.

She moaned into his mouth. He swallowed the sound and wanted more.

She'd lived in dangerous cities. He'd needed to make sure the wrong people stayed away from her. He had.

And when she'd started talking to killers...

Word needed to be spread that no one would hurt her. When she'd been walking straight into hell, the right—and wrong—people had needed to know that she belonged to the devil. You did not fuck with what the devil claimed.

His mouth tore from hers. He began to kiss a path down her throat. Her nails bit into his upper arms. And he decided that he'd like a little bite, too. His mouth pressed harder to her throat. He licked. Nipped.

She gasped and pressed closer. Her nipples were tight, aroused, and they thrust against his chest. He wanted them in his mouth. He wanted to spread her out in the limo and drive deep into her. He'd wanted her for so long and, he'd *tried*, damn well *tried* to stay away.

But she'd come to him. Entered his bar. Walked up to him.

Kissed him.

And sealed both their fates. Because once you had a taste of the thing you craved most, you couldn't go back. Couldn't put the damn genie back in the bottle and pretend that you hadn't just been granted your most desperate, desired wish.

Everything had changed when she kissed him. And now...

No. Not like this. Not our first time.

His wandering hands had been sliding down toward her delectable ass. He yanked them back up to her hips. Curled tightly around her waist and lifted her up and off him. Deliberately, Beau put her back in the seat next to him.

Her lips were red and swollen from his mouth. Her eyes were wide. Dazed.

He could still taste her.

And he'd left the faintest red mark on her throat. His fingers slid over that mark, then fell away. *Mine.*

"I...think I understand how this works now." Her voice. Husky. Sexy as sin. She sucked in her lower lip, then let it go. "When I make a statement that isn't true about you, you kiss me to say it's a lie." A slow exhale. "You're saying you did not knock out Everett and cuff him and—"

He kissed her. Fast. Deep. "You're delicious." He backed off. How long would his razor-thin control hold with her? "And you've got the basic point of the game." Only it didn't feel like a game.

It felt like a dangerous temptation. Because he didn't want to stop with just a kiss. He also didn't want his first time with her to be in the back of a moving limo with Royal up front. The jerk would never let him hear the end of it if Beau pulled a move like that, not with Avalon.

She was too important.

"Okay. Okay." Her hands fisted.

No, he couldn't have that, either. He reached for her left hand. Opened it up. Smoothed his fingers over the faint marks left there by her short nails. "You don't need to be afraid of me. I would never hurt you." The last thing on his agenda. No, correction, hurting her was not on his agenda at all. It never would be. But protecting her? That would be the first item. Always.

Her head dipped as she looked down at their hands. Her hair slid forward and hid her face from him. "I should be scared of you."

His other hand moved under her chin. He lifted her

head up. And pressed a soft kiss to her lips. "Everyone else can be afraid, but not you." *Never you.*

"You're...the stories said you're a crime boss."

He couldn't look away from her. "Stories say lots of things."

"You...you aren't kissing me. That means the stories are true."

He'd been many things over the years. "All my businesses are legitimate now." *Now* being a very important word. "And I haven't killed anyone." *Yet.* He kept the *yet* to himself. If he got his hands on the bastard who'd left her to die in that house of flames all of those years ago, Beau knew exactly what he would do.

And no one would ever find that body. It was, after all, much harder to convict when there was no body. Juries tended to have a whole lot more reasonable doubt when there was no dead person.

"You're going to hunt the man who was driving the car last night, aren't you?"

"Damn straight, I am." Beau had plans for him, too. And if the bastard turned out to be the same pyro who'd torched her home in New Orleans so long ago...

Hell will feel like a blessing after what I do to you.

"You're doing all of this because you feel...protective of me."

Sure, they could go with that. It was true enough. When it came to her, his protective instincts were one hundred percent in overdrive. "I don't like bastards who hurt or try to hurt women. Really pisses me off." The limo slowed again. This time, he knew they were nearing her hotel.

"Do you think the man last night was the same one who torched my home all of those years ago?"

The game wasn't played with questions. It was played with statements. And he'd already been on the receiving end. His turn to see what she would reveal. "You go face to face with killers all the time because you have a darkness inside of you. One I suspect was born on a long-ago night when the heat of New Orleans got too intense for us both."

Once more, she pressed her lips together. Not a denial. Or those lips would be on him.

The limo came to a full stop. Would Royal have the sense to give them more time? Probably not. But Beau needed more. "You talk to killers because you are trying to understand your own dark urges."

"I don't have dark urges."

His hand rose. His index finger tapped against his lips. *Come on, sweetheart. You know what I get.*

Her chin lifted and she...darted forward to press a very chaste kiss to his lips. *Liar, liar.*

But it was a start. "You want vengeance, sweetheart," he rumbled. "Nothing wrong with that. Some prick burns my home down around me, and you can absolutely bet I'd want to incinerate his world."

No kisses. No lies.

He heard the faint click of her swallow. "No one could ever find the arsonist in New Orleans. The cops looked. I looked. And the arsons stopped. When the fires stopped, the investigations stopped."

No fires equaled a cold case. Luckily, he knew some people who freaking lived for cold cases. And he would get to those people, soon enough. "You and I both know the pyro could have—probably *had*—just moved on from the city. Maybe he got spooked when you escaped the fire. Maybe he needed you to burn and you didn't." Now his hands were the ones to clench. "So he fled. But guys like him don't stop. I bet you learned that in all your chats with killers."

"They have to be made to stop." Her gaze darted to the side of the limo. To the window. "Compulsions usually drive them, and you can't ignore a compulsion. Not when it is too strong."

The limo had parked right in front of the hotel's gleaming, double doors. Royal stood just beyond the window. Waiting, not interrupting. For the moment. He was also keeping the eager doormen back.

"I tried to find crimes that I could connect to him in other places," Avalon revealed. "But most arsons—it's *hard* to prove arson in the first case! Lots of arsons go undetected. And the US is huge. There are so many fires each year."

"Over a million."

A flash of surprise came and went on her face. What? Did she truly think he hadn't investigated, too?

"One of the things I learned early on in my career is that serial killers have signatures. This guy? He killed three people in New Orleans. It was never just about the fire. It was about death, too. He moved that bookcase in front of my door. He trapped me in my room."

Beau remembered shoving the bookcase. That heavy, freaking bookcase.

"I didn't realize the window had been nailed shut. Not until you told me recently. I thought it was just stuck. It was an old house, after all. Historic. Things in old houses get stuck and warped all the time."

"I felt the nails."

Her lashes fluttered. "In order for the nails to be there, he had to be in my house before that night. It...it was the sound of the bookcase grinding over the floor that woke me, you see. I heard it. The sound scared me, and I woke up. No way in the world I would have missed him being in my room and nailing my window shut."

Beau had realized the same thing long ago. "It was a premeditated attack."

"It was personal. My bedroom. Me. He wanted me to die. Someone hated me so much that they trapped me in my room and wanted me to burn alive."

Some sadistic bastard will pay.

"I've been hunting him." Avalon's quiet confession. "But I can't find him."

"You won't stop until you do." Something he'd suspected about her for a long time.

"I won't stop."

Neither would he.

The limo door opened. "We're here," Royal announced. "Been here a while. But I was trying to give you time to, uh, finish up. If you needed to do that."

"Shut the door, Royal," he ordered. "We aren't finished."

"Good for you. Glad to see dreams are coming true. I'll just tell these assholes honking behind my ride to calm the hell down." Royal shut the door.

"Does he..." Avalon's voice lowered. "Does he think we're having sex?"

"Probably."

"I've *never* had sex in a limo."

"I know."

She jerked back. "Right. Because you know so much about me. Way too much, Beau. Scarily much."

"You hold back with your lovers, Avalon. You don't let people get close. You keep the secret part of yourself—that part with the wilder, darker urges—you keep her chained up."

No kiss. No lie.

"You don't have to do that with me." *You won't hold back with me.* "I can handle dark. And I excel at wild."

Her delicate nostrils flared.

He slowly extended a hand toward her. "Want to hunt with me? I have some resources that can prove invaluable."

She didn't take his hand. But she did look at it. With way too much focus. "The flunkies you mentioned before?"

"I do prefer the term friends." To be clear. "Our first order of business will be finding the jackass who was driving the car last night. Then we focus on your past."

"And what if the past is tied up in the present? What if the person is one and the same?"

Then they had only one hunt, not two. He kept his hand extended. "I think we'll find out everything we need to know. I also think you believe I can help you far more than the cops can."

No kiss. No lie.

But her hand reached for his. Her soft, silken fingers curled around his. "Aren't you going to say..." Avalon asked with a tilt of her head, "that our partnership will just be business? No sex? No ties?"

Hell, no, he wasn't saying that. What was he, an idiot? "Screw that shit. You want to have sex with me, then we'll fuck until you can't move."

Her mouth dropped open.

"And we'll still stop the bad guy." His fingers curled around hers. Not too tightly. He'd have to be careful never to hold her too tightly. If you held something too tightly, it might break. "I'm the best multitasker you'll ever meet."

A faint smile curled her lips. Her dimples almost winked at him. He wanted to see those dimples. He wanted to see a real, full smile spread across her face and light up her eyes. And, what Beau wanted…

He would get.

Sooner or later.

"Trust me," he urged her.

"If I do, will it prove to be a terrible mistake?"

"I've saved your life twice now." More than that. Unnecessary info. Overkill. "If you can't trust your hero, who can you trust?"

"I trust you." She nodded. Then leaned forward and kissed him.

A kiss.

Because her words were a lie.

* * *

THE SCENT of the river teased his nose. A pretty enough spot. Tourists certainly seemed to think so. But since it was the day and not the night, the bar known as LeBlanc's wasn't bursting at the seams.

In fact, it appeared dead empty.

Once upon a time, the building had been a warehouse. Then it had been abandoned when the business failed. The owner had gone to jail for some smuggling crime. Beau LeBlanc had come along. Stolen the place for a paltry sum, then set about reimagining the location.

A bar now, at least, on the ground level. The line to gain entrance would stretch down the road when darkness fell.

But darkness hadn't fallen, not yet.

He slipped toward the back of the building. He didn't see any security cameras. Probably because someone like Beau wouldn't want footage of certain individuals who visited him. Just in case, though, because maybe he was missing something, he tugged down the ski mask he'd brought along. Then he advanced toward the door and made short work of the lock. He had plenty of skills that had come in handy over the years. Lock picking had been something he'd mastered as a kid. It was necessary to be able to get in and out of locations very easily.

The door didn't even squeak when he opened it. An alarm began to beep. A damn inconvenience, but one that he could handle. And, moments later, he did handle it, just as he handled shutting off the sprinkler system.

Silence reigned again.

Behind the mask, he smiled. Beau would need a new alarm installed. *By the time I'm done, he'll need one hell of a lot more than just a new alarm.*

Then he turned and headed through the staff area. Past all of the boxes of booze. Some expensive. Some cheap as hell. Then he was behind the bar. The counter gleamed. His gaze swept the area. Chairs had been neatly stacked on top of the tables. All of the lights were off, but sunlight drifted through the windows and allowed him to see perfectly. Lots of gleaming, shining wood. Some cool bricks on the back wall. A nice enough place. But what he really liked...

His turned and focused on the items behind the bar. All of those wonderful whiskey bottles. After all, LeBlanc's was known to have some of the very best whiskey in town. His gloved hand reached up and curled around one bottle. Twenty years old, huh? He took off the top. Inhaled through the mask. Kentucky bourbon whiskey. Special reserve.

He bet it would burn like a beautiful bitch.

Whistling, he began to pour the whiskey along the bar's countertop. It splashed and flowed so wonderfully. He was going to—

"What the hell are you doing?" A voice barked.

He dropped the bottle. It shattered onto the floor.

A big, dark-haired bastard stood about ten feet away. He'd come in the front door. And he was lunging forward fast.

You can't stop me.

He reached into his pocket. Pulled out his gold lighter. The bastard couldn't see him smile behind the mask. But when those flames ignited, oh, but his smile sure stretched from ear to ear.

Chapter Eight

Avalon climbed out of the car. Royal waited a few feet away, and he glanced at her. Mirrored sunglasses hid his stare, but his lips had curled into a mocking smile. "Have fun?" he asked.

"Fuck off," she replied sweetly.

He laughed. "No wonder he's so obsessed with you."

"*Royal.*" A definite snap filled Beau's voice as he followed her out. "Do not poke the bear right the hell now."

Royal shrugged. "I was—"

A ringing cut through his words.

A ringing that came from Beau's phone. She looked back to see him pull it from his pocket, frown at the screen, then immediately shove the phone to his ear. "Look, Lane," Beau fired off, "not a good time. I'll call you right back."

"The new BFF," Royal explained.

She hadn't asked. But Royal's words had pulled her attention back to him.

"Don't worry. No one comes before you," Royal assured her with a faint smile still lingering on his lips. "But you should know the man has a serious tendency to pick up dangerous strays. Don't say you weren't warned."

Her eyes narrowed.

"*What?*" Beau blasted. "Fucking hell. Yes, yes, I am on my way. Dammit, he got *away?*" Rage now. Dark and seething.

Royal lost his smile. Even as his smile vanished, she was whirling to look back at Beau once more.

Beau's face had twisted into lines of absolute fury. Dangerous. Deadly. "Yes, the bar is damn important. I'll be there as fast as I can." Then, growling, "Thank you. But don't you dare get your ass burned for that place. Ophelia would murder me if you did." He shoved his phone back into his pocket. Locked his stare on Avalon, then ordered, "In the hotel, now." He waved toward one of the doormen. "Dominic, escort her up."

Wait, he knew the doorman by name? Apparently so, because the dark-haired guy instantly bounded forward with an "Absolutely, Mr. LeBlanc," response on his lips.

"Royal, we need to get to my bar, ASAP." Beau spun back for the limo.

She grabbed his arm. "What is happening? Who got away?"

"The SOB who just torched my bar."

Her heart seemed to drop straight to the pit of her stomach. "What?"

"Dominic, get her up to the room!"

Dominic crept closer. "If you'll just come with me, ma'am."

"Dominic, please go back to your post. I appreciate the offer, but I am not going anywhere with you." A crisp response from her. Then she lunged past Beau and jumped into the limo. "Royal, could you please haul ass? We need to get to Beau's bar. Now."

She saw Royal rush to the front of the limo.

Beau didn't get inside. He did lean low over the open door and glare at her. "Sweetheart, what in the hell do you think you're doing?"

"Going with you?" That should be obvious. "We literally just shook on our deal like five minutes ago." Why did this need an explanation? Fear and adrenaline pumped through her. "We both know this isn't random. My house was set on fire last night. Now your bar? *Come on.*" She leaned forward and snagged his wrist. "We are wasting time. The arsonist is getting away!"

Beau finally jumped into the limo. He yanked the door shut behind him. "The bastard already got away. Lane chose to save my bar and the sonofabitch fled." Fury vibrated in every word. Such raw rage. "We will find him."

She caught his hand. Curled her fingers around his fist. "Yes, we will."

* * *

THE LIMO PULLED TO A STOP. Beau was out of the door before Avalon believed that Royal had even fully braked the vehicle, and she was right on his tail. She hopped out and saw the fire truck with its lights blazing. Firefighters were already inside LeBlanc's. The scent of smoke hung heavily in the air.

"Can't go inside!" A bark from one of the firefighters as he hurried past. He was in full gear, decked from head to toe, and his mask bounced over his head as he rushed toward the entrance of the bar.

"I can go any damn place I want," Beau snapped back.

Uh...

A man stalked toward them. Tall. Dark hair. Soot covered his white dress shirt and khaki dress pants. As she stared at him, recognition flooded through her. "OhmyGod."

"Hardly." A mocking response from a nearby Royal. "More like the devil. But you do you, sunshine." He saluted her. "I'm going to search the periphery." Then he vanished.

But the devil closed in. The devil, otherwise known as... "Lane Lawson," Avalon said.

He'd stopped right next to Beau. Actually, he'd stopped right in front of Beau. The better to block Beau's path and stop him from running into the bar. Yet at her words, Lane's head turned toward her. His head inclined. "Avalon Trahan."

She blinked. "I've been trying to get an interview with you for weeks."

"And I've been denying that interview. Will continue to do so, by the way."

Lane Lawson.

The man had been a suspected serial killer. One of the best profilers in the business had gotten Lane locked away—only later, that same profiler had worked to prove Lane's innocence. And when Lane's sister had been threatened, Lane had broken out of jail to help her.

Eventually, Lane had been cleared of all charges. The real killer had been identified. And Lane had become a celebrity in true crime circles.

And he was standing in front of Beau. Covered in ash.

This was Beau's new BFF? The one Royal had mentioned when he was warning her about Beau's tendency to pick up dangerous strays?

Lane's gaze had returned to Beau. Grimly, he said, "The

prick was right behind your bar counter. He disabled your main alarm, but I guess he didn't know about the secondary system you had in place. I was upstairs in the PI office," Lane added. "I got the alert on my phone and rushed down as fast as I could."

"I got the alert, too," Beau muttered. "But I was... distracted and didn't realize it at the time."

She'd been the distraction. Good thing she wasn't the blushing type.

"I entered your place," Lane told Beau. "He was pouring your freaking twenty-five-hundred-dollar whiskey on the counter."

"Sonofabitch."

"You know how I love that shit."

Beau nodded grimly. "Me, too."

"The prick had on a mask. Black gloves. When he saw me, he dropped the bottle and lit up the bar." At his sides, Lane's hands fisted and released. Fisted and released. "The fire separated us. He ducked back through the service door, and I could have either rushed out and chased after him, or...dammit, man, I know how much the place means to you. Another few minutes, and with all that alcohol, LeBlanc's would have been *gone*."

Beau grabbed his arms. "You don't take risks like this. Next time, *let it burn*."

A shake of Lane's head. "No."

"*Yes!*" A yell that came from behind Avalon. She spun around and saw a gorgeous woman with black hair glaring daggers at both Lane and Beau as she jogged toward them.

Beau let go of Lane. The woman closed in. She marched right up to Lane. Elbowed Beau out of her way. "You put out this fire? You did this?"

Lane shrugged.

"With all the alcohol in that joint, you saw the fire raging and you stopped to—what? Grab a fire extinguisher? To save the day?" Her voice rose more with each word.

"Pretty much, yeah." His hands fisted. Released.

The woman threw herself against Lane. Held him tightly. His arms immediately flew up to curl around her. "You don't ever take a risk like that again," she ordered. "Didn't you hear what Beau said? Seriously, try taking advice from him. *Don't do it. Not ever again.*" A tremor shook her body. "You think a man is taking care of a little paperwork. You stop to pick him up some lunch because you're amazing like that. Then you get to the parking lot and see a giant fire truck and hear that *he* put out the fire." She tilted back her head and glared up at Lane. "I hate heroes. They suck ass."

Lane's lips twitched. "You love me, so you can't hate all heroes."

She hugged him tighter. "I swear, I thought I was getting the bad guy. You misled me."

"Your office is upstairs, baby," he murmured. "No way was I letting it burn."

"*Our* office." Her quick correction. "And someone had better start giving me answers. *Now*." Another squeeze against Lane, then she let him go. Well, she technically grabbed his right arm, locked it around her shoulders, and then threaded her fingers with his as she cuddled close to his side and faced off against Beau and Avalon. Her eyes swept first to Beau—he was glaring at the bar—then to Avalon. Recognition filled her furious stare a moment before she nodded. "You." Directed at Avalon. "Start talking. I like full sentences and lots of description."

"I..." Where was she supposed to begin?

Police sirens shrieked.

Avalon jumped. "Beau saved my life when I was a teen—"

"Not ancient history," the woman cut in crisply. "We all know that part. Why is Beau's bar smoking *now?*"

They *all* knew about her past? Avalon filed away that important detail. She parted her lips to respond—

"Because some soon-to-be-dead dick set her home on fire last night." Beau's gaze was still on the door of his bar. "And I think he's trying to send me a message. Stay away or your world will burn." His gaze whipped to the dark-haired woman. "I don't take well to threats."

"No." The woman's hair slid over her shoulder. "You're cool like that."

"My world will *not* burn." He stalked to Avalon. His eyes glittered as he glared down at her. "Nothing is going to scare me off. I can't be threatened."

But she was scared as she stared up at him. Her hand rose and curled around his right shoulder. "I don't want you hurt." He'd already been hurt enough, for her.

"Fuck pain. It's just part of life."

The woman cleared her throat. "It can also be part of death so...yeah. Let's not fuck it. Let's avoid it at all costs."

A muscle flexed along Beau's jaw. "That's Ophelia," he told Avalon. "She's the best PI you will ever meet."

"Ohmygosh, stop," Ophelia murmured. "You'll make me blush." A brief pause. "I was kidding. Do go on. I am amazing." She stepped away from Lane and advanced to Beau's side as she studied Avalon. "So you're the one."

Behind her, Lane sighed. "This is going to shift from bad to worse."

Ophelia's assessing gaze swept over Avalon, but her response was directed at Lane. "Doesn't it always? Except in our case, of course. Because once you teamed up with me, love of my life, things in your world went from nightmarish to heavenly."

Avalon's temples were throbbing. She let go of her grip on Beau's shoulder.

She caught the fleeting smile that curved Lane's lips as he dipped his head toward Ophelia.

"He's my partner," Ophelia explained. "In life. In business. In everything. And seeing as how I take it ever-so-personally that someone just tried to burn down my PI office—"

Beau's growl cut through her words. "I think the guy was trying to burn down *my* bar."

"Yes, but my office is on top of your bar so now I'm extra pissy and thoroughly invested in the case."

Beau frowned at her. "Like you weren't invested before?"

"I was. It's personal now."

Beau nodded. That muscle flexed again along his killer jaw. "Damn straight, it's personal. It will be even more personal when I dump the prick's body in the river."

Ophelia's eyes widened. She threw a fast glance toward the cops who'd gathered and the firefighters who rushed around the scene. "Seriously! Stop it! We've talked about this before." Her voice had lowered to an angry whisper. "We don't announce to cops what we will do with the bodies of the bad guys. How many times do I have to go over this with you?"

Avalon rubbed her temple. "This isn't a joke." She backed away from them. "His bar could have burned to the ground. A man was killed last night. I was attacked." Another step back.

Ophelia's head tilted. Lane closed in and looked extra grim. Beau's eyes kept glittering.

"I'm shaking apart on the inside and you all—" Avalon darted a glance at each one of them. "You're being so flippant. Joking about dead bodies. This is real. We have to find the arsonist and stop him before he hurts someone else."

"My humor isn't for everyone." Ophelia's stare never wavered. "Believe me when I say that I'm on your side. In fact, Beau had us working your case for the last few weeks."

For the last few weeks.

Her heartbeat pounded faster. "Excuse me?"

"Lane and I have been digging and trying to find patterns. We do believe the original arsonist left Louisiana after the attack on you failed all of those years ago. We've discovered more arson-murder crimes that we believe were his work."

A dull roaring filled Avalon's ears. "You're been working my case? For weeks?"

"It's what Beau hired us to do. Didn't he tell you?" Ophelia asked. A little furrow appeared between her delicate brows. Her full lips—painted a bold red—pulled down with a hint of dismay.

"I just talked to Beau for the first time in years... yesterday. No, day before yesterday?" She rubbed her temple harder in an effort to dull the throb. Everything had been happening at a fast and terrifying speed. "How could I have known about what he'd done weeks ago?"

Ophelia slanted Beau a glance. "How, indeed."

Beau looked back at his bar. Automatically, Avalon followed his stare and saw the figure of a firefighter advancing toward them. The firefighter removed his mask and helmet to reveal a sweat-soaked face.

Tan skin. Late twenties, maybe early thirties. Sweat plastered his dark hair to his forehead. "Scene is currently contained." His stare swept them. Landed on Beau. "You're Beau LeBlanc."

Beau nodded.

"I'm Lieutenant Wesley Vaughn. Been to your place a few times. LeBlanc's was always a great spot to unwind." A quick grin came and went on his face. "Very glad to report that the fire seems to be out for now. We had some rekindling when we first arrived on scene, but we took care of it. Additional rekindling—a reflash—is always a risk in a situation like this one, and with all of that liquor in such close proximity, we are gonna want to be extra cautious." He grimaced. "I've told the crew we need to move the liquor to a safe location. No way do I like having all that booze close with the threat of another reflash hanging over our heads."

"Uh, yeah." Ophelia waved her hand. "For those of us who are not fire professionals, when you toss out words like rekindling and reflashing—you're talking about the fire starting again? That happens? It can just flare to life?"

A grim nod. "Heat and embers remain. Fire can easily reignite. We're often recalled to scenes because we have to fight the same fire again."

"Great." Ophelia's hand dropped back to her side. "Just great."

"It's not great, ma'am," he responded, voice very serious and his expression earnest. "It's actually a very dangerous situation. Both for me and my fellow firefighters and for any civilians who might be close by." A low whistle escaped him. "When you have a fire in a bar like this—a place with so much accelerant just waiting to burn—you have yourself one extremely volatile situation."

None of what he was saying reassured Avalon in any way.

"When can I go inside?" Beau asked.

"No time soon, I'm afraid. It's going to be an arson scene. An investigator will need to come out and the cops..." He motioned toward them by lifting the helmet he still clutched in their direction. "They're gonna have plenty of questions. You'll have water and smoke damage in the interior. I'll warn you now—your place will be closed for a while."

"I'll reopen." Absolute certainty from Beau.

"Figured as much. I'll look forward to it happening." Wesley's attention shifted to Lane. "What you did was brave. But it was also dangerous. With that much alcohol and the fire raging..." His voice trailed off. "I don't like digging bodies out of the ashes. Or what's left of bodies. Next time, just get out and call for help once you're clear. Buildings can be replaced, but people can't." Someone called his name, and he turned away.

But even as he turned away, the cops began to close in. Not just uniforms, either. Avalon recognized two familiar faces. Detectives Lynn Baker and Campbell Cunningham had arrived on the scene. Their eyes were already on Beau.

"Those two have the look of hunters closing in on prey," Ophelia muttered. "Someone want to clue them in to the fact that Beau is the victim here? And by someone—I mean I'm volunteering."

"It's okay," Beau told her quietly. "I can handle them."

And the detectives were right there, so the handling had to begin immediately.

Chapter Nine

"Two fires within twenty-four hours." Campbell shook his head as he came to a stop near Beau. "What are the odds of that?"

"Pretty damn high when you're being targeted by a freak arsonist," Beau returned without missing a beat. "Oh, and to save you some time, let me just go ahead and tell you that I was with Avalon when LeBlanc's was being torched."

He'd been kissing her. She'd been kissing him. Definitely *with* her.

"The prick broke into my bar. He would have burned the place to the ground, but my friend stopped him." Beau motioned toward Lane.

Campbell fired a glance at Lane. "I am well acquainted with your *friend*."

Lane raised one brow. "The perp you're after is approximately six-foot-two. Looked around one hundred eighty pounds. Fit. Strong. Caucasian." He lifted his hand. Tapped his inner wrist. "He wore gloves and a ski mask but when he was pouring Beau's very fine whiskey on the countertop, I caught a glimpse of the skin right here."

"And Beau will have him on video." A shark's smile from Ophelia. "He recently added new video surveillance equipment to the outside of the bar. No way we didn't get our guy on the footage." She pulled out her phone. "You can't see the cameras unless you know where to look. They're too well hidden. But they do the job." She tapped her phone's screen. Hummed a little. Then she flipped the phone around.

Avalon leaned forward. She stopped breathing when she saw the figure. He already had on his mask as he approached the rear door. He walked with intent. Never hesitated.

Ophelia kept staring at the screen. "Damn. That is fast work on the lock. This guy is no amateur when it comes to the B&E scene."

In the video, he'd already gained entrance. Fast was an understatement.

"We'll need that video," Lynn announced.

Avalon's gaze tracked back to the front of the bar. More firefighters had spilled out. She saw Wesley talking to a uniformed cop. Wesley looked back at the bar's entrance. He stepped toward it.

"Absolutely," Ophelia's smooth reply to Lynn. "And we'll need complete cooperation with the police as we conduct our own investigation and—"

Fire shot from the windows of LeBlanc's. A loud blast filled the air. Glass shattered. Voices rose in screams. Heat seemed to lance over Avalon's skin. Her eyes were on Wesley as he fell to the ground.

And LeBlance's *burned.*

A fire that was raging wild and hard. Avalon opened her mouth to scream, and she felt hard arms curl around her stomach. She was yanked back against a powerful body.

"Fuck that!" Beau's snarl. "We're out of here, now."

Wesley was on his feet. Shouting orders. The firefighters leapt into action. One of them grabbed the end of a long hose and began shooting water at the building.

"Rekindling, my ass," Lane snapped. "What is happening? That felt like a freaking bomb blast!"

A blast—a full-on inferno—*that* was happening. LeBlanc's was burning right in front of her horrified eyes.

And Beau was hauling her away from the scene.

"Beau!" Avalon twisted and squirmed in his grasp.

He just tightened his hold. "You heard the lieutenant. People can't be replaced. You can't be. Nothing can replace you."

He was at the limo. Royal had the door open. When in the world had Royal reappeared?

Beau dropped her into the limo. She started to shoot right back out. But Beau caged her with his hands on either side of her body. "He's here."

She knew it.

The fire kept raging behind Beau.

"I think he planned for me to see the place go up. The sonofabitch. He wanted me to watch it burn. Maybe he'd even set up explosives somewhere inside. Hell, I don't know. But I *felt* that blast. There had to be more than what Lane saw. The place is a fucking trap. He got me here. He got *you* here." Beau shook his head. "You're leaving. Now."

"I'm *in* this! Dammit, we talked about a partnership—"

He kissed her. A furious, hungry, desperate kiss. Then, against her lips, he vowed, "My world will not burn."

"Beau—"

He backed away. Left her in the limo. "Get her to safety," he told Royal.

Behind Beau, she could see the thick, gray smoke rising in the air. And the flames. There was no missing them.

More sirens wailed.

His world *was* burning. Because of her. "I'm sorry," she whispered.

He slammed the door. A moment later, the limo pulled forward. She peered through the window and watched as Beau walked toward the blaze. A firefighter appeared to shove him back. The firefighter wore a mask and helmet, so she couldn't see anything about his features.

Water sprayed at the blaze.

Then the limo turned a corner, and she couldn't see Beau or his bar any longer. She lurched toward the front of the limo. Her fingers shoved at the small button that would lower the divider that separated her from the driver. With a little whir of sound, the tinted glass slid down.

"Hello, Avalon." Royal was as cool as you please. As if they weren't fleeing a fire that had detonated like a bomb.

"Beau has been investigating my old arson case. He had those people with him—Lane and Ophelia—they are helping him. They have been working on my case for weeks."

"That doesn't sound like a question."

"It wasn't. And, for the record, your response didn't sound like a denial."

"It wasn't."

"So he *has* been working on my case."

"The man just can't give up some things."

Her breath hitched. "He's been watching me."

"I think Beau prefers the term 'protecting' you. Less stalkery."

"Am I supposed to be afraid of him or grateful to him?" How in the world was she supposed to feel about Beau?

Royal turned the vehicle to the right. "I don't know. Do you see a giant red flag waving in your direction? Or, oh, my bad, could it be giant red *flames* waving toward you? Have you noticed those?"

She leaned closer to the small window that she'd created between them. "He's your brother."

"And my boss. And my friend. And the guy I'd bleed for in an instant." He pulled the car to a stop and angled back to look at her. "I really don't fucking like it when people set his bar on fire. Beau cared about that bar. The things that Beau cares about? They matter to me. *I don't like LeBlanc's burning.*"

She wet her lips. "I don't like it, either. I also don't like being put on the sidelines. Beau and I literally just made a deal to work together."

Royal sent her a sad smile. "Oh, Avalon. You have so much to learn about him." He inclined his head toward her. "First thing, he isn't putting you on the sidelines. He's protecting you. He's lost too much in his life. You are the one thing he can't afford to have taken away."

"You...act like he...he has me. We just got in each other's lives again—"

He quirked a brow. "Really? That's what we're going with? Try that story with someone who doesn't know what the two of you were busy doing in the back of the limo."

"His bar is burning because of me."

"No, the bar is burning because of some twisted prick with an addiction to fire. And the prick is screwing with the wrong man. He'll learn from his mistake soon enough. As for you, you have a choice, Avalon. And it's a choice you are going to have to make very, very quickly."

She swore she could still smell the smoke. "I don't know what you're talking about."

His fingers tapped against the steering wheel. "Sure, you do. You know what Beau is. You know what he's been doing."

Watching. Protecting?

"And you know you can either walk the hell away. *Run* away."

She waited. Only there was nothing else. "Uh, you get when you say that there is a *choice,* you actually have to give the second option."

"Why? You know it. You knew the first option before I voiced it."

Her eyes narrowed.

"Run," he repeated. "That's option one. As for option two...Well, you can run or—"

"Or stay with Beau," she finished.

He sent her a tight smile. "Not about staying. It's about what happens if you stay. Just what do you think will happen if you stay with Beau? You think he's gonna remain in the shadows of your life now? Gonna keep his hands off the way he's done for so long? Gonna be content just knowing you're safe?"

She didn't think she wanted his hands off her. They felt far too good *on* her body. And maybe that was part of the problem.

She also didn't think that was something Royal needed to know. "Beau wants me to trust him."

"Um." His fingers tapped against the wheel in a faster rhythm. "Tell me your choice. You staying? Am I taking you back to the hotel? Or you want me to drop you off at the airport so you can run like hell?"

"I'm not running." Not from Beau.

"Thought that would be the choice. Call me psychic." He checked the road and drove forward. "By the way, for what it's worth, I trust Beau with my life. Figure I should, since if it wasn't for him, I'd be dead."

Her arms curled around her stomach. "I know exactly what that's like." *Without Beau, I'd be dead, too.*

* * *

As if he would have left without accomplishing his goal. Oh, hell, no.

The firefighters battled the blaze. There had been so much chaos at the scene. They hadn't even noticed when he'd slipped back inside.

Beau was watching his precious bar burn.

Sure, the firefighters were working hard, but they weren't gonna stop this fire anytime soon. The point had been proven.

I can destroy what you value. And all you can do is stand there and watch the flames.

It was hard not to let his grin spread. Beau had fisted his hands at his sides. His buddy—the dark-haired prick to Beau's right—kept trying to pull him from the scene.

But Beau was watching the fire. He seemed locked in place.

It was a beautiful show. Some people didn't get that. They didn't understand just how spellbinding the flames could be. They twisted and they danced, and they consumed.

And if you don't stay out of my way, then next time, it will consume you. But Beau wasn't the one he wanted. The man should consider himself lucky to get this warning.

Avalon Trahan was the target. The flames had been hungry for her—they'd wanted her for years. Beau should have let her burn the first time.

Or the second.

The third time will be the charm. Wasn't that the old saying? The third time would definitely be his lucky charm.

The flames danced, and they burned, and they destroyed.

Chapter Ten

His hand curled around the door to her bedroom. He turned the knob and soundlessly pushed open the door.

Avalon lay sprawled in the king-sized bed. The suite had a separate bedroom for her. She was safe there. Protected.

He needed her protected.

So many hours had passed since the blaze at his bar. Beau had watched the firefighters try to salvage LeBlanc's. The smoke had turned to dark black as it drifted in the air. He'd been told to leave the scene. Over and over.

He hadn't left. He'd watched the fire.

Now he watched her.

Small, delicate. Her body nestled beneath the covers. Her hair fanned out over the white pillowcase. He'd only wanted to watch over her. After her parents died, she'd been alone. Unprotected. Too vulnerable. Beau had wanted her to be safe.

He'd never intended to actually enter her life or talk to her. He'd just wanted to know she was protected.

Yeah, he got that he had a problem. More like an *obsession*.

But he wouldn't have approached her. He would have stayed in the shadows. And, once he'd unmasked the arsonist who'd tried to kill her back in New Orleans, once she'd been free of the past...*once the bastard was in the ground*...Beau would finally have ended his watch.

Plans had changed. Everything had changed.

She'd come into his bar. She'd kissed him.

And then a fire had destroyed the life he'd been building.

"Are you going to stand in the shadows much longer or are you going to walk toward the bed?" Her voice drifted from the bed and had him jerking. "Just curious. Trying to decide if I should go back to sleep or if you're about to kiss me like you can't live without me."

Light spilled in behind him, enough light so that she could see his outline easily. He narrowed his eyes and realized that—

Avalon is staring straight at me.

"I was..." He stopped. His voice had come out too gruff. Deep. Growly. And what exactly had he been doing? *I was just thinking that I'd kill to keep you safe. No hesitation. And that I do want you more than I want my next breath.* Nope. Couldn't say shit that would freak her out too much. "I just...just was checking on you."

"Because that's what you do. You check on me."

He didn't speak.

"Apparently, a lot."

Guilty.

"It's like that Chinese proverb, isn't it?" Her voice drifted to him. "You saved my life, so now you think you're responsible for it—for me."

No, that wasn't what he thought. He'd explained things to her. Tried to, anyway.

"You made me leave LeBlanc's." Avalon sat up in bed and pulled the sheet with her. "That was not an appropriate partner thing to do. We'd literally just had a conversation about working together. Then, bam, you throw me in the back of a car."

He stepped to the side. The light poured through the doorway and fell on her. That was when he realized she wasn't wearing anything beneath the sheet. Her shoulders were smooth. No shirt to cover her. No bra. No nightgown.

Silken skin.

"There was nothing there but fire." His voice came out too rough yet again.

"Wrong. You were there."

He took a step toward her. Caught himself. "The fire is contained. Wesley said the bar area itself was a total loss. Some of the offices and storage space on the first floor were salvaged. And Ophelia's office on the second floor was mostly safe."

Mostly.

Good thing she has backups of all her files at home.

"You're safe," Avalon said. "That's what matters."

What mattered to him was that she was safe.

And he took another step toward the bed.

"You can't do this," Avalon told him flatly. "You *can't.*"

His body tightened as he took the rejection. *You knew coming to her was a mistake. She doesn't want to be with someone like you.* "I was—"

"You can't say we're partners in one breath, and then shove me in a limo and tell me to get my ass gone in another. That's not how things will work between us. I'm not a sitting-on-the-sidelines type of person, and I told your buddy Royal that very fact."

Yes, Royal had mentioned that detail to him. He'd also mentioned... "Royal told you to run from me."

One hand held the sheet to her breasts. "I recall he mentioned that was an option, yes."

"You aren't running."

"No. Actually, I was sleeping until about, oh, three minutes ago when a man slipped into my bedroom. Had a crazy moment when I first opened my eyes. I was terrified that someone was coming to hurt me."

Shit. "I'm sorry—"

"Then I realized it was you. What's really crazy is that *every* time I get scared, or even worried or...hell, whenever I'm uncertain, I feel like you're there."

I am.

"I feel like you're watching me or coming to get me and that everything is going to be fine. That I'm not alone." She eased to the side of the bed. Swung her legs over. Kept the sheet. Most of the sheet. But he could see her trim calves. Her sexy thighs. "I think you're a big red flag, Beau."

He nodded. "Probably."

Avalon rose. She pulled the sheet with her, and as she stalked toward him, the sheet trailed her like a wedding train. "I also think you're a man I want very, very badly."

"You attracted to red flags?"

"I'm attracted to you." She stopped right in front of him. "Ground rules."

Nope. "I'm not a rule type of guy. You must have me confused with someone else."

"There is no confusing you with anyone else. An utter impossibility."

"Now you're just trying to stroke my ego."

Her head tilted to the side. Her hair fell over her shoulder. "I plan to stroke quite a few things."

Sweet hell. "Careful." A rasp of warning. "You don't want to push me too far."

"Why? You gonna let that control break and do something other than *watch me?*"

Yes.

"Ground rules," she repeated. "No sidelining. If things get dangerous around us, you don't get to go all controlling and try to tell me what to do. I only agreed to leave today because I had things to handle."

It was hard to concentrate on what *things* she might have done when she was only partially wrapped in a sheet as she stood in front of him. "I'm not going to let you be in danger." That was his one rule. "You're protected. That isn't up for debate."

"You're an arrogant asshole, you know that?"

"It's been mentioned a time or twenty."

"Have you ever thought that, oh, I don't know...*maybe I don't want you in danger, either?*"

He frowned. "Why would you care about what happens to me?"

"Because I just do!" Her delicate nostrils flared. "You don't face danger alone. I don't face danger alone. There. Done. Got it?"

He got that there was always a way around rules. You just broke them. And he also got that he needed to circle back to something she'd said before. "What things?"

"Excuse me?"

One tug, and he could have the sheet on the floor. *Do. Not. Tug.* "What things did you have to do today?"

"Oh, I had to handle the little matter of arranging a

meeting with a convicted serial killer. You were suspicious of Everett Thomas. So was I. You wanted to get in the room with him. So did I. I pulled strings, and voilà, we'll be meeting him tomorrow morning at nine a.m."

His back teeth pressed together.

"I have connections. I used them. I couldn't very well battle the blaze at your bar." One hand rose and curled around his forearm. "Though I wish I could have. I'm very, very sorry about LeBlanc's."

Her touch had warmth pouring through him. Her eyes shined with her sympathy. She actually seemed to care about him.

What the hell was he supposed to do with that?

But then she pulled her hand back. "Ground rule one. No sidelining. I don't sideline you. You don't sideline me. We don't ditch each other in dangerous situations."

"I was protecting you."

"What if I wanted to protect you?"

He frowned at her. Who the hell would want to protect him?

"You have a tendency to see fires and rush right into them." A shake of her head. "Super bad trait. Without me at your side to hold you back, who knows what madness you could face?"

"I rush in..." He stopped. It wasn't like he rushed into every dangerous situation he saw. And as for the fire, he'd rushed in once before. He'd done that—

"For me?"

He stared into her eyes.

"You rushed into the fire all those years ago in order to save me. You didn't know who I was. You rushed in because you heard someone screaming for help. You can play the villain all you want with the rest of the world, but villains don't run toward the fire when they hear a scream. Villains stand back, and they enjoy the blaze. Heroes are the ones who help."

He'd never enjoyed the flames. "That's too one-dimensional. Sometimes, you can save one person and then turn around and cut the heart out of someone else."

Her eyes widened. "Ground rule two. No heart cutting. You don't cut out my heart, and I won't cut out yours."

His eyes narrowed. As if he would ever do anything to physically hurt her. He'd sooner cut off his own hand.

She let the sheet fall. "In other words, don't break my heart, and I won't break yours."

He should have told her that he didn't have a heart. That it couldn't possibly be broken. And if his every single fantasy wasn't currently naked in front of him, he would have mentioned that very important point.

But...

Avalon.

Was.

Naked.

And he wanted to touch. And taste. And devour.

And most of all...*take*.

"When Royal gave me the choice, I didn't want to go to the airport. I didn't want to leave you. Mostly because...I just want you." A slow exhale from her. "But you're standing there, not saying anything, and I'm basically baring my body and my soul, and you are *not* responding the way I'd hoped. So please, say something. Do something."

He did. He touched. His hands curled around her shoulders, and he hauled her closer.

He tasted. His mouth locked onto hers.

He devoured. Beau could not get enough of her taste.

Avalon was driving him absolutely insane, and he wanted more and more and more.

He would take. Take until she screamed his name.

His hands slid down her body. Down the curve of her back. Down to the lush ass that he wanted. And he pulled her against him even harder. Silken skin. Naked woman.

Avalon.

He could fuck her right where they stood. Ditch his jeans. Thrust into her. Pound hard and fast and deep. He could—

Make it good for her. No, better than good. Has to be great. He needed to drive her wild. Past the point of no return. He needed her begging and moaning and drowning in the pleasure he gave her. Only then could he let go of his control. Only. Then.

He lifted her up.

She gasped against his mouth, and her arms curled around his neck. A few steps and they were at the bed. Carefully, tenderly, he lowered her onto the mattress. He kissed her lightly, then pulled away. His gaze traced over her body. Every perfect inch.

"Uh, Beau? Not to tell you your business, but this works way better if you're in the bed with—" Avalon stopped. Swallowed.

For a moment, what could have been fear flashed in her beautiful, green eyes as her gaze met his.

He knew she'd seen the true depth of his need for her. He was freaking holding on to his control by a thread. "Don't worry, I got this."

A nod. "I, yes..."

He caught one of her ankles. Then the other. Slowly, he maneuvered her to the edge of the bed. Then he spread her legs wide.

"Beau?"

He touched. His fingers dipped into the heat between her legs. Two fingers. Thrusting. Stretching. Her hips surged up against him as he pulled the fingers out and then raked them over her clit.

"Beau!"

He tasted. He bent and put his mouth on her core. That hot, tight center. His tongue thrust into her, and when her hips bucked again, he locked his hands around them and held her in place as he—

Devoured.

His tongue thrust and he tasted heaven and he wanted to eat her right up. So he did. He licked. Sucked. Kissed. Stroked. Worked her clit over and over again and her feverish pants and moans drove him on. He was merciless. So focused and hungry for her that he could not, would not stop until she came.

And she did.

She shrieked and climaxed against his mouth. Her hands fisted in his hair. Not to pull him away but to hold him closer. He lapped her up as she came for him.

Then...

He eased back. Her breasts heaved as she stared up at him.

"That—that was—"

Without taking his eyes from her, Beau stripped. He paused long enough to pull a condom from his wallet. He rolled it onto his dick.

She still sprawled at the edge of the bed. Her legs were still open. Her sex glistening for him.

He hauled her a little closer to the edge of the bed. Still standing, he positioned her, and he *took*. Beau drove as deep into her as he could go. And that was when his control snapped. Nothing had ever felt so good. Nothing could feel as good as Avalon. Tight. Hot. Wet. Driving him to the brink of sanity and beyond. His fingers bit into her waist. Her legs wrapped around his hips. She surged against him even as he pounded into her. The rhythm was too fast. Too hard. Her body was too perfect. He could not get in her deep enough.

His mouth took hers. A wild, voracious kiss. His hips kept driving against her.

Not enough.

So he hauled her off the bed.

She gasped into his mouth.

He whirled. Pinned her against the wall. Then with his hold on her waist, he lifted her up and down. Up and down. Up and—

"*Beau!*" Avalon tore her mouth away and yelled his name even as her hands flew out. Something thudded onto the floor. He didn't stop to look and see what it was.

He was too busy coming inside of her. A deep, endless wave of pleasure poured from him as he held her. Not just taking. Not any longer.

Claiming.

And he knew that he was well and truly fucked.

* * *

BEAU HAD GONE BACK to her. At the very first opportunity. Gone rushing back to the hotel where he knew Avalon hid.

Apparently, Beau had not learned a lesson from the fire that had wrecked his bar. Instead of kicking Avalon from his life, he seemed determined to run back to her.

Like a moth to the flame.

From the darkness, he smiled.

He'd always really liked that comparison. Some things were just drawn to the fire. Even though, in the end, the fire would consume them.

A beautiful tragedy.

That would be Avalon's life. And death.

A beautiful tragedy. Because that was exactly what she deserved.

Chapter Eleven

"Dammit. I meant to do that in the bed."

Her breath heaved in and out. Her heartbeat pounded so hard that Avalon could feel it shaking her body. Sweat slickened her skin. And she was pretty sure she'd just left claw marks on Beau.

His head lifted. The room was mostly in shadows. Darkness. Some light spilled through the open doorway. At one point, Avalon vaguely remembered knocking over a lamp. She also remembered coming. Hard.

At least two times.

Maybe three.

And by *hard,* it hadn't been some nice pop of release. It had been an orgasm that blasted through every cell of her body and left her quaking and shaking with aftershocks of pleasure. Left her wanting to say...*More, more, more please. So much more.*

Instead, she was trying to transform her still heaving pants into normal breaths and trying to make sense of what Beau had just said. Something about the bed?

"First time shouldn't have been against a wall," he muttered.

Her legs were still around him. Maybe she should let them fall? But, nope, he was moving her now. Carrying her back to the bed. And pulling out of her.

Dammit.

He covered her with a sheet. Then went to the bathroom to ditch the condom, and the condom ditching was important. His brief exit also allowed her to finally get control of her ragged breathing and racing heartbeat. *Holy crap. That was the best sex of my life.* Hands down. Not even close. More like...*Leaving everything else in the dust, that's how great it was. In the dust. No comparison.*

And he was back.

"I should apologize." He stood by the side of the bed. All naked and sexy and with muscles bulging. And speaking of bulging, his dick was fully erect. Again. Already. Wow.

"No...apology necessary." She sat up. Did she sound normal? Or still way too breathless? "Who apologizes for mind-blowing orgasms?"

He reached out. His fingers skimmed over one nipple.

She hissed at the stab of pleasure.

"I wanted to explore all of you," he said.

"Please, help yourself." Like she was going to stop this ride anytime soon. Uh, no.

He sat on the edge of the bed. One hand pushed against the mattress on her left side. The other pushed down just past her right hip. Beau leaned over her. All intense and dark and brooding. "I need more condoms."

"Ch-check the nightstand drawer. I...may have taken the liberty of getting a box from the gift shop earlier." Another item on her to-do list.

He tensed.

"I knew I wanted you," she said, voice soft. Husky. Sensual? She would have never, ever described her voice as sensual until that moment. But she totally sounded like she was trying to seduce him again. Because she was.

"You didn't run."

Back to that, was he? "No way I'm running."

"Even if you find out things about me that scare you?"

Her hand lifted and pressed to his cheek. "I did my research on you."

"A few hours on a computer isn't going to tell you what you need to know."

Definitely not. Because the stuff on the computer had hardly been reassuring. Her hand trailed down his cheek. Down...to his right shoulder. There was still only a little light spilling into the bedroom, so she couldn't see the scars clearly. But she could feel them. Twisting marks left from the burns on the front of his shoulder and then curling around to the back.

"Avalon..."

She leaned forward. Her lips skimmed lightly over the old wounds. "I'm not scared of you." She'd been looking for him, for years. He didn't get that, did he?

And while she'd been looking...

He'd been watching over her.

Avalon had thought she was alone. But he'd still been there. And he wanted to find the man who'd taught her to fear years ago.

She pressed another kiss to one of his scars.

"Sweetheart, don't."

"I hate that you hurt." A flash of a younger Beau filled her head. The handsome boy in the hospital bed. Battered.

But with the most amazing eyes she'd ever seen in her life. So determined and dark.

"It doesn't hurt anymore. Promise."

Another kiss. "I can't ever forget that night," she confessed against his skin. "Sometimes when I try to sleep, I still wake up screaming for you. In my nightmares, we're going through the window, and I'm afraid that we won't survive."

His hand slid down and curled under her chin. He tipped her head back. His lips took hers. Carefully. Tenderly. "You think that you're the only one with nightmares?"

Her hand fluttered lightly across his scars.

"I wake up, and I can swear that I hear *your* screams," he told her gruffly. "You're in the fire, and I can't get to you."

"You *did* get to me."

"Some sick sonofabitch is after you again." Anger. "I am going to stop him."

"We are." Her vow. Because the sick sonofabitch wasn't just after her. He'd targeted Beau, too.

Beau kissed her again. Harder. More need. Lust. Less care.

She didn't need care. She wanted passion and pleasure. The heat they created together, not the memory of a fire that wanted to destroy them. Her hands shoved against the sheet so she could get it out of her way. Then she was straddling him. Her legs curled around him, and the head of his cock thrust toward her. It would be so easy to take that head inside.

"Condom," he growled.

"Drawer," she growled back even as she began to kiss his neck. His body was taut and so powerful against hers.

She felt him stretch and knew he was snagging another condom.

Her mouth kept feathering over him. Her hips rocked against his cock. Then her fingers trailed down to grab his heavy dick. Long. Hard. Thick.

She stroked him. Pumped. And wanted to taste him.

But...

He'd lifted her up. Off him. Yanked on the condom and had her spread beneath him on the bed.

In basically a blink of time.

Avalon peered up at him. "You, ah, move fast."

"I should go slow with you."

Not exactly what she'd meant.

"But I can't. It's like I haven't already had you once." His hands had slammed into the mattress beside her. "I need in you again."

She wanted him in. By all means, *go in.*

His cock pushed against her opening.

"Consider this your invitation." She arched against him.

He slammed deep. And there was no more talking. Because he'd been right—it was like they hadn't just had sex. Like pleasure hadn't just rocked Avalon to her core. Her body was just as hungry and aching. She was just as desperate as before. A cry broke from her lips as he filled her, and there was no more control. She arched and twisted. They heaved together.

He caught her legs and lifted them over his powerful shoulders so that he could plunge in even deeper. She started to scream as the pleasure built, but his mouth swooped over hers, and he drank in the sound.

One of his hands had flown down between their bodies. He relentlessly thrummed her clit. Over and over as he thrust in and out. The bed slammed into the wall, and

Avalon came so hard that she thought she might actually pass out.

"Fucking...*perfect. I feel you squeezing me as you come.*" His guttural snarl. And then he was coming, too. She felt the surge of his hips. Her eyes opened to see his shadowy form above her. Powerful. Dark.

"Finally..." Another hard thrust into her. "*Mine.*"

* * *

HE HAD NOT BEEN in control.

He had *not* played that cool.

More like, he'd been so desperate for her he'd fucked her up against a wall. *The first time. The second time I actually used the bed.* Even as he'd basically shouted that she was his.

But maybe she'd missed that part.

Darkness filled the room. Beau was pretty sure that Avalon slept beside him. Her breathing was nice and easy. Her silken body relaxed against his.

All he wanted to do was keep holding her. And never let go. But his freaking phone was vibrating with a text. He could hear the damn thing, and if he didn't get his ass out of that bed soon, Avalon would hear the sound, too. She needed her rest.

And, he, hell, had it been twenty-four hours since he'd slept? Longer? He needed to crash, too. Especially since he now had an early morning appointment with a serial killer.

Without waking her, he slipped from bed. Naked, he scooped up his discarded jeans—and the phone that vibrated in the back pocket. He eased from the bedroom, shut the door behind him, and made his way into the sitting area connected to the suite. His gaze darted to the piano.

Had she played it that day? She was really wonderful on the piano. He'd caught one of her recitals before she went to college.

His phone vibrated again.

Setting his back teeth, he hauled the phone out and swiped his finger over the screen. "Royal," Beau muttered as he put the device to his ear. "What is it?" *Better not be another fire.*

"You want more guards on her tonight? The first shift is ending, and I'm checking in for new orders."

He looked back toward the closed bedroom door. Extra guards had been at the hotel that day. Royal had stayed close, too. *Because I thought the bastard might target her.* "I'm staying the night. No one will get in her suite without going through me." He'd like to see the bastard try.

A pause. Then, "Got to ask, is reality better than your fantasies?"

"Don't be an asshole."

"I'll take that as a resounding yes."

"Take it as me telling you to fuck off."

Rough laughter. "Love you, too, man." But the laughter faded. "I'm sorry about the bar. I know how much the place meant to you."

"Just wood and booze. It can be replaced." He turned to look at the bedroom door. *She can't.*

"Guessing our extracurriculars are on hold for a bit?" A delicate cough from Royal, when he was far from a delicate man. "Until we put this particular bastard in the ground, that is."

Beau's spine straightened. "We're gonna slap a fucking red bow around him and bury him so deep that no one will ever find him."

Another pause. This one lasted a bit longer than the first. "You don't...quite sound like yourself."

Because he'd just admitted to planning to kill someone? "You know me best, Royal." Better than so many others.

Even though the story they gave the world was a lie.

Royal wasn't his brother—not by blood. Not a half-brother. Not even a stepbrother.

"I think you know," Beau continued grimly, "that I sound *exactly* like who I really am."

"Be careful."

Ah, was that real worry in Royal's voice? Sounded that way. "I know what I'm doing."

"I don't think you do." Gruff. "I think you're pissed as hell right now. I think this prick wants you that way. When rage blinds you, you can make mistakes. He is playing with you. Pushing all your buttons."

"No, he's fucking burning what belongs to me. Not pushing a damn button." His gaze remained on the closed bedroom door. "No one fucks with what's mine."

And the door opened. Soundlessly. It swung open.

Avalon stood there, with the sheet wrapped around her. Her tousled hair fell over her shoulders. Her eyes locked on him.

You touch what belongs to me, and I will annihilate you. "Got to go, Royal. We'll talk again soon. And, remember, no extracurriculars until I'm back at your side." He hung up the phone. Dropped it on a nearby table and walked to Avalon.

She yawned. Sleepy. Sexy. "What extracurriculars?"

"Community service work." He scooped her into his arms. "Royal just loves cleaning up this town. He's a Boy Scout like that."

Chapter Twelve

It wasn't Beau's first trip inside a maximum-security prison. Not his first, not his second. Hell, he really wasn't sure how many visits he'd paid.

The first time he'd ever stepped foot in one? *That* visit he distinctly recalled. He'd been eight years old. He'd come visiting with his mother because she wanted him to meet his father. The bastard hadn't given two shits about his scrawny kid, though. Tattoos had covered his father's arms. His fingers.

And tear drops had been carefully etched just beneath his cold, dark eyes.

Beau had told his mother that he never wanted to go back to that place.

And, yet, he had. Not to see his father. He'd never seen that man again. But, other times, he'd returned. To see other people. Sometimes, he'd gone to help. Sometimes, he'd gone to terrify.

Of course, the cops had even worked to get him locked up a few times.

Beau hated the sound of a cell door closing. He never wanted to be locked in a cage again.

The DA side-eyed him as Beau stood near the back wall in the room. Beau just sent him a wide grin determined to show none of the emotions rocketing through him. He knew that Douglas Baptiste was not happy to see him, and that was putting it very, very mildly. Understatement of the century. Not like Beau didn't remember the guy. Douglas had been an up-and-coming prosecutor when their paths had first crossed.

Douglas had wanted to send Beau away for murder.

Beau hadn't felt like being convicted of the crime. Especially because he hadn't been guilty. Had he beat the shit out of the guy when the prick got rough with one of his waitresses? Hell, yes. Done. Had Beau murdered the man? No, someone else had finished the job. A killer who had never been caught.

Luckily, Beau had been cleared. Thanks to Ophelia. The woman truly was one hell of a PI. And, now that she'd paired up with Lane Lawson, the two were pretty unstoppable. One of the reasons Beau had gotten them involved with Avalon's arson case weeks ago.

Long before she strolled into my club.

"Tell me again why he has to be here," Douglas muttered. He jerked on his tie. The blue and gray tie was wrinkled to hell and back because of his nervous jerks.

Two silent guards remained in position near the lone door in the room. The prisoner hadn't been brought in yet. But Everett Thomas was on his way.

"He's here because he's with me," Avalon replied. She sounded all casual and calm, but he knew she was just hiding her real emotions, too. He'd seen her nerves back at the hotel suite as she prepared for this nightmare of a meeting.

Douglas glowered.

Beau winked at him.

The glower got worse.

"You agreed to let him be here." A crisp reminder from Avalon. "You're aware there was an attack at my house—I *told* you about it yesterday during our very long phone conversation." Avalon did not look up from the papers in front of her. "Beau is acting as my bodyguard."

"Bodyguard," Beau repeated. "My eyes are on her." That was certainly true. He'd been watching that sweet ass of Avalon's for quite a while.

"Where I go, he goes," she continued after flickering a glance in Beau's direction. "And considering that one of our suspicions is that Everett Thomas might have ordered someone to torch my place, I needed to be here in order to interview him again."

Douglas stopped tugging on his tie and pointed at Beau. "Your place got torched, too. I heard all about it from some cops and an arson investigator. What's the theory, bodyguard? You going to tell me that you think Everett hired someone to torch LeBlanc's, too?"

He didn't respond.

Avalon did. "LeBlanc's was one of the bars that Everett specifically mentioned to me when I was here last. Perhaps he believes Beau is the one who, uh, wrapped him up for the police and Everett wanted some vengeance. Seeing his reaction to Beau's presence should be quite telling."

The DA took a step toward him. "Did you do it?" he demanded.

Beau let his eyes widen. "Do what?"

"Knock out Everett Thomas and leave him for the cops to find?"

"Why in the world would I do something like that?" *Because the prick needed to be stopped before he hurt someone else? Because Everett Thomas is a freak who should never see the light of day? Because the cops were going to let him slip through their fingers?* Beau shook his head. "Just doesn't seem like something that would interest me. I already have plenty of hobbies. Getting into the gift-wrapping business holds no appeal for me."

The door opened. The prisoner shuffled in. His wrists and his ankles were manacled. His gaze immediately went to Avalon as she sat with her back perfectly straight at the table.

A flash of hunger filled his eyes.

Oh, the hell, no. Beau stiffened.

A wide smile curved Everett's lips. That smile froze when his gaze drifted and landed on Beau.

Beau sent him a very grim smile of his own. "Hello, there, Slasher."

Everett swallowed. He also backed up a step and almost hit the guard who'd followed him inside. *Three guards in the room now.*

"What's happening here?" Everett's voice cracked in the middle of the question.

Douglas advanced toward him. "An additional Q&A session. We can certainly have your lawyer present, but the last time you spoke with Avalon, you waived—"

"*I only want to talk to her!*" His nostrils flared. The orange prison jumper made his pale skin look all the more garish under the light. "No one else." He lifted his cuffed hands—as much as they would lift because a thin chain connected the cuffs around his wrists to the manacles around his ankles—and he pointed toward Beau. "Not him! He needs to get the hell out!"

Beau kept his smile in place. He was not going anywhere.

"We're a package deal," Avalon informed Everett crisply. "Where I go, he goes. And vice versa. So if you want to have another chat with me, you'll do it with him watching."

Douglas moved to stand in front of Everett. The DA completely blocked the other man from Beau's line of sight. "There a reason you're afraid of Beau LeBlanc?" Douglas asked the prisoner.

Beau couldn't see Everett, but he could hear the man's ragged breathing.

Avalon turned her head. She peered at Beau. Quirked one brow. That little quirk clearly asked, *So, what's this about?*

He shrugged. How was he supposed to know why serial killers acted crazy? Wasn't that more her thing?

"You *obviously* know him, Everett," Douglas's voice held heavy suspicion. "How do you know Beau?"

"He came to my bar a few times," Beau responded as he kept his voice low. Almost lazy. He allowed his drawl to thicken a bit as he added, "Liked to have a good time at my place, didn't you? Everyone loves LeBlanc's. But, I'm afraid I've got some unfortunate news for you on that score. Some asshole torched my bar last night." He took a step to the side as he delivered that news. The better to see Everett's reaction.

And Everett—the prick—his eyes lit with delight. A flash that was quickly extinguished. But not quickly enough.

The sonofabitch knows something about the fire.

"I do hope no one was hurt," Everett murmured. "Fires. Never liked them much. Have you seen what they can do to a human body?" He shuffled forward a half-step. The manacles clanked. "The scars they leave behind on those who survive their kiss—those scars are hideous. Twisted. Red. So rough. Never to be smoothed away. Never to fade. The fire touches you, and it claims you." He dipped his head toward Douglas. "I will sit for the Q&A. After all, it would be horribly rude to leave. Especially when Avalon wants to write my story so badly."

One of the guards pulled out the chair that was opposite of Avalon. The guard secured Everett into the seat. Locked the chain that connected his bound hands and feet to a hook on the floor. Everett frowned briefly, but when the guard moved back, the furrow along his brow and the faint lines near his mouth smoothed away. "I knew you would be back," he told her with a pleased nod. "Decided to help me prove my innocence, didn't you? I certainly appreciate your assistance. With so many people on the outside calling me a monster, it's good to know that you believe in me."

She straightened the papers on the table. Then her hands dropped to her lap. Her hands fisted.

Sweetheart...

"I can't prove something that isn't possible, Everett. As I said at our last talk, I happen to believe you're guilty as sin. Add me to the list of individuals who think you're a monster."

Everett threw back his head and laughed. The sound seemed to grate as it echoed in the room.

Douglas strode closer to Avalon's side.

"I do love to talk about sin with you," Everett said. His gaze drifted over her. "Oh, the things I could do to you..."

Beau immediately surged forward. "*Watch it.*"

"Isn't that what *you* like to do?" Everett asked with a confused smile and a wide-eyed blink. "Watch...her?"

Oh, you sick prick. You want to play? Let's play, Slasher.

"I've been lonely in this hellhole." Everett's smile turned upside down. "Do you know they keep me in solitary? They do. For so many long, empty hours each day. I don't enjoy being alone. I like having...friends to talk with me."

Douglas crossed his arms over his chest. "The time in solitary was for your own protection. You do understand that many of the inmates here want to rip you apart?"

"Not everyone is a fan." A roll of one shoulder from Everett. "But some are."

Douglas peered at Everett as if the prisoner had lost his mind. "You tortured and stabbed multiple women. Dismembered them. You don't have fans. You have people who want to see you strapped to a table while a needle is plunged into you. The world can't wait for your execution date."

Everett's Adam's apple moved in a quick bob. "That can be appealed. Especially when my innocence is—"

"You're guilty." From Avalon. Cold and flat. Beau had the feeling she'd been studying her prey very carefully. Her hands were still beneath the table. From his position, he could see her small fists, but he didn't think anyone else could view them. Her spine was straight. Her shoulders squared. Her focus seemed to be entirely on the man in front of her. Avalon's profile showed no fear.

No emotion at all.

"Not only did you kill those women, but you've been playing more games, haven't you, Everett?"

She called him by his given name. Beau had

deliberately addressed him by the name the media had attached to the bastard.

Slasher. Just like a freak from the horror shows. Because he'd slashed his victims to pieces. Women who'd been about Avalon's height. Who'd had similar builds. Two blondes. Two redheads.

Those were just the victims that the authorities had confirmed. Beau was certain there were many, many more. He believed Avalon suspected the same thing.

But at Avalon's question, Everett blinked, as if confused.

"Which friends have you been talking to, Everett?" Avalon prompted quietly.

Everett darted a glance at Beau. Then he paled even more.

Beau was sure the prick had just seen the promise of death that waited for him. "The guards need to take you out for more walks in the yard," Beau murmured. "You're starting to look like a ghost, Everett." *I will damn well make you into a ghost.*

"Other inmates?" Avalon queried when Everett just sat in silence. "Or...since you have been in solitary, maybe it wasn't inmates. Maybe it was a guard. Have you been chatting with some friendly guards, Everett?"

Beau realized her repeated use of Everett's first name was deliberate. Maybe a way to disarm him?

Meanwhile Beau intended to keep calling him Slasher because that was exactly what the piece of shit was.

"Fans can come in all shapes and sizes," Everett finally told her. He shrugged. The chain clanked.

"Unfortunately, they can." Her hands remained beneath the table. "My home was recently torched. My home, then Beau's bar."

"Oh, no. That's just terrible to hear." But even as he said the words, Everett's tone was off. Because his tone held delight, not sympathy.

You sick sonofabitch.

"A man was waiting in my bedroom when I got home a few nights ago."

Everett leaned forward. Eager. Practically salivating. "Tell me everything."

It took all of Beau's self-control not to drive his fist into Everett's face. That stupid, pretty-boy face that had lured women to their death because he'd been smiling and flirting and had seemed so harmless.

Screw that. One punch, and Beau could break the guy's nose. His jaw. He could leave him in a puddle of blood on the floor. *I can make you scream. Just like you made those women scream.*

Avalon pulled in a slow breath. "He caught me in my bedroom. Grabbed me in a painful hold and told me that I was going to burn. I'd burn while I was alive."

Everett licked his lips. "He hurt you. I bet—I bet he hurt you—"

She leaned toward him.

Beau snapped his teeth together. *Do not get touching close. If that prick touches you, sweetheart, all bets are off. My fist will be in his face two seconds after he touches your skin.*

"I shoved my taser against his skin." Avalon paused barely a beat. "He pissed himself in front of me."

Everett jerked. His face scrunched in disgust.

Aw, was that not part of the story he'd wanted to hear?

"Then Beau appeared." A soft laugh slid from Avalon. "He had the guy begging for mercy one minute later."

Everett backed up against his seat. Fear flickered in his gaze. All traces of delight had vanished.

"The intruder—he was just a punk kid. But one who somehow had my alarm code. He got in, but we got *him.* And he was talking plenty by the time we were done with him. Telling us all about how he'd been hired to break in and scare me. That he was following orders."

Everett's breath rasped out.

Beau advanced a slow, deliberate step. He was so close to the table now.

Everett's gaze immediately snapped to him. "Get back! I-I don't like you so close!"

Why? Because I'm not some woman who is about seventy pounds lighter than you? Because you can't hurt me? Beau stared down at his prey and didn't back up so much as an inch. "You enjoy hurting women, don't you, Slasher?"

Everett pressed his lips together. But his eyes said...*yes.*

"Fire isn't your way, though. You like to slice your victims with your knives. Penetrate their bodies with the blades."

Avalon fired a quick glance his way, then snapped her head back toward Everett.

"That's why I know this meeting is a fucking waste of time," Beau added with a growl of disgust. "Because if you'd wanted to get at Avalon, you wouldn't have got some kid to use fire as a way to scare her. You would have wanted her skin sliced open." Another slow step forward. Now he was right at the table and towering over Everett. "You would have wanted a knife plunging into her again and again." *His* hands fisted.

He hated saying this shit. But Avalon had given him a script before this little meet and greet from hell. She'd seemed so certain of the way things needed to play out.

Avalon had been absolutely convinced they could break through Everett's control if they both just said and did certain things...*but I hate what I'm saying. And all I want to do is rip that bastard apart.*

"Told you already," Avalon grabbed her papers and shoved them into her briefcase. A few papers had been scattered on top of the table. Purely for show. Avalon setting her scene. "He doesn't have the power or reach to do something like that. Everett is helpless in here. He can't possibly be tied to any attack on me—"

"I know what happened to you, Avalon."

She stopped shoving in the papers. Her head lifted and she stared across the table at Everett. Her lower lip trembled. "Wh-what?"

The stutter was a good touch, Beau would give her that. *Or is it real? Is she scared?*

"Lost little girl..." A taunt from Everett. "Were you scared when the fire came and you couldn't get out?"

Beau started to raise his right fist.

Avalon gave a small, barely perceptible shake of her head.

"I bet you were terrified." Everett laughed. "Did *you* piss yourself back then? Trapped alone in that bedroom and just not strong enough to get out?" Once more, delight filled his stare. "What were you, fourteen? Fifteen? My first victim was around that age. So much fear when you're so young. She screamed. I bet you screamed, too."

Help me! Avalon had screamed.

"But you got out when you shouldn't have. The trap had been set. The fire lit. You were waiting to die. But a hero came to save the day. One who should have just stayed busy with his fucking Jag." Everett's neck inched forward, like a turtle's head coming from its shell. "There won't be anyone to save you this time."

Ice flooded through Beau's veins.

"*Are you threatening her?*" A sharp question from Douglas. He'd been avidly watching the byplay, but now he straightened to his full height. "You don't get to threaten—"

"I'm not going to touch her. I can't. I'm locked away inside this hellhole. Solitary. All alone. No friends." His head turned toward Beau. "You won't be there."

You can't kill him in front of the DA. "Guess you didn't hear the lady before. Where she goes, I go." And if that meant into the fire, *through* the fire, so freaking be it.

"Does your shoulder still hurt?" A tilt of Everett's head to the right. "I bet it does. The skin is all twisted and warped, isn't it? Because that's what I've been told the fire does. It reshapes you. Changes you. You become someone brand new when the fire takes you." His tongue snaked over his bottom lip. "Who did you become? A scrawny gang member turned into...what?"

He knows too much. "I became the man who is going to kick your ass." He lunged forward. Grabbed the bastard by the shoulders. Wrenched Everett up as far as those chains would allow. "*You were warned,*" he breathed, the words low enough for only Everett to hear.

All the color bleached from Everett's face. And there hadn't been much color to begin with.

But guards were shouting.

Douglas was barking commands.

Two of the guards went for Beau. They hauled him back and away from Everett even as the prisoner cried out, "*Assault!* You saw him! *Assault!* DA, you charge this man with assault!"

"Get LeBlanc's ass out, now!" Douglas demanded. "Sonofabitch!" He ran a hand over the top of his head.

The guards hauled Beau toward the door.

He looked back. Avalon still sat at the table. Spine still straight. Fisted hands in her lap. No emotion showed on her face.

Douglas was rushing after the guards. Two were taking him out. That left only one in the room with Avalon and Everett. The guard who'd trailed Everett into the room. *One guard.* Fuck that. "*Don't leave her alone!*" he bellowed.

Douglas froze. Glanced back.

Avalon had been whispering to Everett. And whatever she'd said...

"*Take me out!*" A wild yell from Everett. "Forget him—take me back to solitary! Get me out *now!* Get me *out* of here!"

The guards dropped their hold on Beau, and they grabbed Everett.

Chapter Thirteen

"THAT WAS A COMPLETE WASTE OF TIME." DOUGLAS slammed the door shut. He kept one hand on the frame and his back remained angled toward Avalon.

Her heart raced. Her palms were soaked with sweat. And she wanted to get the hell out of that room, that prison, but... "We learned quite a bit, actually."

"From that shit show? Seriously?" He straightened. Whirled. Glared at Beau. "Do you have any concept of what the word *control* means?"

Beau shrugged.

Avalon thought Beau had displayed admirable control. And incredible trust. When she'd told him how this scene needed to go down, he hadn't hesitated. Well, he had hesitated on one point...

No fucking way do I leave you alone with the guy.

She'd tried to tell him that she wouldn't be alone. At least one guard would remain with her, if her plan went correctly. She'd just wanted a moment to speak with Everett without others hearing her. She'd *needed* that moment.

And she'd gotten it.

While the guards and Douglas had been distracted by Beau, she'd whispered to Everett, *He's tying up loose ends. He killed that kid who was waiting in my room. Drove over him with a car. You know who he is. Do you think he'll let you live with that knowledge? Or do you think your friend will find a way to get to you?*

She'd seen terror take over Everett's expression. The killer hadn't been able to get away from her fast enough. "He knows who the arsonist is."

"Uh, how the hell would he know that?"

Her hand tightened around the handle of her briefcase. "Did you know that Everett Thomas was born and raised in New Orleans?" Her question was poised for Douglas, but her gaze darted to Beau.

No surprise showed on Beau's face. She'd come to realize that he had already done plenty of background work on the players in this drama. Interesting.

Something else that was scarily interesting? The details about Beau that Everett had just revealed. Details Avalon hadn't known. *What Jag? And Beau had been in a gang back then?*

How had Everett known those facts? Were they even facts or had he been spouting BS?

"Of course, I knew," Douglas fired even as her mind swirled.

Her question hadn't been for him, though, not really.

Douglas jerked his head down in a nod. "I've long suspected Everett may have claimed other vics in New Orleans. He left the city when he was around eighteen. Maybe nineteen. Things aren't one hundred percent clear. We do know he eventually moved to Atlanta. That's where authorities eventually found Virginia Long's body."

"I lived in New Orleans for a very long time, too," she

said. "Since his conviction, Everett Thomas has refused most interview requests, including those from some very powerful hitters in the industry. But he agreed to see me. I found that quite odd."

Douglas blinked.

"I could only conclude that Everett agreed because, for some reason, he wanted to see me."

"You're similar in appearance to his vics." Douglas tugged on his tie. "Thought that was enough to whet his interest. He'd been away from his prey for a while and was jonesing to see someone like you again."

A growl came from Beau. Predatory. Dangerous.

"Look, I don't like it, either! The guy is a freak, okay?" A rough expulsion of air from Douglas. "But I think—I know—there are more vics. Avalon is great with the killers."

No, I'm not.

"If she could get him to slip up and reveal info we could use to find more vics, then him drooling over her for a bit would be worth it." Douglas grimaced. "Avalon, you knew the score before you walked through the prison doors. The bodyguard—boyfriend—whatever he is—he may not like things, but you knew the game even before you started to play."

"Yes." She had. "I wanted to know who'd caught him." It certainly wasn't every day that a civilian captured a dangerous serial killer. Except...*Everett was the second killer who'd been gift wrapped.* Her gaze did not stray to Beau as she told Douglas, "In our first meeting, I could tell the way Everett watched me that he was curious about me. He *knew* all about my past." That had certainly just been confirmed. Everett *had* slipped up and revealed too much. *I believe he even knew about the bookshelf that had been moved in front of my door. I could open my door, but I couldn't move the bookshelf that blocked my path. I wasn't strong enough.* Everett had specifically referenced her not being strong enough to get out. Her heartbeat quickened. "I think he knew the man who set the fires in New Orleans when I was a teen."

But Douglas was clearly not on board. "That's a huge jump to make, Avalon. There's no reason to believe that Everett might have a connection to the arsonist just because the man happened to live in the same city!"

She had plenty of reason to believe that jump.

"He knows that I saved Avalon." Beau's voice.

That deep, dark voice slid through her.

"My name was always kept out of the media because I was a minor back then. Hell, I didn't even give my real full name to anyone at the hospital. I've always been good at lying."

Douglas twisted his tie.

"He knows that I have scars from the fire. How the hell does he know that?"

Douglas didn't have an answer.

Avalon had suspicions. She knew Beau had those same suspicions.

"The bastard knows all about me and about Avalon, and now," Beau's voice deepened even more, "I have to wonder if he came to my bar those times because he was watching *me*. He knew about my past. You heard the bastard. He was curious to see what the fire had made me. What I'd become."

Douglas squinted at him. "So, just what are you? Because Avalon assured me that you were playing on the side of the good guys right now."

Beau stared steadily back at him. "I'm always playing on Avalon's side."

"I want a list of every guard who has been given duty with Everett." Avalon's mind churned through possibilities. "We need to cross-reference those individuals with Slater Wade, the man who was killed outside of my home. There's going to be a link, I know it." Excitement and adrenaline pumped in her blood. "I think a guard is passing along info for Everett. We connect the dots, we find a phone record, we find an email...*something*, and we will have a real lead." It was happening. She knew it. Finally.

Douglas opened his mouth. Closed it. "You're not serious. You think a guard—*here*—is working with a convicted serial killer?"

She inhaled. "Yes." *Believe me, Douglas. Believe me and—*

"Fuck. You get that this is conjecture. Practically jack and shit, right? Not like I have enough to take to a judge or show any jury in the world right now."

This wasn't about a jury or a judge. Yet. This was about trying to find the link that would break open her past.

"The law works in certain ways. Steps have to be followed. Procedures."

"I'm just asking for the names of the guards who have access to him. The warden will give you that info. You don't need a warrant." She waited. *Come on, Douglas, come on.* "Just go talk to the man."

"Pretty sure you tried to prosecute me for less than jack and shit once upon a time," Beau recalled.

Douglas stabbed a hand in Beau's direction. "I had a roomful of witnesses who saw you fighting the dead man! You threatened his life!"

"I told the bastard if he ever raised a hand to a woman again, it would be the last mistake he made." A shrug from Beau. "And speaking of mistakes, not trusting Avalon right now will be *your* huge mistake. Go chat with your warden buddy. Get a list of names. Let's see if there's a connection to Slater Wade. What the hell do you have to lose?"

She could have kissed Beau right then.

When Douglas swore and stormed from the room...

He's doing it! He's getting us a list of the guards!

Avalon bounded toward Beau. She grabbed his shoulders and hauled him toward her. "You were perfect!" Avalon told him.

Then she kissed him.

* * *

"THIS ISN'T the way to solitary." Everett felt sweat slide down his back. Stupid fucking hot prison uniform. Stupid fucking meeting.

She doesn't know anything. I'm safe.

He'd kept his secrets for years. Kept his friend close.

She doesn't know.

But...

The kid was dead. Shit. Shit.

Didn't mean anything, though. The kid had just been a tool. Meant to be disposed of sooner or later. Everett was different. He'd been in this thing from the very beginning.

They'd grown up together. Experimented together. Perfected together.

I started with water. You watched me. But the water was cold, and I couldn't hear any screams when the vic was under the water.

Everett liked the sound of screams. The screams were half of the fun.

Water and fire. Such opposites.

171

Fire crackles like a scream. And the vics scream so loudly when they burn.

A lifetime ago. That was when it all began. Two kids shoved together. Two souls that understood.

Not fucking problems. Visionaries. That is what we were.

And...

He wouldn't turn on me.

But, Everett was locked up. They'd been apart for so long.

More sweat trickled down his back.

Avalon Trahan should have died long ago. But she'd had guards after the fire. First from her family. They'd yanked her out of her school. Transferred her to a fancy private academy behind a big-ass gate. Bought a new house. Kept those hulking security personnel on her all the time.

Then later...

Others were watching. He'd first noticed the tails on her. Because maybe...maybe he'd thought that he could eliminate an old, loose end for a friend.

But she was never unprotected. He'd warned his friend about that. But someone had not paid attention.

He had to think. He had to plan. Had to get another message out, but the damn guard he needed wasn't there that day. Everett fired an angry glare over his shoulder. He was stuck with those dumbasses.

"Settle down. You're not going back to solitary, not just yet. You get five minutes in the yard."

He stumbled. Stupid chains. "I don't need five minutes." He wanted the quiet of solitary confinement. It let him think. He needed to think.

Avalon was trying to get in my head.

And...she had.

"Relax," the guard assured him. "It will be just you in the yard. Five minutes of sunshine. You know you're supposed to get out each day."

Yeah, yeah, he knew that but…

Another guard opened the door up ahead. The metal screeched. Sunlight glinted. So bright. Too bright. He'd never really liked the daytime. Night was better. Everything was better in the dark.

They took off his ankle manacles. The better for him to walk more than a freaking half-inch at a damn time.

And they…

Left him in the yard.

With his hands cuffed. With the sun shining down on him. Oh, Everett knew he wasn't really alone. Guards watched from up above. But…

Quiet.

Still.

He closed his eyes and remembered the girls he'd loved over the years. He could hear their screams so perfectly. He'd become their nightmares. The last thing they'd seen before death. They'd been so afraid.

He hadn't liked the water or the fire. He'd liked a knife. One gripped in his hand that had become part of him. He'd been the perfect weapon. And he'd been able to hear every single scream with such wonderful clarity.

She won't feel a knife at the end. Avalon was going to be taken by the fire. He knew it was coming. She'd been marked for so long.

She didn't remember him. He'd realized that when he first sat across from her just a few days ago. Oh, sure, she knew him as the Slasher. But she didn't remember…

We met, once upon a time in New Orleans. A day she'd been celebrating. Laughing.

Young and innocent. Had she even realized what she'd witnessed in those few moments? Just in case, she'd been marked for death.

But she'd escaped the fire. Because of Beau. A prick who should have just boosted the ride and gone on his way. Hell, they had even thought about pinning the fire on Beau. He'd been in the right place. At the right time.

We saw you, too.

Except Beau hadn't done what they anticipated. He'd changed everything. Screwed everything.

And now, the past had come back. Only, really, the past had never let her go.

He heard a rush of wind. His eyes opened because the sky had been so bright before. No sign of clouds and why was the wind so loud all of a sudden?

Pain pierced his chest.

"How does it feel, bitch?"

He blinked.

Footsteps thudded. More wind. And pain.

Men swarmed him. Old. Young. All in orange. Dark tattoos on their necks. Arms. Hands. A twisting snake. A roaring dragon. Tear drops on a tanned cheek.

Their arms flew up and down and he screamed and screamed as the pain cut through him.

Distantly, he heard the alarm when it began to blare.

But they didn't stop.

Not even when he begged.

Chapter Fourteen

His hands curled around Avalon's waist. Her mouth was open beneath his, her taste making him mad with need, but this was not the place. Alarm bells were ringing in his head because of the crap that Everett had said.

How had he known about the Jag? I never told a soul about the Jag. And how did he know I was in a gang back then? How did he—

Avalon pulled back. Her long lashes lifted.

And Beau realized that the alarm bells weren't ringing just in his head. An actual alarm was blasting through the prison. Fear filled her green eyes.

"What's happening?"

He grabbed her arm and ran for the door. Even as he reached out to yank it open, Douglas surged inside.

The DA yelled, "Lockdown!"

The alarm seemed to blare louder.

"The whole damn place is going under a lockdown. There's been an attack in the yard. Swarm of prisoners jumped someone." Douglas had yanked off his tie. "Come with me, *now*, before we all get our asses trapped in here for who the hell knows how long!"

Like Beau had to be told twice. He kept his hand wrapped around Avalon's wrist. Adrenaline spiked in his blood. Wasn't this one of the things he'd always feared when it came to Avalon? That she'd be trapped with killers when something bad happened? An inattentive guard who let a prisoner get too close? A riot where there was no control?

He'd spread the word hard at every prison she entered. Made it clear through his connections that she was not to be touched. But he still had enemies. People who might not follow along like they were supposed to.

People like freaking Everett Thomas.

You're a dead man, Everett.

Guards were running forward.

He heard talk of tear gas being deployed. There were more frantic shouts. Metal doors clanged shut. Douglas hauled ass, but the DA kept glancing back to make sure he was being followed by Beau and Avalon, and it was while he was glancing back that last time—that was when he was attacked.

A bear of a prisoner in a garish, orange jumpsuit came out screaming, and he swung what looked like a lunch tray into the side of Douglas's head. Douglas cried out in pain even as he stumbled to the side and slammed into the prison bars of an empty cell.

The prisoner raised the tray again—

Beau plowed into him. He drove his shoulder into the man's chest, and then he pounded his fist right into the prick's groin. Oh, what? Like he wasn't supposed to play dirty? It was the only way Beau knew how to play.

The tray clattered to the floor.

The prisoner grabbed his dick and moaned in pain.

"Douglas? Douglas, are you all right?" Avalon's soft voice.

The prisoner's shaved head whipped up. His eyes locked right on her. Lust. Hunger. A wide smile curved his fat lips.

Beau scooped up the tray. Not really a tray. Felt more like a damn drawer. Where had the prisoner gotten it? Did he even want to know?

I want to get Avalon out of this hell. That's what I want.

The prisoner tried to lunge for Avalon.

Beau kicked him in his already wounded dick and slammed the tray or drawer or whatever it was against the side of the bastard's head. Then he slammed it into the jerk's face. Blood spattered. A tooth might have dropped to the floor.

The prisoner went down hard.

"Guess you didn't get the memo." Beau glared down at him. "No one touches her." He lifted his makeshift weapon again.

"Beau? A little help?"

He whirled instantly and saw Avalon staggering to lift Douglas off the floor. A bleeding and blearily blinking Douglas. She had one of his arms stretched behind her shoulders. The two of them were toppling and about to hit the floor again.

He dropped the makeshift weapon. "Fuck." He also grabbed Douglas. Because leaving him wasn't an option. The DA left alone during a riot? Oh, yeah, that wouldn't end well for the man. "You will owe me for this," he grunted as he slung Douglas over his left shoulder.

Then Beau grabbed Avalon's wrist again and barreled forward on the path they *had* been taking. "DA," he snarled. "Wake that ass of yours up fully. Tell me where to go." Because this was not the route they'd used on the way to the interrogation with Everett.

He had to get Avalon to safety. Right the hell then.

Another door opened. Beau tensed, more than ready to fight another attacker. No one was going to touch Avalon.

But it was the warden. Beau recognized the man because he'd been glowering during the check-in when Avalon and Beau had first arrived at McKinley prison.

"This way!" The warden motioned frantically. "I saw you on the security feed. Get Douglas over here, now!"

He went there but sent Avalon through the doorway to safety first. Then he followed with Douglas. The door shut behind them. Another clang. And another corridor waiting up ahead. But guards were there, too. Rushing up to cover the rear of their group. Beau followed Avalon and the warden. More twists. Turns. Doors that were lined with bars slammed shut behind them time after time, and then... then they were in what looked like an infirmary.

"Put Douglas on a bed. Nurse? Nurse!" A shout from the warden. "Check him out, now!"

A male nurse in white scrubs rushed forward.

Douglas blinked when Beau dropped him on the bed. "Wh-what—" A ragged groan took away the rest of his words.

"You're alive," Beau told him, voice hard. As hard as the rage burning through him because Avalon should not be in the middle of this danger. "You can thank me later. Trust me, I will collect on the thanks. Probably with interest." He spun, caught Avalon's smaller hand in his, and bluntly told the warden, "Avalon is out of here. Now. Show me the exit."

"There's a riot going on!" Sweat dotted the warden's forehead. "A prisoner was just attacked in the yard. A gang swarmed him. Shanked him again and again! We can see the body on security footage, but we can't get to him."

"Body?" Avalon sidled even closer to Beau. "You're sure the victim is dead?"

"With that much blood, I'm gonna say that, hell, yes, the Slasher is dead."

Slasher.

Dead, right after leaving their meeting?

"We're going to use tear gas in the yard. The attackers will disassemble. I've got them on camera. They'll be prosecuted. They will be—oh, fuck, most of them were already in for life, anyway. What the hell will more time do to them?" The warden whirled away. He pointed at a guard. "Moses, get them clear. *Now.*"

Moses—tall, with grim features, dark eyes, and a posture that said he was ready for battle—nodded. Then he started moving, fast.

Beau followed, making sure that Avalon was with him every step of the way. He remained as tense as Moses because he expected an attack to come at any moment. In a lockdown, people weren't supposed to be allowed out, but there was no way Avalon was staying in that prison while hell was breaking loose. If the warden hadn't seen the wisdom in the fact that she needed to flee, then Beau would have just been kicking that guy in the dick, too.

Moses typed in a fast code near a closed, massive steel door. With a beep and hiss, the door opened. "Go!" Moses urged.

Alarms were still blaring.

But they were almost out. Beau curled his arms around Avalon and urged her in front of him. He glanced back.

Moses dipped his head toward him.

Moses Milroy had sure changed one hell of a lot over the years. Once upon a time, plenty of people would have been sure that Moses would be the one who wound up behind the bars. *Being* a prisoner. Not the individual keeping the prisoners in check. But Moses was a proud father of two now. His wife was finishing up nursing school.

They planned to move down to Pensacola in a few months. Fresh starts for them both.

Beau would make sure that Moses was given one damn fine housewarming present when that move came.

Then Beau and Avalon were being checked by more guards. Cleared. Sent out of the prison and into the sunshine as, behind them, chaos still reigned.

* * *

Her hands wouldn't stop shaking.

When the last guards gave them the all clear, Beau opened the passenger side of his car and ushered her inside. He hooked the seatbelt across her, then ran his hands quickly over her arms and legs. "You're not hurt." Not a question.

Her hands fisted in her lap.

"Avalon, you're *not* hurt."

Still didn't sound like a question to her, but she managed to shake her head because she had the feeling he was not going to move until she did something, and she very, very much would like for him to move. To get in the car and get them out of there. *Now, please.*

He slammed the door and rushed around to the driver's side. In moments, the Jag's engine was growling to life.

"He...knew you drove a Jag." Her heartbeat thudded too loudly in her ears. "He's been watching you. Having someone watch you. Everett knew this specific car. He mentioned your Jag." He'd been taunting them. And now he was dead? It wasn't that she felt bad about his death. He'd been a monster. One of the worst killers out there.

But, he'd had answers, dammit. Answers that she needed. And now she might never get them.

"He wasn't talking about this car. The bastard was talking about the ride I was stealing the night you and I first met."

She looked up from her fisted hands. Her stare flew to his hard profile. A muscle flexed along his jaw.

"Didn't you wonder why I was there? In the middle of the damn night?"

"I was..." Avalon swallowed to ease the dryness of her throat. "I was just grateful you were." She hadn't stopped to question why he'd been at the scene.

The engine growled louder as they sped down the road.

"I'm surprised they let us leave," she breathed. She truly was. "They searched us, and they checked the car, I know they did, but I-I thought they might hold us until the facility was secure."

"No prisoners are getting out. You're only out because the last thing the warden wanted was a PR nightmare on the news in which a pretty crime writer got attacked or killed in *his* prison." A growl. Not from the car this time. From him. "You know what you do is damn dangerous. I do my best to protect you, but I can't control everyone. They're fucking *killers and rapists*. The worst bastards out there. *You* can't control them. You can't play your games with them. *Dammit, what if I had not been there?*"

"But you're always there." Her nails bit into her palms. "Aren't you?"

That muscle jerked harder in his jaw.

"You do your best to protect me..." She let those words—his words—linger between them. "You knew the guard who led us out of the prison. Moses. I saw the way you two looked at each other."

He didn't deny her words. Didn't confirm them either.

"You *knew* him," she repeated.

"Yes." A hiss.

"But you know others in there, too, don't you? Maybe some guards. Maybe some prisoners." Everything was slipping into place for her. "You've got connections everywhere, don't you?" The implications of his true reach stunned her. "I once asked if you were a crime boss, and my God, I think you are."

"Told you before, my businesses are legitimate."

"*Now*. What you said was that your businesses are legitimate *now*. A very important qualifier—and *would you slow down? You're scaring me*. Just because a car can go this fast doesn't mean it should!"

Immediately, he slowed. They were on a long, lonely stretch of road that led to the prison. No houses nearby. No businesses. Because who really wanted to be neighbors with a maximum-security facility that housed the most dangerous criminals in the state?

And Beau knows them. Beau knows so much he didn't reveal to me. "I trusted you."

"Did you? Because I thought your trust was a lie. Isn't that why you kissed me right after saying you trusted me? Our little lie game." Angry words. Mocking.

Avalon sucked in a shuddering breath. "I fucked you

last night. I don't fuck men that I don't trust. You know so much about me, so really, shouldn't you know that?"

"You were just in danger. There were too many of them, and I didn't think I could get you out. I'm not thinking clearly. I have to get you away from here." His knuckles whitened around the wheel. He huffed out a breath. "And I'm not a crime boss."

She could feel his rage in the car, but she could also feel her own fury and Avalon wasn't about to back down. She wanted the full truth from him. "You've been watching me for years. Getting other people to watch me. When I go in prisons, do you have eyes on me then?"

"You don't get to have sit-down chats with the worst predators out there without me having contingency plans in place. Bad shit happens. Just like today." He slanted a glance in the rearview mirror. Automatically, Avalon whipped around to make sure they weren't being followed.

They weren't.

"I wanted to make sure you were safe," he gritted from between clenched teeth.

"Because I'm your good thing. Right. Been over that. You've been stalking me because I'm good and you are—"

"I've been watching over you because I've been in love with you since I was sixteen years old! Fuck! Fuck!" A hard shake of his head. *"You were just in a prison riot. You could have been ripped apart.* Douglas was on the floor. That big, burly bastard was coming at you. My contingencies weren't going to save you. I had stayed away all this time—thought it was better for you. Thought you deserved better than me. *But if I hadn't been there today, what the hell would have happened to you?"*

Her breath exhaled slowly. She opened her fisted hands. Stared down at the small half-moon marks that had been left by her nails. "Simple. I would probably be dead. So, what does that make? The fourth time you've saved me? The fifth? Maybe the hundredth? What the hell am I? Lois Lane while you're some undercover Superman?"

"You're everything! *Everything*. And that's why I'm so absolutely insane where you're concerned."

Chapter Fifteen

HE'D SCREWED UP. BEAU REALIZED THAT EVER SO important fact. A major, game-changing screw up. But when the alarm had started blaring in the prison, when chaos had been reigning and that big bastard in orange had turned his attention on Avalon...

Beau may have lost his control.

May?

Okay, dammit, he had. He'd completely lost his control. Thoroughly screwed up. And, yes, he'd even screwed things so badly that he'd admitted a truth that he'd tried to keep from even himself.

I love Avalon.

Sonofabitch.

She hadn't said anything after his big confession. Dare he hope that she'd somehow missed it? Beau cut her a quick glance. He found her eyes on him.

Nope, she hadn't missed a thing.

She was going to kick his ass to the curb. Get one major restraining order. And never look back.

"This isn't the way to the hotel." The first words she'd spoken in fifteen minutes. Yes, he'd been watching the clock.

"I'm not taking you to the hotel."

"But if you don't take me to the hotel, then how will your friends Percy and Dominic be able to keep watch over me?"

He sucked in his left cheek.

"It was the chocolate croissants that tipped me off about Percy. And the fact that the cops were extremely pissed that he'd delayed them from seeing me for so long. Let me guess, you told your buddy Percy I needed rest? That the cops couldn't see me until at least...oh, eight a.m.?"

Was it wiser to stay silent? Or plead guilty?

"And I realized Dominic knew you because you called him by name. I think you were stressed, and you slipped up. Detective Cunningham wasn't wrong about you, was he? He was actually telling me the truth. You have flunkies everywhere."

They weren't being tailed. They'd left the prison far behind. He swung the car into a vacant lot, let the engine snarl, and turned to her. "Really don't like that term. I have *friends* who help me out. And, for the record, Detective *Cuntingham* is pretty much wrong about everything."

She stared back at him. "That's not funny."

"Wasn't supposed to be. He really is wrong about every damn thing. And the nickname works. Once you get to know him better, you'll see it's accurate, not funny." He exhaled. How to explain things to her? "I have...friends who want to pay me back for favors they think I did for them."

"Because you *did* do favors for them. Tell me about Dominic."

"This really isn't the time. We need to get back to—"

"Your place? Because you aren't taking me toward the hotel. Are you taking me home?"

Home. "Yes."

A nod. "And you'll reveal all of your deep, dark secrets to me there?" Her gaze watched him. Waited.

He didn't speak. Lying to her wasn't so easy. Everyone else? Sure. A snap. But not Avalon. He was finding it exceedingly difficult to stare into her green eyes and lie.

"I want your deep, dark secrets."

Hadn't he just given her one? He'd told her he loved her. And he did. In his dark and twisted way. Not like he was the guy who'd show up with flowers and wine and take her out to a fancy dinner while they danced the night away.

Instead, he was the man who would have a small army at the ready to protect her from danger. The man who would threaten killers so that they'd cooperate with her questioning sessions and never put so much as a finger on her. He was the man who would stand in the fucking shadows, his heart feeling like it was being cut out of his chest, because he didn't want to touch her life and ruin it. He'd let her go on dates with some other assholes just so she'd be *happy*. "I damn well hated them."

"Excuse me?"

His eyes squeezed closed. "I'll tell you what I can."

"Dominic. Let's start there."

"Dom's younger brother was busted on a B&E not too long ago in Atlanta. Good kid. Fell in with bad people. I'm sure you know the story." He opened his eyes and glanced around the area, just to be sure they were safe. *We need to get out of here.* "Short sentence, but Dom wanted to make sure the kid didn't get roughed up or come out trapped in some gang that had forced him to swear allegiance while on the inside. I talked to some people. Made sure he had the right protection in place."

"You collect dangerous strays."

"Excuse me?" His turn to choke out the words. "I'm talking about people. Not animals!"

She shook her head. Her hair slid over her shoulder. "Something Royal told me."

Royal. Right. *Not* a story he wanted to touch at the moment.

"How did Royal get into your life?"

And, of course, she would zero right in on him. "This isn't the place. We're going *home*." Home. Where he could be sure she was safe. Where he could close the doors and lock out the rest of the world. The world was angry and dangerous and bloody. He knew that. Had always known it. But Beau wanted to make it better for her. All these years, he'd just wanted to make things better for Avalon.

Unfortunately, he was just screwing up more and more.

"When we get home, I want to know about the Jag you were stealing so long ago."

He drove out of the lot.

"I want to know about the gang."

The gang. Right. Another nightmare.

"I want to know why you disappeared from the hospital without a word."

That one was easy. "To keep you safe."

He caught her swift inhale. And then, softer, he heard her say, "And I want to know if you really do love me or if I'm just some twisted obsession that you have."

His jaw locked.

He drove them home. The Jag snarled.

* * *

Warden Curtis Flint stared down at the body of the dead inmate. The blood had pooled around him. Pooled. Splattered. Gone every dang place.

Everett Thomas's eyes were closed, and sure, protocol dictated that their emergency medical team still try and save the man, but, clearly, no saving was going to happen. You couldn't save the dead.

"How many times was he stabbed?" Douglas asked. Douglas was on his feet, with a bandage around the side of head. Weaving a bit. He'd told the DA to stay back. But Douglas was one stubborn bastard. Something he admired.

Curtis angled his head to try and count. "I see at least... fifteen?" Probably more. Three shivs had been dropped on the ground when the prisoners were rounded up.

"Why was he out here?" Douglas's low question went just to Curtis. "I thought he was being taken back to his cell."

"Each prisoner is entitled to time in the yard. Even those in solitary." His head turned so that he could meet Douglas's suspicious gaze. "The question we should be asking is...why the hell were those other inmates out here?"

Inmates who'd seemed to come with one goal. *Kill Everett Thomas.*

"Guess they weren't fans," Douglas muttered.

No, they clearly had not been.

And neither was I.

He didn't think anyone was going to be mourning Everett Thomas's death.

* * *

"You HAVE a murder board in your den."

Beau dropped onto the oversized couch and watched Avalon as she slowly closed in on what was, indeed, a murder board. One he'd carefully crafted with help from Lane and Ophelia. And a few other players in town.

Players that Avalon had not met yet. It had truly been a team effort.

She wore black pants and a black top. Black ballerina flats. He'd bought those clothes for her—and the black bra and panties that she also wore. She hadn't said a word about him knowing her exact sizes. But she was clearly aware of his...oh, how had she phrased things?

Twisted obsession.

"These are the first three houses that burned. The houses that were hit before mine in New Orleans. The houses and pics of the victims." She tapped the large, black-and-white photos that showed the aftermath of the fires. "A forty-year-old wife and mother died in the first fire. A seventy-year-old retired grandfather died in the second. And a newly married twenty-five-year-old male perished in the third." Her fingers trailed to the fourth picture. The aftermath of her fire. Only the skeleton of the house remained. Blackened. Charred. "And I would have been victim four."

He remained on the couch.

"Do you think they were trapped inside their homes, too? They were all home alone. Something that I have always thought linked the crimes. We were all in the houses by ourselves." She wrapped her arms around her stomach. "Different ages. Male. Female. Different races. Usually, serial killers have a victim type. But, then again, there aren't exactly a whole lot of serial killers who use fire as their weapon of choice." She swung to look at him. "Arsonists like to watch buildings burn. They like to watch the fire grow and twist. I always felt like this person just wanted to watch us suffer."

Beau slowly exhaled. "I believe they were trapped, yes. In Darius Cramer's file..." The grandfather. Grieved so much by his family. "There was mention that the windows in his bedroom were nailed shut. The investigator noted it in passing. The house was going through renovations, so he suspected that Darius had been working on the windows before the fire." A shake of Beau's head. "That's not what me and my team think."

"Your team." She rocked forward onto the balls of her feet. "Do elaborate. What does your *team* think?"

"Ophelia and Lane went to New Orleans. They found the old arson investigators. Two worked the cases originally. They dug up all the old case files for Ophelia and Lane. They talked for hours. They..." An exhale. "We believe no one was random. The victims were all deliberately selected. Targeted. All the attacks occurred between midnight and two a.m. No one else was in the homes. Just the vics. Neighbors weren't even around at the first two scenes. The fires were caused by an accelerant that was poured throughout the home. In your case..." His nostrils flared. "I remembered smelling gasoline when I got up the stairs. He'd soaked your house."

She shuddered.

"Lane and Ophelia found at least two other cases after yours. Not in New Orleans. One was in Birmingham, Alabama. About a year after you graduated high school. A girl your exact age—she was the victim then. Found in her bedroom. Trapped inside. Dead."

She jerked.

"Then three years after that, another woman was the

victim of a similar fire in Nashville. First responders were called to the scene at one thirty-three a.m. They rushed in to try and help her. Too late." His gaze drifted to his murder board. "Zoe Dagger's photo is behind you."

She looked back. Shivered. "She...she kind of looks like me."

There was no "kind of" about it. "I don't think he had a type before he set the fire at your place. But after you got away, I believe he did."

"He's been burning me over and over? Those poor women have died in my place?" She choked back a sob. "I *hate* this."

He surged off the couch. Beau could not just sit there and watch her pain. It ripped him apart. His arms curled around her, and he yanked her against him. She struggled for just a second, and he was already preparing to let her go when she suddenly locked her arms around him and held on as if she'd never let go. The same way he was holding her.

"I was scared," Avalon confessed. "So scared in the prison. Scared when we were running through all those corridors. Scared when I was in my bedroom and that jerk in the mask was attacking me. Scared when I was a teenager." Her head tilted back. "I am so sick of being scared." A tear tracked down her cheek.

His hand lifted. Caught the tear. He hated it when she cried.

"Everett was the key. He knew things about our past." Another tear slipped from her eye.

Tenderly, he wiped it away.

"He knew about the Jag. About your gang involvement. He knew so much."

Yes. "Because he knows the killer." The only conclusion

Beau could reach. Correction—*knew* the killer. Past tense because Beau was sure Everett was being loaded up into a body bag about now.

Her head turned. Her lips skimmed over his hand. The briefest of caresses, before she backed away. "Tell me everything. No secrets. *None.* Understand? You tell me everything you've been holding back, or I walk."

"You'll be afraid."

A broken laugh escaped her. "Didn't I just cover that I'm already scared all the time? And I'm sick of it. Nothing you can say is going to make me fear more." She blinked away tears. "I *hate* crying."

"I know." Soft.

"Because you know everything about me?"

"Not everything. I feel like I could be with you for a hundred years, and I'd still not know enough."

"Do not say freaking sweet things to me right now. *Talk to me about the past.*"

There was certainly nothing sweet about the past. "I was in the Garden District that night because I was supposed to boost a Jag. I was inside the vehicle, ready to ride into the night, and then I smelled smoke. Heard the crackle of fire. Heard a voice calling for help."

This time, she was the one to swipe away the tears on her cheek. She wiped them away even as she stiffened her spine.

"I went into the house to save you."

"Why?"

"Because you wanted my help." Simple. *Because you were going to die, and I couldn't just stand there.* "I hadn't done that before. Helped someone, that is. Mostly, I just tried to help myself." A shrug. "My old man was in prison. Serving two murder convictions. He still is, by the way. My mom left me in a church when I was ten. Found out that she died three weeks later of a drug overdose."

"Beau…"

His shoulders tensed. "It is what it is."

"No. It's not." She surged toward him.

But he lifted his hand. "Sweetheart, you touch me again, and you're not gonna be hearing the rest of the story right now. You'll be getting fucked. Because you might want to offer me comfort—and believe me, I do appreciate it—but I want you. Always have. Always will. And I'm riding one insane blast of fury and adrenaline due to what happened at the prison. My control is razor thin. So, just…thanks for the sympathy. But it's really better if you keep your distance." *Safer for you, sweetheart.*

She froze in place. Was that a flash of pain in her eyes? Sonofabitch.

I'm the sonofabitch. He cleared his throat. "Where was I? Oh, right. Saving this terrified teenage girl. We were on the third floor of her house. I'd realized someone locked her in to die, and all I wanted to do was make sure that we both didn't get burned alive. I had this crazy idea to climb down the old pipe or gutter or whatever the hell it was near her window. But it broke. And we fell. And when I woke up in the hospital, for the first time in a very long while, I wasn't alone."

"I was at your bedside."

He nodded. "Every time I opened my eyes, you were there. Your parents were there. People were coming in and saying how grateful they were. How much of a hero I was." His lips curled down. "Like the hero could admit he was only in the right place because he'd been in the middle of stealing a fancy ride. I already had a rap sheet at that time.

Lots of fake IDs. Giving a false name was easy. But they still tracked me down."

"They?"

"I was supposed to deliver that car, sweetheart. You don't just tell a gang that you changed your mind. Thanks, but no thanks." A mocking laugh slipped from him at the very idea. "Certain individuals came for me when you went home one night. I barely got out of that room with my life." They'd come to kill him because they'd been so sure he would talk to the cops about their operation. At the time, the car theft ring they'd been working had been absolutely huge. But it hadn't just been about cars. It had been about drugs. Weapons. *Pick your poison.*

Beau cleared his throat and continued, "They were gonna pump me full of drugs. I wouldn't wake up when they were done with me. Maybe they thought it would look like I died of my injuries or some shit. Maybe they didn't care what it looked like. But I wasn't going out that way. I fought them, even with that stupid cast on my leg. Then I got out."

"You left me."

Never. "They look for weaknesses. I couldn't let them hurt you in order to get to me."

"I-I didn't matter. You'd just met me."

"You always mattered. From the moment I met you."

Her lashes swept down to cover her eyes as Avalon seemed to find the floor oddly fascinating. She must, the way she stared so hard at it. But she murmured, "You mattered, too. From the moment I met you."

Did she have any idea how badly he wished that was true? But she wanted the whole story, so he'd keep giving it to her. "I had to get out of that gang. Sever ties. But it wasn't easy. There were things I knew I'd have to do. Power I'd have to gain." A dark part of his life that didn't need to ever touch her. "When I could be clear, I was gone from that life. Done. But I wasn't alone. When I left New Orleans, I took Royal with me. He'd been in the same gang, only I knew he didn't belong there. Royal was like me. Hell, so much like me."

"Brother from another mother." Her gaze had lifted to study him once more. "That's what he said."

She didn't understand. "I told you that my mother left me. She abandoned me in a church."

Her eyes were so wide.

"When he was two years old, he was found wandering around Royal Street."

A swift inhale.

"That's why he mocks about us being brothers—brothers from two mothers who'd abandoned us. Royal has no idea what became of his mother. I know mine died. I also know that he was a torn-up kid who needed someone to watch out for him. I took him with me when I left, and we've been in and out of each other's lives ever since." Royal had so much darkness inside of himself. So much pain. For a while, Beau had been afraid of what Royal might become.

I tried to help him. To channel him. Beau was still trying. Some days, Beau thought he might be helping his friend. Other days, he worried that he was just putting Royal on a path straight to hell.

"He's...your bodyguard."

Occassionally, maybe. But mostly, "Royal is his own thing. He has his own business interests. His own goals. But, yeah, he'll do some bodyguard work for me because he is one of the most dangerous bastards I know. Royal is also my family. I don't care about blood. He has been with me through every nightmare I've faced. He knows how important you are to me. When I need someone that I can absolutely trust with your safety and I can't be there, he steps in."

"You've seriously been…guarding me all this time."

She was sugarcoating. "Yeah, let's just call it guarding instead of stalking. Way more PC."

"Beau—"

He stepped back. "I was going to stop." That had been the plan. "Once we'd unmasked the arsonist. I never intended to actually enter your life. I wasn't even going to talk to you."

Her delicate jaw seemed to harden.

"I've watched you. Saw you go out with other men." Had wanted to rip those men to freaking pieces, but he hadn't. Because… "I want you happy. That is all I've ever wanted, and I know you can't be happy with someone like me." He swung away and stared out the window. Darkness stared back.

Didn't it always?

"Beau, I believe this is the part where you should ask me what I want."

"You want to be safe. You want to be free."

"I actually *want* this really arrogant asshole of an ex-gang member."

Beau's shoulders tensed.

"He's this really intense guy who may or may not have been a crime boss. He recently had his bar burn right in front of him, but instead of being enraged about losing something that mattered so much to him, he's basically moving heaven and hell combined because he's trying to protect me."

Beau looked straight ahead. In the window's glass, he

saw more than darkness. He saw Avalon's reflection as she edged up behind him.

"Want to hear some crazy stuff?" she asked him.

Always.

"I think I *knew* you were in my life."

He shook his head. No, she hadn't.

"I never saw you. Or your goons."

They hadn't been goons.

"Because if I had, that would have freaked me the hell out."

He hadn't gotten close enough to freak her out. And he'd tried to be so careful but... "Everett knew I was watching you. I think he might have come to LeBlanc's because he was studying me." *But how did that work out for you in the end, Slasher?* While Everett had been in LeBlanc's, he'd become prey.

Another dark story Beau would have to tell Avalon.

"When my parents died, I felt so alone. I didn't know what I was supposed to do. Where I was supposed to go. My past haunted me—it still does—and I was so uncertain all the time and then I just...I swear, I could feel you."

He shook his head.

But he saw her reflection, and he saw her come closer.

"When I walked into LeBlanc's, I saw you behind the bar, and I could have sworn the whole world stopped spinning for just a moment. Not the boy I remembered, but a man I absolutely recognized with every part of my being." She was right behind him now. Her hand rose and pressed to his shoulder. Lightly skimmed over the scars that marked him. "When we were kids, you were willing to die in order to protect me."

He spun toward her. Caught her hand. "I'm sure I warned you about touching me."

She smiled at him. Those dimples—those damn dimples had his heart aching. "I am scared of many things in this world. I'm pretty sure I just went over a rather extensive list for you. But you know what wasn't on the list? Or *who* wasn't?" She rose onto her tiptoes. Her lips brushed over his jaw. "You."

He should have been at the top of her list. Hadn't she heard what he'd confessed?

"We aren't kids any longer." She kissed his jaw again.

His hand remained locked around her wrist. He could feel the frantic beat of her pulse beneath his touch.

"But I still know that you'd die to protect me, wouldn't you?"

"Killing is more effective than dying, but, yeah, sweetheart, for you, I'd do both." In a heartbeat.

"And you've been hunting my arsonist."

"I suspect my hunt is what has spurred him into action again." Dammit. *My fault.* "Ophelia and Lane think that they might be able to tie a few more arsons to him. They were going to head out of town to chase down those leads, but then LeBlanc's went up in flames."

"We don't need to head out of town in order to find him. He's here."

"He was clearly telling me to back the hell off." A giant message as his bar burned.

Another kiss. This time, on his neck. Over the pulse that raced even faster than hers. "You aren't going to back off."

"No."

Her tongue licked against his skin. Then she sucked.

His eyes closed.

A sensual bite followed. One that had his dick shoving

hard against the zipper of his jeans. *I warned her. Why didn't she listen?*

"What are you going to do?" A soft taunt from Avalon. "Catch him, cuff him...and then slap a bow on the bastard?"

His eyes flew open.

"Because that's what you have been doing, isn't it, Beau? You've been hunting killers and leaving them tied up for the police. Tied up with a pretty, red bow."

Shit.

Chapter Sixteen

S**HE EASED BACK AND STARED UP AT BEAU. WHILE SHE** waited for him to speak, Avalon counted the passing of time by the hard beats of her heart that seemed to echo in her ears.

One.

Two.

Three.

Four...

"The bow was Royal's idea. Bastard has one sick sense of humor."

Her breath expelled in a rush. "You're hunting killers! You are *seriously* hunting killers." She staggered away from him.

His fingers—the fingers that had just been holding her wrist—flexed and curled. Flexed and curled. Then he dropped his hand to his side. "Sweetheart, you write books about killers. You go into prisons and have casual sit-down conversations with them." He grimaced. "All I do is bag them and tag them. Can't we just view this as me giving you more business?"

"Beau!"

"Oh, come on! The cops weren't even close to catching the bastards! The first prick—Owen Bell? We caught him following a co-ed home. He had a syringe in his hand, and he was literally running up behind her in an alley. What were we supposed to do?" A shake of his head. "Royal and I knew that women had been going missing after leaving bars in the area. We were worried that someone was roofying them. We were wrong about that. He wasn't doing it *in* the bars. The prick waited until they were alone, and he straight up drugged them with enough horse tranquilizer that they were *out*. Helpless. This is *my* town now. That shit wasn't gonna keep happening on my watch."

In and out. In and out. She breathed in and out. Deeply. Hard. "You could have called the cops."

A shrug of his right shoulder. "We did. After we'd secured Owen. Not like we killed the guy in cold blood."

"Did you *think* about killing him?"

"I didn't." A prompt reply.

But she realized there was more he wasn't saying. *Did Royal think about killing him?*

"As for Everett Thomas, he'd been hunting along the southeast. The Slasher's crimes were all over the Internet. Ophelia and Lane were digging into his past vics and... Look, I've got another buddy in town, Saint. Saint likes to solve cold cases." His lips twisted. "Bastard used to be an insanely good bounty hunter. Don't ask me how I know that, by the way."

"I don't have to ask. I'm guessing Saint might have hunted you down—or Royal down—at some point?"

He smiled. That killer smile of his that rocked its way through her whole body. "Told you, Saint is a buddy. I've actually had him helping out on your case, too."

Who wasn't working on her case? Other than, you know...*me.*

"You'll meet him eventually. Though I should warn you, he's a lot. So is his wife, Alice. She has a great speakeasy in town, by the way. Stellar."

Alice. "Are you...talking about Alice Shephard?" The name Alice hadn't just rung a bell. It had set off major alarms. When Avalon had first moved to Savannah, she'd wanted to interview Alice Shephard. The woman had been a suspected black widow. But Alice hadn't exactly been in a cooperating mood. Then hell had broken loose in Alice's life. And—

"She *was* Alice Shephard. She took my buddy's last name when they got married. And I'm not the least bit surprised that your crime-obsessed mind would know about her. I'm certain that you'll have fabulous chats with Alice in the future. I'll be sure to take you in her speakeasy at the first opportunity so you can become fast friends, but for now, are you about to take out your phone and call the cops? Sorry, but it feels like a good question to ask. Trying to decide if I will be sleeping in a jail cell tonight or not. It's important to know."

She blinked. "The cops?"

"Yes. Because I've confessed to you. I attacked two men. They deserved it, one hundred percent, but Detective Cunt—sorry, Cunningham might not see things in the same light."

She had to unclench her teeth and get Beau to focus. "You didn't tell me how you figured out Everett Thomas was the Slasher."

"I put together pieces that I'd learned from hearing Saint and Ophelia and Lane talk about the Slasher cases. Then Everett started nosing around my bar. I noticed he paid a bit too much attention to one of my waitresses. The way he watched her..." The faint lines near his mouth deepened. "Predatory. And he tried following her when she'd go into the back. Then he put his hands on her even as she told him to back the hell off. When I got in his way and told him to get the fuck out of my place, he said some things to me that put me on high alert. Crap about how a woman's screams were the best music he'd ever heard." His hands weren't loose at his sides. They'd fisted. "Who the hell says that? He told me some twisted BS about how he'd found the best way to hear screams. Water muted them. Fire fought them."

Water muted them. Fire fought them. She backed up a step.

"When he said fire, I suspected that he was taunting me. At first, I thought he might have been your arsonist. Royal and I tore into his world. But instead of being the arsonist..."

"You found out that he was the Slasher."

A grim nod. "We watched him. We studied him." His eyelashes flickered. "We didn't tell the others. Saint, Ophelia, Lane—none of them have any idea what happened. When Royal and I realized Everett was gonna run, we stepped in. Is it really that big of a deal? All we did was stop the man from slipping away."

"*All we did.*" Her mouth dropped. She snapped it closed. "You understand how insanely dangerous what you did was?"

"Everett and Owen were hurting people. You wanted us to just stand there and do nothing?"

No, he wouldn't do nothing. He hadn't just done nothing when it had been her life on the line. "My God." Another step back. "I was wrong. You're not Superman."

She gestured toward the *mansion* that surrounded her. A mansion and a murder board and a man who hunted down killers. "You're Batman."

"That shit is not funny."

"What you're doing isn't funny! It's dangerous!" How many times would she have to state the obvious to him? "You're pulling some vigilante justice and—" Now she leapt to him. She grabbed his arms and held tightly. "You could get yourself killed! What am I supposed to do if you get killed? What is my life supposed to be like?"

Thick hair tumbled over his forehead. "I wasn't in your life until recently. You'll be fine without me. Actually, I think your life would be *better* without me in it."

She didn't breathe. Not for a moment. She just glared. "Don't you *ever* say that again." A hard inhale. Exhale. Inhale. "I have looked for you, I have dreamed about you, I have wanted you in my life for *years*. And the last thing I want is for you to vanish again on me. You're not getting killed. You're not getting tossed behind bars. You are staying with me." Her nails dug into the fabric of his shirt. "Do you hear me?"

"Yeah, I do. It's a good thing I don't have nearby neighbors. They'd hear you, too."

"Beau!"

And the mask he wore—that flippant mask he'd had on even as he revealed his secrets—shattered right before her eyes. Need, hunger, desire—they all flashed on his face. Craving. *Hope.* A desperate hope. His hands curled around her waist. "You're not calling the cops?"

"You are *not* going into a jail cell. But we are going to have a serious talk about you discontinuing this particular extracurricular activity! That's what you called it before.

You basically confessed right in front of me when you were talking to Royal, and I didn't even realize it."

His eyes blazed down at her. "I think Everett knew the arsonist who set your fire."

"Yeah, I got clued in on that, too." Everett had been the key.

"I had nothing to do with his death."

What? "I didn't accuse you of being involved." She'd never even thought it.

"I needed him alive. You needed him alive. He could have led us to the killer."

His mask was still gone. Beau stared at her with such a voracious need. She sucked in a breath. "I taunted him. Just like I said I would. I warned him that the arsonist would be coming after him, and he was afraid, Beau. I saw his fear." As clearly as she could see Beau's need. "I agree with you. He knew the arsonist. And that's a big lead for us. We have to look back at Everett's associates when he was in New Orleans. We have to delve deep and create lines in our lives. My life. Everett's. See if a link shows up."

"I'll text Ophelia and Lane. They can turn up intel faster than anyone else I know." He let her go. Stalked away and fired off the text.

She rocked from her heels to the balls of her feet, then back again. Rocked and waited and... "Do you really love me?"

He finished the text. Dropped the phone onto the couch. "There is nothing in this world I love more." His head angled so that he was staring over his shoulder at her. "Does that scare you?"

"No." She licked her lips. "I believe I told you already that nothing about you scares me."

He turned to fully face her. "Maybe the way I want you should make you afraid."

Never. "How do you want me?"

"I want to fuck you until you're screaming for me. Until we forget everything else. Until you don't remember any other man but me. I want to own you because, sweetheart, you own me. You have for years." Guttural. Possessive. Predatory. His chin lifted. "Sorry." Beau cleared his throat, but when he spoke again, his voice was still a growl. "Too much adrenaline. Too much need. I'll go take one real freaking cold shower, and we'll figure out our next move after that. I'm sure we'll be hearing from your DA buddy soon. The world will come crashing in on us." He swung away and began to pace toward the hallway.

Did a cold shower wait down that hall?

"The DA. Cops. The warden. I'm betting our phones will be ringing off the hook." He stopped and his hand pressed to the wall near him. "Make yourself at home. Actually..." Another glance over his shoulder. "My home is your home. I bought the place because I wanted to have something nice to impress you with. That is, if we ever actually crossed paths in a normal way."

"I don't think we do normal." She hadn't moved from her position near the window. "That's not who we are."

"Right. Not normal." His smile was sad. "There's a piano in the study. A whole cabinet full of your favorite chocolate in the kitchen. Go play music. Rest. Pace. Do whatever you want, but please don't leave the house. I'll be back when I—screw it. I'll be back when I stop wanting to take you until we're both boneless on the floor. I do have control. It's just always weaker where you're concerned."

Her control was pretty much nonexistent when it came to him.

"Security here is top-notch. You're safe." And with that, he headed down the hallway.

For a moment, she continued to stand exactly where she'd been. But curiosity filled her. She headed back to his murder board. Studied the pictures. Felt sadness tug at her as her gaze darted to the victims.

When she wrote her books, the victims were always the worst part for her. The most painful aspect. Getting into their lives. Learning about the people who mourned them. Seeing the pain that had been left in their absence.

She'd already learned about the vics from the fires in New Orleans. She'd talked to the family members. Heard the echo of sorrow in their voices.

But the arson victims Beau and his team had discovered after her fire...

Her stare lingered on them.

They were new to her. Their pain was new.

Slowly, she retreated from the pictures. Avalon found herself trailing through his house until she wound up in the study. In front of the piano.

Her mother had been the one to first teach her how to play music. They'd sat together at their piano for hours. Her mother had been able to play so effortlessly. So beautifully.

Avalon pulled out the bench. She sat down. Ran her fingers over the keys.

She thought of the victims.

The fire.

The killer still out there.

It's the same person. All the arsons are tied to the same man. I know it. The arsonist stalking me now is the same one from all those years ago.

She started to play. Her fingers moved slowly at first. Hesitantly.

She thought of Beau. Of how much she'd longed for him.

Of the bar he'd lost.

Of the way he looked at her.

Hunger.

Desire.

Her fingers played faster.

And she thought of the way she wanted him.

Her fingers flew over the keys.

* * *

THE ICY WATER hadn't helped. Heat seemed to churn beneath his skin, and he was certainly far too well acquainted with fire. Beau turned off the water and stood in the massive shower, dripping, as he tried to figure out what the hell he would do next.

Not pounce on Avalon. Get your control back. Get it back now.

And then he heard the music. Not soft and gentle. Hard. Driving. A crescendo of power and demand.

Avalon was playing his piano. Correction, her piano. He didn't know how to play the damn thing. He'd bought it for her ages ago.

He grabbed a towel. Knotted it around his waist and, still dripping, he followed the music. He just wanted to see her playing. A memory to keep close after she left.

His bare feet hurried toward the study. He paused in the doorway.

She leaned over the grand piano. Her fingers moved— no, they *flew* over the keys. The music was beautiful. Dark and fast and heavy. Soaked with passion. And it pulled him closer and closer to her as the music built in a frenzy. It was a frenzy that he could feel all the way to his soul and then—

She slammed her hands onto the keys. A crash of sound. "Doesn't help." Breath heaving, Avalon shot to her feet and spun toward him. Her wide eyes swirled with so many emotions. Too many to name. "Did the shower help you?"

Nothing could make him stop wanting her. The shower had been a bad idea. Now he was practically naked, and she was right there.

"The piano didn't help me. That's okay." She edged around the bench. "I know what can help us both." She grabbed the towel that he'd knotted at his waist. Avalon yanked. It hit the floor.

A second later, so did her knees. She knelt right before him. Her silken hands went to his cock.

"Uh, Avalon?" Such a bad idea. Her mouth. On his dick?

Heaven.

Hell.

"Avalon—"

Her lips closed around him. *Heaven. Paradise. Wet. Soft. Her tongue sliding over my dick. Her sucking me. Pulling me deep.*

His hands clamped around her shoulders.

She sucked him in deeper. Her fingers were pumping the base of his cock even as her mouth opened wide, and she took him inside.

He thrust against her mouth. Could feel the orgasm rolling forward and building up so fast because this was Avalon. His Avalon. Her mouth on him. Her mouth—

"No!" He wrenched back. *Too many clothes.* She wore far too many clothes. So he basically ripped them off. She helped. Her shoes went flying. Her black pants. Her panties. She stayed in her top and bra, and he had Avalon in his arms in a flash. In his arms, with her legs curling around his waist, and his dick pushing against the entrance to her sex. She surged against him.

He rammed home into her.

They banged into the piano. The keys crashed. He lifted her up higher. His hands were tight around her waist as he lifted her up and down. Up and down. She cried out, then leaned forward and clutched him with a wild grip. "Yes! Beau!"

She was so hot around him. Insanely tight. Wet. He drove in and he realized...

No condom.

Beau froze. With his dick fully lodged in her tight, wet heat, he stopped moving.

Her breath—his—filled the air.

"Beau?" And she clamped her inner muscles around him. A fast clamp. Release. Clamp.

Sweat beaded his brow. "No...condom."

She bit down on him in the spot where his shoulder met his neck. "I'm on birth control." Her inner muscles clamped around him again. Squeezed his dick. "Just had a full checkup. I'm safe."

So was he. But...

"I like you this way," she whispered and sealed both their fates. "Makes you feel even more mine."

The keys of the piano crashed again. He'd staggered against the piano because she'd almost made him erupt then and there.

Soft laughter from her. Laughter that had her body squeezing his dick all the more.

Keeping his hands on her waist, keeping her legs locked around him, he moved toward the fireplace. Too freaking hot for that thing, but he bent and stretched her out on the lush rug in front of it.

She still wore the black top. Her bra.

He was still balls-deep in her.

His right hand lifted. Grabbed her blouse. Buttons went flying.

The blouse hung open so he could see her black bra. He shoved it out of his way. Her tight, gorgeous nipples thrust toward him. He had to take a nipple into his mouth. Lick it. Suck it.

Her hips surged eagerly against him. "Beau!"

He sucked harder. His hand slid between their bodies. His thumb strummed her clit.

He bit her nipple.

"*Beau!*" She bucked beneath him.

His thrusts became even harder. Even wilder. Deeper. He took her other nipple into his mouth. Laved it with his tongue. Pistoned his hips against her. Over and over. In and almost out. Only to drive in deeper. Deeper.

Her body tensed. He looked up in time to see her mouth open in a wide circle. Her eyes squeezed shut, and she came for him. A hard clench of release around his dick as her face went slack with pleasure and she moaned his name.

Good.

Not good enough.

Not enough to satisfy him. He was too far gone.

He thrust through her orgasm. Pounded into her again and again, and when he felt her climax fading, he pulled out of her.

"Beau!" Her eyes flew open. "You haven't—"

He would.

He flipped her over. "Put your hands on the floor."

She did.

He lifted her onto her knees. Positioned her perfectly. Then slammed home.

This time, they both moaned.

His hands slid around her body. One hand went to cup her breast. To tease her nipple. To squeeze it. One went for her clit. To rub hard and fast. The same way he thrust. Hard and fast.

Hard.

Fast.

She shoved her sweet ass back against him as she came a second time.

And he exploded with her.

* * *

SHE ROSE ON SHAKY LEGS.

Beau had pulled out of her. Cursed. Promised to be right back.

Then he'd vanished down the hallway.

She was still busy trying to cope with a mind-breaking orgasm. And her legs weren't feeling quite steady enough. She staggered a few steps. Her hand flew out. Slapped down onto the keys of the piano.

A clang of music.

"Sweetheart..."

Completely naked, she looked back over her shoulder.

He watched her with lust burning in his eyes.

"Can you take me again?" He had a cloth in his hand.

She nodded. Her hands started to lift from the piano.

"Stay right there." A sensual order.

Her hand slapped down again. The music burst out. A fast, sharp cry.

He walked up behind her. "Part your legs."

She did. Those shaky knees of hers shook a little more. The warm, wet cloth pressed between her thighs. She gasped and rose onto her toes.

Music pounded again. Rougher.

"Just trying to make sure I didn't hurt you." The cloth was so warm. So soft as he stroked it between her legs.

"You didn't." Enough pleasure to make her weak, yes, absolutely, but no pain, not from him.

Her head tipped forward. Both of her hands were on the piano. One on the keys. One gripping the frame for dear life.

The warm cloth slid over her clit.

She hissed out a breath.

Then the cloth was gone. His fingers weren't. His big, long fingers were sliding between her folds. Stroking her. Playing with her.

She stared down at the white and black piano keys.

"Play a song for me."

What? No, no way, he could not be serious. Not at this moment. No way at all could he actually want her to try and play the piano *now*.

"Play for me, and I'll fuck you."

Her fingers flew over the keys. She had no idea what she was doing. She just stroked those piano keys mindlessly.

Two fingers sank into her. His thumb scraped over her clit. The most delicious scrape. Rub. Tease.

"You're not playing."

No, she was moaning and shoving down on his fingers.

He withdrew his fingers. His mouth pressed to her neck. His teeth scored her. "Play for me."

Once again, her fingers flew blindly over the keys. She didn't know what she was playing. Didn't even think it was a song. She just wanted his thumb to stroke her clit harder. And those wicked fingers of his needed to come back inside of her.

"Rise onto your toes. Higher. Like this." He pulled her up. "Good." His hand slid over one ass cheek. "I want you too much.'"

She wanted him too much. Was that dangerous? Probably. Did she care? Nope.

His fingers dipped into her. She rose up even higher. Choked out a breath.

He kissed her neck again. Sucked the skin. "I want every part of you."

"Then..." One hand slammed onto the keys. The other grabbed for that frame again because it was either grab it or fall. No way could she *play* right then. "Then take every part!"

And he did.

He plunged into her. Her right hand slapped against the keys. Her left gripped the frame tighter. His thrusts were merciless and so deep. They rocked through her whole body, and she ground her hips against him. She loved what he was doing to her. The wild plunges. The primal growls. The thud of their bodies coming together.

The frantic strokes of his fingers over her clit.

She came with a scream. A sharp, echoing cry because there was no build up to the climax. It just stuck with the force of a hurricane.

And he was with her. A long, hot blast filled her as he came. And, somehow, his release just spurred on her pleasure. Had her gasping and rubbing her hips against his feverishly because this was what sex should be.

It should consume.

It should ignite.

It should possess.

It should leave you broken and panting and aching with throbs of pleasure because it was so intense and powerful that it would obliterate you...

He pulled out.

She whimpered in protest.

But he lifted her into his arms. "You are my beautiful music."

That was...Her eyes squeezed closed so he wouldn't see that she was tearing up again.

And I think you might be my everything, Beau.

For the first time, she began to feel...afraid of him. No, not of him. Afraid of how he made her feel.

Chapter Seventeen

"How do you feel about a little breaking and entering?"

At the question, Avalon paused. She'd just been stepping out of the shower. Water droplets skated down over her delectable body, and her wet hair trailed over her shoulders.

He lifted up a towel.

She took it. Slowly dried off and wrapped it around her body. "Is this just a general...do I think B&E's are wrong sort of thing? Or are you asking specifically if I feel like breaking into a house with you?"

She'd covered her nipples when she wrapped the towel around her body. A crying shame. "The prison riot made the news." He'd watched the story while she showered. "One inmate is listed as being killed."

"Everett."

"That's what my money says."

She eased forward on the bathmat. "You didn't answer my question."

"I have a specific B&E in mind. Seeing as how we're

217

partners, I thought I'd extend a participation invitation to you." He scratched his jaw and tried to keep his gaze *on her face*. "Don't want to be accused of sidelining you again." He also didn't want to let her out of his sight.

After the attack on Everett...

You pulled strings, didn't you, you bastard? You realized that Everett might be a weak link. You torched my place. You got Everett killed. What is next? The SOB had accelerated at an alarming rate.

Beau feared the "next" move would be a direct attack on Avalon. He was pretty sure she was the bastard's end game.

Not on my watch.

"I appreciate not being sidelined. And thanks so much for the offer of committing a crime with you. Before I accept or decline, though, do you mind telling me whose house we'll potentially be entering?" Steam drifted from the open shower.

"Slater Wade's rental house."

Her eyes narrowed. "Isn't his place still a crime scene?"

"Probably." Most likely. "But wouldn't you like to see if we can discover something the uniforms might have overlooked?"

She pulled in her lower lip. Studied him. And Beau knew the answer even before she said, "Damn straight, I would."

"Great." He backed up a step. Two more. Kept his hands behind his back. "There are fresh clothes for you in the bottom drawer of my dresser." He spun away.

"Beau."

"Yes?"

"How are there fresh clothes for me in the bottom drawer of your dresser?" A sweetly asked question.

"I, uh, got some new clothes for you after the fire at your

house." He glanced back at her. *Stay focused on her face. Not the little towel that could be so easily removed.* "Remember? I had that bag waiting in the limo. I kept a few things here, too, just in case..."

"In case we wound up having frantic sex and you ripped my blouse?"

In his fantasies, oh, yeah. But in reality... "I kept them just in case the hotel wasn't safe enough, and I wanted you closer."

"That is both sweet and alarming."

"Yep, that pretty much describes me when it comes to you. Now I've been good as long as I can be. You're naked, and...*it's you*. I always want you. But I'm trying not to pounce again. I'll go wait in the den while you dress. Then we'll do some B&E fun." He faced the front and took a quick step forward.

"You'd really break the law for me in an instant, wouldn't you?"

Now he glanced back once more. His beautiful Avalon. "Sweetheart..." He sent her a smile. "I would kill for you in an instant."

"Both sweet...and alarming." Her lips pressed together. "Want to know something else alarming?"

He waited.

"I would do the same for you." Soft.

* * *

A FIRE TRUCK raced past them with its siren blaring. Beau had pulled the Jag off to the side of the road when he'd first caught sight of the vehicle's flashing red lights behind him. As the wail of the truck's siren died away, he carefully merged back into traffic.

"I'm getting a really bad feeling," Avalon muttered as her hands flattened onto the dashboard.

So was he.

But he kept driving slowly. He turned the corner up ahead. Then took another right. He was following the directions that his phone was giving to him. Directions that would take him right to Slater Wade's rental.

Another turn. A left one, this time. And...

"Sonofabitch," he rasped. He braked the car and stared at the flames shooting from the small house.

"I think the bad guy beat us here," Avalon murmured.

He watched the flames. Watched the firefighters run in and out of the house. He was pretty sure he caught sight of Lieutenant Wesley Vaughn as the man stood beside a parked fire truck and held his helmet tucked under one arm. Looked like Wesley was barking commands to the men hauling the hose toward the house.

Smoke blackened the sky above the small structure. "Really getting tired of this shit," Beau groused.

"Call me psychic, but I don't think we're going to find a whole lot of evidence left inside that place."

"Psychic," he called.

Her hand reached over and squeezed his as he gripped the steering wheel. "I know where the fire was more contained. Another place we can look that might have clues for us."

Beau raised a brow as he waited for her to continue.

"My house," she told him, even as her gaze swept once more to the twisting, heaving fire. "The fire didn't get to spread too far in my home. Maybe there is something there that can help us. Something Slater dropped. Something the arsonist left behind. Or if there isn't anything in the house, let's try talking to my neighbors. Maybe one of them saw something."

Lots of options. He knew she needed to act. And not just wait while the world kept burning.

He glanced back to make sure the road was clear behind him. Then Beau threw the car into reverse. Whipped around. He hauled ass out of there, but when Beau peered in his rearview mirror, he blinked.

A firefighter—in full mask and turnout gear—was in the middle of the road. The firefighter seemed to be staring after them. Just staring.

Beau braked. The car screeched. "Sonofabitch."

He jumped out, instincts screaming, but...

No firefighter was staring after him. All of the firefighters were swarming toward the house. No one was watching them.

But I swear, one was. One. Was.

"Beau?"

He climbed back into the car.

"Uh, want to tell me what just happened?"

Once more, he looked into the rearview mirror. "You can't tell jackshit about them when they're in their masks and turnout gear."

"I think they wear that for protection. Fireproof stuff, you know."

"You can't tell who you're looking at. You can't tell if the person behind the mask is even a real damn firefighter."

"What?" She squirmed and glanced back.

"You get the uniform. You get the mask. You blend right in." His mind was going a hundred miles an hour. "One minute, the fire at my bar seemed to be out. The next, the place was igniting like a bomb went off inside of it."

"You heard Lieutenant Vaughn. Reflashing can happen."

Sure. Another arson could happen, too. "What if someone went in and restarted the fire? All of those people in uniforms...we don't know who the hell belonged there and who didn't. I was so sure the bastard was watching my bar burn. What if he was watching and wearing a firefighter's uniform? No one would have even looked twice at him." Such an easy way to get close to the fire.

Silence.

Great. She was probably going to tell him that he was being crazy. But...

"What if..." Avalon's voice was halting. "What if he *did* belong there?"

He slanted a fast glance her way.

"The people who know the most about fires?" She pressed her lips together. "They're firefighters. What if—all along—the bad guy has been someone that the rest of the world thinks is a hero?"

He pushed the gas pedal down harder and said once more, "Sonofabitch."

* * *

"Firefighters!" Beau slammed the driver side door of the Jag and stalked around to Avalon's side. He yanked open her door even as he kept the phone pressed to his ear. "Dammit, Lane, I know you heard me the first time!"

Avalon climbed out of the car. Her gaze darted from him to the dark house that waited about thirty feet away. Her house.

A yellow line of tape—CAUTION DO NOT ENTER

—stretched from one column on her porch to the other. The tape flapped lightly in the hot breeze.

"We both know that you and Ophelia have access to not-quite-legal means of acquiring intel. I need you to look back at the fires in Louisiana and see which firefighters might have responded to all the calls. See who was on the scenes. Then see if any of those names match up with the firefighters who responded to the blazes that took the two victims that we have *after* New Orleans."

When she stepped away from her car, he slammed the door shut. Her gaze remained on the front of her home. She'd loved that house. Loved the big azalea bushes on either side of the porch. Loved the giant oak near the slightly jagged sidewalk.

"And, yes, cross-reference everything. See if any names from New Orleans happen to pop up at any of the stations here in Savannah. Though, hell, we all know how easy it is to change a name." He hummed. "Maybe we need to get physical descriptions of the firefighters and compare those."

As she started to advance toward the house, Beau moved in perfect time with her.

"What do you mean, I'm asking for a miracle?" His voice rose. "I will pay for the miracle. Name the price. Ophelia knows I'm good for it, and so do you. Yes, yes, dammit, I get that firefighters are the good guys. But what if one *isn't* so good? Think about it. Think about *my* blaze at LeBlanc's. Everything was calm. And then—with all the firefighters right there, all the masks covering them—hell came calling."

She heard Lane blast out a retort to Beau's words, but she couldn't quite make out what he was saying.

Avalon crept up the porch.

Beau's hand flew out and curled around her wrist. One

hand on her. One hand around the phone that still pressed to his ear. "Here's an idea," he spoke quickly into the phone even as he held her. "I bet they have old pics of the station crews over in New Orleans. Get the pics. Get someone to email you the ones from—" He broke off. "Yeah, buddy, I *get* how long it has been, and, again, I'll pay for the miracle. If we can get names, if we can get photos, we might be able to get *him*. I will pay anything to bury him."

She tugged her arm.

He didn't let her go.

"Thank you," he groused into the phone.

Her head turned. Her gaze met his.

"Hell, yes, I'm watching her. Got my eyes on her right now."

He actually wore sunglasses, so she couldn't see his eyes, but she felt his stare.

"Yes, I was with her at the prison." A pause. "No, I don't know how the hell that scene went down in the yard. I want to talk to Moses when he's off his shift and see what he's heard. My gut is telling me someone ordered a hit on Everett. Someone with enough pull to get multiple inmates to attack. I swear, it feels like a gang hit to me."

And Beau would know about that. A shiver skirted down her body.

"Everett *knew* the identity of the arsonist. And the arsonist got too scared that Everett would give him up. So he sped up the SOB's execution date."

The wind blew against her, but it didn't feel so hot any longer.

"We're checking her house. No, no, it's not a B&E if it's *her* house. What am I? A criminal? Uh, huh. Right. Look, I've got to go. Call me when you know more. And, man?

Thanks. Thanks to you and Ophelia." He hung up. Shoved the phone in the back pocket of his jeans.

How to phrase this delicately? "You're being very optimistic to think that they will be able to turn up records from so long ago."

"I'm an optimistic kind of guy."

Her brows lifted. Since when?

"Lane and Ophelia already talked to the arson investigators who were in charge back then. They have contacts. One of their contacts can get them the information that they need. And if the current contacts don't work, Lane and Ophelia are resourceful. I trust them to uncover what we need by other means."

She realized he meant that. Total faith. "They're your friends."

"Damn straight."

"And so is Royal."

"Right. And if you can't get your friends to break the law and help you catch a killer, then who can you count on?"

Avalon shook her head. "Beau..."

"Let me go in first. Could be dangerous in there. Don't know if the fire did any structural damage. As soon as possible, I want a construction crew out here. I will have your house built back so well that you'll never know this happened. I swear it." He took off his sunglasses and hung them on his shirt. Beau brushed past her, ducked under the yellow tape, and made his way onto the porch. "The front door is still broken. What is this shit? Couldn't the cops at least patch it up? Anyone could get inside, at any time."

Not so reassuring.

She slipped under the tape, too. Avalon followed him inside the house. And, at first, things weren't bad at all. The foyer looked mostly normal. Sure, the chandelier was covered in soot and there was a heavy, smoke smell in the air but...

She made her way to the den. Froze in her tracks. Her piano had burned. Her books were ashes. And her white bookshelves that she'd carefully painted? What remained of them was a scary, darkened husk.

"Rebuild," Beau promised, voice grim but determined. "We absolutely will rebuild. Picture it the way it will be, sweetheart. This will be gone."

So many things were already gone. The piano that she'd loved. The books that she'd had since she was a teenager. She and her mom had bought most of those classics after the fire. Because the first fire—the one in New Orleans—had also taken away her cherished books. And her mother's beloved piano.

That monster fire had taken the whole house.

This time, the fire had been limited to the ground floor. Primarily to the den. The books were gone. The photos on the shelves that she'd had of her family were gone. Pictures from childhood—gone. And the piano. Gone.

She turned around, frowning. "The things that mattered the most to me."

Beau was near the remnants of the piano. At her words, he frowned over at her. "I can get everything back."

She knew he wanted to, but...the childhood photos? They'd been given to her by her grandparents. All of her other photos from when she'd been a kid had been lost in the Garden District fire. Yes, they could buy more books. They could buy another piano.

Don't get hung up on this stuff. He lost his bar. Beau isn't bitching and moaning when he lost the thing that mattered most to—

Her breath caught. She spun back to stare at the bookcase. "He took the things that mattered most to both of us. Targeted. Deliberate."

A loud creak came from upstairs.

Her head whipped back as she looked up.

Another creak.

Was the ceiling about to cave in? Beau had mentioned being worried about the structure of the place but—

He was running for the stairs. "Beau!" she called out.

"Someone is up there!" Beau paused only long enough to yank a knife from his boot. He'd had that strapped to his ankle?

Avalon snapped her mouth closed and gave chase behind him. His feet pounded up the stairs. So did hers. Whoever was up there had to hear them coming. At the landing, Beau didn't hesitate. He immediately turned for her room. The door was partially open.

He shoved open that door fully. She heard a gasp. A thud. Avalon rushed inside.

Beau had a dark-haired man pinned to the wall. The man wore blue coveralls, black safety shoes, and a safety helmet tilted to the side on his head.

Beau's knife was at the man's throat. "Who the hell are you?" Beau demanded. "And what are you doing in her house?"

Chapter Eighteen

The intruder's eyes doubled in size. Blue eyes that were about to bulge right out of his head. "S-searching—"

"Searching for what?" Beau scanned the bedroom. "You leave something behind in the house the first time you were here, bastard?"

The tiniest shake of the intruder's head. If he'd shaken more, the knife would have sliced him.

"Arson..." A gasp.

"Yeah, we fucking know that," Beau snapped right back.

"In...investigator!"

"Beau." Avalon touched his shoulder. "Pull back the knife. I think he's saying that he's the arson investigator."

A quick nod. "Yessssss." A long hiss. Like a balloon deflating.

"Show me the ID," Beau snapped. But he did pull back the knife.

With a shaking hand, the man pulled out his wallet. Flipped it open and handed it to Beau. Swearing, Beau finally stepped back and shoved the knife back into his boot.

"OhGodOhGodOhGod." The dark-haired stranger sucked in a gulp of air. He shoved his shaking hand through his hair.

Beau handed her the ID. A driver's license was on one side of the wallet and a card identifying the man as arson investigator Colton Ross was on the other.

"Your car wasn't out front," Beau snapped.

Colton snatched back the wallet. When he did, Avalon saw the raised scars on the inside of his right hand.

Fire burns. Long healed.

"I pulled up around back because I didn't want nosey neighbors coming to grill me. This is a *closed* scene." Colton's gaze darted from Beau to Avalon then back to Beau. "You just assaulted me!"

"Uh, correction," Beau returned without missing a beat. "I just stopped someone I thought was an intruder."

"I identified myself!"

"Be a little faster next time," Beau advised.

Colton's eyes narrowed.

"This is my home," Avalon interjected because someone needed to calm things way, way down. Fast. "We didn't realize anyone else was here. I-I came with my boyfriend because I just needed to take a look around." She eased closer to Beau's side. "When we heard noise on the second floor, we thought the arsonist had come back. I'm sure you can understand—in light of what happened here— that we were both afraid."

Colton's lips tightened. The investigator looked to be in his mid-thirties. Close-cropped, dark hair. Blue eyes. A slightly hawkish nose and a hard jaw. "I'm sorry for what happened to you, ma'am." The south came and went in his voice.

A flicker of familiarity slid over Avalon.

"But this is a crime scene. You do not have the all clear to be here. I haven't finished my work."

"The fire was on the first floor. Why are you up here, in her bedroom?" Beau wanted to know.

Blue eyes blinked.

"Technically," Beau added as he sized up the other man, "a crime did occur in this room. This is where Slater Wade was lying in wait for Avalon."

She glanced toward the windows. Her gaze darted around the room. She had a flash of herself fighting the masked attacker. She'd been on the floor. Kicking back at him. Her gaze shifted to the chair near the door. A chair that had fallen to the side. Her taser had been in the purse that she'd put on that chair. Avalon had been so desperate to get the taser. She'd reached it, used it, and Slater had jolted.

Her stare slid over the floor. She could see the fight so clearly in her mind. Every instant felt etched in her memory. *More like burned in my head.*

"There was no fire up here, though," Beau continued in a grim tone laced with suspicion. "So what are you looking for in this room?"

Avalon inhaled and pulled in the heavy scent of smoke. The smokey smell was everywhere.

"I believe in being thorough," Colton responded curtly. "I don't half-ass any of my jobs. Not the scene here, and not my next target, your bar."

Target? Her shoulders stiffened.

"I'm very good at my job. But I can't do it when knives are being shoved at my throat." Colton straightened to his full height. A height just a little shorter than Beau's. "You two need to leave, now."

Getting kicked out of her own house...okay, fine

correction—her *arson scene of a house*—was not the way she'd thought this search would go.

"You lead the way back downstairs," Beau invited, and she knew he was just as suspicious of the investigator as she was. "And we'll go."

Colton groused but turned and began marching out of her bedroom. He didn't glance back.

She did share a long look with Beau.

"Oh, damn straight, baby," he breathed as his head dipped toward her and his lips skimmed over her left ear. "We'll have Lane and Ophelia investigate him the minute we get back to the car."

Clearly, they were on the same page.

Beau put his body between hers and the arson investigator's as they headed down the stairs. But she craned her head, and she was able to make out the letters on the back of Colton's coveralls. *Fire Inspector*.

Once on the ground floor, Colton crossed his arms over his chest and waited. His impatience was clear. His left foot even tapped against the floor. When Avalon climbed off the last step, her gaze darted toward the den, and then back to him. She hated to leave without more answers. "The fire started on the bookcase."

His nostrils flared. "I'm not supposed to discuss this case with civilians. I'm supposed to write my report, present it, and then—"

"It's clear that the fire burned the hottest there. When we were upstairs that night, I remember hearing a really loud whoosh." No other way to describe it. "The sound scared the hell out of me." She'd actually already been scared as all hell, but at that distinct sound, terror had crawled through her.

I'd heard that sound before. A very, very long time ago.

Because the night of the fire in New Orleans? She'd heard that same, terrible *whoosh* as fire raced its way through her home.

Sympathy flashed on Colton's face. Was that a crack in his armor? A chink she could use to her advantage?

Her lips curved down. "This is my second fire. I lost everything in the first one. I've tried to learn about fires since then."

His right hand rose. Straightened his helmet.

"You start by looking for the origin of the fire. That's step one, isn't it?" She edged toward the den. "The bookcase looks like the origin. It burned the hardest."

"Hottest." He slipped toward the den, too.

"Because an accelerant was used on the bookshelf?"

His gaze was on the bookshelf. A quick nod. Barely perceptible. "Burn pattern starts there." Once more, his right hand lifted. A flash of the scars on his palm before his fingers curled in—all except for the index finger that pointed toward the shelf. "You can see it span out. Accelerant was thrown at the shelf. Found pieces of a broken bottle. Would have led to the whoosh sound you heard."

"Like a...Molotov cocktail?" Avalon asked carefully. That was the one used in all the movies.

"Don't know what kind of accelerant was in the bottle. But I believe he hit twice. One hit there." A point of his index finger at the bookshelf. "One there." His finger swung toward the piano. "Very targeted. Honestly, if he'd wanted the place to go up, there were a lot of better ways to do it. All this did was cause localized damage." His hand dropped to his side. "This info will be in my report." A sniff. "And I'm not saying more. Not until I turn that file over to the detectives."

"Which detectives would that be?" Beau asked casually. "So many work at the PD."

"Cunninghan usually works on arsons with me. Always has ever since he came to town a few years ago. He'll get the report first."

"Thanks so much for the information." Beau inclined his head toward the investigator. "And my apologies for the mishap with the knife."

"Mishap?" Colton grunted. "That was no mishap. That was assault."

Beau's eyes narrowed. "After the attack on Avalon, I'm sure you can understand I don't take lightly to strange men appearing in her bedroom. I'm afraid I had a bit of a flashback. Instinct took over."

"Your instinct is to attack?"

"When I think she's in danger, absolutely."

Avalon twisted her hands in front of her body. "It was a mistake. My boyfriend is just extremely protective."

Colton's stare swept to Avalon. He nodded. "Yeah, all right. I get it." Colton swiped his hand over his neck. "No harm done." His shoulders squared. "But you two need to leave, now."

They'd pushed as much as they could. "Thank you for the help," Avalon said.

A curt nod.

She and Beau headed for the broken door.

"I-I know it's hard."

Colton's voice stopped her. She looked back.

"Being trapped in the fire. I know how hard it can be." He'd lifted his hand again. He opened it toward her. "I don't go in the fires any longer. I lost my best friend in one. Tried to pull him out but..." His hand clenched. "You make it out of a fire once, you consider yourself damn lucky. You make it out of a fire twice, and I'd say you need to go buy yourself a lottery ticket."

She and Beau had both made it out twice.

"Don't go for a third time." Colton's gaze dipped to Beau. "It won't be the charm for either of you. It might just be a death sentence."

* * *

Beau shut Avalon's car door. He walked slowly around the front of the Jag and tossed a wave to the arson investigator who stood on her porch and watched him.

Colton didn't wave back. Shocking.

Colton did pull out his phone and make a call. Yep, that guy was not going to be forgetting the scene with the knife anytime soon. That "no harm done" bit? Total BS.

Beau opened the driver's side door, slid inside, and even before he'd pulled his door shut—"So, at the end there, was he threatening us," Avalon asked as she gave a little wave to the watching investigator, "or trying to offer friendly advice so that we stayed alive?"

The engine growled to life. "Very hard call to make." *But I'd probably go with option one.*

"Uh, huh."

He got them on the road and away from her house.

"You think he's phoning Cunningham?"

"Oh, I am one hundred percent sure of that." Now that was hardly a difficult call to determine.

"Did you know that Cunningham worked the majority of arson cases in town?"

"Not until about five minutes ago, no, I didn't know that very important fact. Makes sense, though, seeing as how he was the detective questioning you the morning after the fire at your house."

"Cunningham probably knows a lot about fires. How to start them. How to get away with setting them."

Beau dipped his head forward. "Again, I am now one hundred percent sure of that fact." He turned to the right and pulled to a stop on a small cul-de-sac. Quickly, he fired off a text to Lane and Ophelia. He definitely wanted to know more about their arson investigator. The arson investigator had set off Beau's inner alarms for a variety of reasons. *No sign of your car. You were digging in the bedroom. You never told me why you were up there. And I swear, I heard the twang of New Orleans in your voice once or twice.*

"You did pull a knife on him," Avalon noted. "Maybe that's why he wasn't quite so cooperative at first."

She'd gotten the guy to open up. By being all casual and non-threatening. Batting those gorgeous eyes of hers. Pulling on his sympathy. *If* the man had actually been sympathetic. Beau didn't trust him for a second. At this point, he was sure most of the world was just hiding behind a mask. "Don't like that he was in your bedroom."

"Maybe he was being thorough."

"Yeah, or maybe he was checking to make sure Slater hadn't left anything behind that could tie back to him. Maybe—" Beau's phone rang, cutting through his words.

At first, he thought the call might be from Lane or Ophelia. A response to the text he'd just sent. But, no, the pic flashing on the scene was of Kai. What the hell did his bouncer want at this time of the day? Kai worked nights. Normally. When there was, you know, a bar to actually work at.

What is happening now?

His finger swiped over the screen, and he put the phone to his ear. "Kai, you had better not be calling to tell me that something else is burning. Because I am not in the mood to hear that news."

"Detectives spent the last hour grilling me," Kai responded flatly. "I came to LeBlanc's in order to take a look around. Thought I'd make sure we didn't have anyone trying to break inside and steal anything."

"Uh, is there anything left to steal?" Doubtful.

"Not much. Sorry, boss. Shit's gone to hell here."

Beau grunted. He'd figured that out when he watched the place burn. "No employees were hurt. That's what matters." The fire had been during the day, when the bar was usually closed up tight. The arsonist had counted on no one being there.

But you didn't count on Lane, did you? He was upstairs. He almost caught you. Almost. So the arsonist had fled the scene...

Or had he?

"You always take good care of your staff." Kai exhaled on a hard breath that carried over the phone. "That's why I'm here now. You gave me a place when I needed it. I don't buy any of the bull that Detective Cunningham was spewing. I know you didn't burn down your own bar just to collect insurance money."

Beau's left hand rose to squeeze the bridge of his nose. "Tell me that's not the theory."

"What's he saying?" Avalon asked.

Beau lowered the phone and put it on speaker. "Oh, just the usual," he answered Avalon. "That jackass detective suspects I burned down my bar for insurance money."

"I told him it was bull, boss." Anger vibrated in Kai's voice. "And I don't think the pretty lady detective with the red hair bought that theory, anyway. It was mostly Cunningham. Heads up, I don't think he likes you."

"Shocking," Beau rasped. *Detective Cuntingham hates me? The feeling is mutual.*

"He was questioning me hard, but then he got called away. Something about a dead body being found at another fire? I mean, damn, how many fires are we gonna have in this town? When I decided to move here from Hawaii, no one said it was the arson capital of the world."

Beau looked over at Avalon. "It's not." Someone was just very busy and very dangerous.

She nibbled on her lower lip, then asked, "Did you happen to hear where this fire was?"

"Sweetheart," Beau whispered. "We already know." They'd passed the scene earlier.

"I just heard the name Slater mentioned," Kai recalled. "Does that help any?"

"It does." Confirmation of Beau's suspicion. Now, next question, who had died in Slater's house?

"What else can I do?" Kai pushed. "You need extra eyes on your girl? You want me to take a bodyguard shift? I know how protective you get of her, and with these blazes going down, you have to be about to lose your mind."

Not his mind. His control.

"Name it," Kai urged. "Tell me what to do and I am on it, boss."

"I have eyes on her." Straight on her. "You keep eyes on the bar. And if you see an arson investigator arrive at LeBlanc's, you let me know, got it? Text or call right away."

"Done."

"Thanks, man. Appreciate it. And do me one more favor? If you see a fire, run away from it. Not into it." Beau exhaled as he hung up the phone.

"Who died in the fire at Slater's?" Avalon's low question. "And when is this going to stop?"

When we make it stop.

But before he could say another word, Beau heard the shriek of a siren. One that seemed to be coming closer. "Let's get home." He needed to think. To plan.

To have her somewhere safe.

He started the car. Got out of the cul-de-sac.

But he kept hearing the shriek of sirens.

And, soon enough, he saw the flash of blue lights in his rearview mirror. Hell. He'd known this might happen. "Avalon..."

She'd already whipped around to stare behind him. "I see them."

The cops were closing in. There were lots of ways he could play this scene. After all, it wasn't his first time to be hunted. But it was his first time having her with him during a hunt. "Ophelia is a lawyer."

"What?" Her head was still turned to gaze behind them. "I thought she was a PI!"

"She's both. She's *my* lawyer. You'll need to get her to come to the station when they take me."

"No one is taking you anywhere!"

Oh, but they were. He slowed down because he wasn't about to get involved in a car chase with Avalon in the passenger seat, even though he knew the Jag could leave the patrol car in the dust. Her safety always had to come first for him.

"I'll let them take me in. It has to happen." If he ran,

every cop in the area would chase him. And innocent men weren't supposed to run.

I've never been one hundred percent innocent.

"*Why* would they want to take you in?"

He was sure there would be plenty of reasons. "Trust me, okay? I want you to call Ophelia as soon as they cuff me. And I want you to take my phone—right now—and I want you to send a text to Royal. He's my first contact in the phone."

She grabbed for his phone. "What do I tell him?"

"Code Avalon."

"*What?*"

"He'll stay with you until I get free."

"You don't know that they are arresting you!" But from the corner of his eye, he saw her fire off the text.

He pulled the vehicle to the side of the road. "I've been through this routine a time or twenty, sweetheart. I know how it will go down." After rolling down the driver's side window, he put his hands flat on the dash. "Trust me. Trust Ophelia. Lane. Royal. The people I just listed, but no one else, got it?"

"Beau..."

"And remember that I love you."

Her mouth dropped open. He would have liked to kiss that beautiful mouth, but two uniformed officers were racing toward his car with their guns drawn.

"Beau LeBlanc!" A shout from the closest cop. "Come out with your hands up!"

He sent Avalon a wink of reassurance. "Totally have this under control."

"You totally do not." She'd gone pale.

"Stay in the car, sweetheart. Please." He opened his

door. "I really want to call my friend Ophelia," he announced as he climbed out. "Don't want to chat without my good buddy. And, by the way, I have a knife strapped to my ankle."

The cops leapt for him.

Chapter Nineteen

"HE HASN'T DONE ANYTHING!" AVALON FELT LIKE AN absolute broken record as she paced in front of Detective Lynn Baker's desk. "I'm telling you, Beau was with me all day! He didn't—"

Lynn's sigh cut through her words. "I know he was with you. Colton Ross said you were present when Beau assaulted him with a knife."

Her stomach dipped. "That was a misunderstanding." She'd insisted on going to the police station. Beau had been cuffed right in front of her. Cuffed and pushed into the back of a patrol car. "We were at my house. We thought the arson investigator was an intruder!"

"He wasn't an intruder. He was a man doing his job. *You* shouldn't have been there. Beau shouldn't have attacked him with a knife." Lynn's gaze was steady. "Colton called in the attack the minute Beau left. An APB was put out for Beau, and...here we are."

At the police station. With Beau being booked and questioned and Avalon about to go out of her head with worry and frustration.

"Don't you think it's about time you saw him for what he is?" Lynn asked. The detective winced. "I get it. Truly. You are hardly the first woman to fall for the wrong man."

"Beau isn't wrong."

"From where I am sitting, there is very little that is *right* about him." Lynn held up her hand and began ticking off issues. "He was at the prison when the riot went down and an inmate died. Don't tell me that's not suspicious. One word from Beau—one whisper—and he probably set the whole thing in motion."

"No." Avalon shook her head.

"And do you know how much insurance he has on LeBlanc's? The man is set to get a windfall."

"He already has plenty of money. I've seen his house."

"Yeah, well, just where do you think Beau got all his cash? You actually think he earned it the old-fashioned, honest way?" Mocking. "Come on, you are smarter than this."

"I am smarter than this. You're right. Smart enough to know Beau didn't have anything to do with the riot. He was protecting me when chaos reigned at the prison. He protected the DA. Beau carried him out of there when Douglas was attacked."

Lynn's brows rose. "He did what?"

"He—"

A knock at the door. Before Lynn could tell the visitor to come in, the door swung open, and Detective Campbell Cunningham popped his head inside. "I'm starting the interrogation. You in, Lynn?" Then his gaze collided with Avalon's. "What are you doing here?"

"I'm waiting to take Beau home. This is a misunderstanding."

A sharp bark of laughter escaped the detective. "He's

not going home. He's going to a cell. Or hell, maybe that is home to him."

"I get the nickname," she snapped. "I really get it now."

"I don't know what damn nickname you're talking about. But I've got a dead body. I've got people who *saw* Beau's Jag leaving the scene of the fire today—"

Her eyes widened. "I was with him! We were just—" She stopped. Right before she accidentally said...*We were just planning my first breaking and entering*. Nope. That would not be helpful to admit at this point in time.

"You were what?" Campbell pounced.

"I wanted to do a sweep in front of Slater Wade's house. But we saw the fire, so we went back to my place."

"Learn to lie better," Lynn urged her as the detective rose from the seat behind her desk. "Or maybe, learn to hang around with people who don't make you have to lie in the first place. Now, for the last time, leave the station, Avalon. You aren't seeing Beau. And, yes, Cam, I am *in* for the interrogation."

* * *

THE INTERROGATION ROOM DOOR OPENED. Campbell Cunningham entered first. Face looking all intent and angry. Stomping steps. Badass attitude like he was about to do something incredibly important.

Lynn followed. Softer steps. Gaze just as hard. Plenty of suspicion on her face.

But it was just the two of them. No one else. Odd. "I thought my friend was coming," Beau murmured.

"I told Avalon she wasn't going to see you." Lynn pulled out the chair across from him. "Don't you think you've done enough to that woman? You really want to make her an accessory to your crimes?"

"What crimes would those be?" His hands were cuffed in front of him. Overkill, really. "It would be ever so helpful if you spelled them out for me."

"You assaulted an arson investigator!"

Oh, starting with that, were they? "I thought he was an intruder. When he identified himself, I immediately backed off." Beau shrugged. "Is that it? The big crime? Because I have to say, that was certainly easy to clear up."

"You forced him to reveal details about the investigation!" Campbell accused.

Beau narrowed his eyes. "Only if by 'forced' then you mean...asked him and he overshared? Then, yes. I suppose you could look at it that way."

"You were interfering in a criminal investigation!"

He'd been trying to hurry along the criminal investigation. "I was escorting my girlfriend to *her* house." That was the story they'd given the arson investigator. And someone had certainly been fast at calling the cops.

And getting me locked away.

But hadn't he suspected—as soon as he saw Colton with that phone on the porch—that this would happen?

Campbell pulled out the chair next to Lynn. The legs screeched over the floor. "Does the name Max Donway mean anything to you?"

"It means zero to me."

Grunting, Campbell sat in the seat. "You sure about that?"

"If the name is supposed to ring a bell, it doesn't. Want to clue me in on its significance?" The detectives thought they were grilling him.

He was busy grilling them. No sense wasting a good opportunity for intel.

"Sure, sure, happy to do it." Campbell watched him like a hawk. "Not too long ago, Lieutenant Wesley Vaughn—you met him before, didn't you? At the fire that occurred at LeBlanc's?"

"That name is familiar," Beau allowed. He watched Campbell just as closely even as he wondered...*Who the hell is Max Donway? Just spit out the info already.*

"Max Donway was a guard at the McKinley prison."

Beau did not change expression.

"Believe you were present there today, weren't you? Terrible thing, that riot."

"Terrible," Beau echoed. He didn't blink.

"Interesting story..."

He was waiting to hear one.

"Seems that Max Donway was one of the guards present in the room when Avalon Trahan had her first chat with Everett Thomas."

Shit. That was actually interesting. "How do you know that?"

"Because I talked to DA Douglas Baptiste not ten minutes ago and he told me."

Lynn's gaze darted between Beau and Campbell.

"Max Donway didn't show up for work today," Campbell revealed. "Another interesting element to add to our mix, isn't it? He's not at work on the day a group of prisoners magically get out of their cells and kill Everett Thomas."

"Don't know that there was magic involved." Beau could hear the ticking of the clock on the wall. "Don't remember anyone yelling abracadabra at me."

Campbell's eyes narrowed.

"But how about we get back to Lieutenant Wesley Vaughn," Beau said. Keeping the detective on track was an effort. "I believe you were about to tell me that he did something, ah, not too long ago, I believe it was?"

"He pulled Max Donway's body from the fire at Slater Wade's rental house."

Beau still did not change his expression. Didn't so much as let his breathing alter.

"Burns were over ninety percent of the prison guard's body, and he was stone cold dead."

"With that many burns, I'd actually think he was hell hot." Mocking words even as his heart seemed to squeeze in his chest.

Campbell leapt right back to his feet. "You sonofabitch! A man is *dead.*" His eyes blazed. "And I think I'm staring straight at his killer. One remorseless bastard who likes to play with fire."

* * *

AVALON MARCHED past the check-in desk at the police station. Ophelia was supposed to be on her way. They'd talked twice on the phone, and Ophelia had assured her that she would be arriving any moment.

Hurry, please hurry. If Ophelia was really Beau's lawyer, shouldn't she be in interrogation with him? How could the cops even talk to Beau without her being present?

Avalon peered through the glass doors but saw no sign of Ophelia. Avalon spun around and collided with—

The firefighter?

Tall, dark hair. In a blue firefighter's t-shirt and some kind of blue cargo pants. Shadows lined Lieutenant Wesley Vaughn's eyes. A smear of ash stained his left cheek.

"Sorry," she murmured quickly. "I didn't see you there."

He swallowed. Nodded.

She started to step out of his way but stopped. "Is everything okay?" Because he looked like he'd seen a ghost.

"I like saving people. That's why I do the job. To save. To help." His voice came out so hoarse. As if he'd been screaming. Or battling a fire. "I don't like pulling the dead from the rubble. They stay with you. You never, ever forget them." A long exhale. "I-I was giving my statement to Detective Cunningham. I need to go."

And she was still blocking his path. "Someone died today?"

He nodded. "So many burns…" A shake of his head. "I have to get back to my station. Need to check on my crew."

She eased out of his path. But even as Wesley hurried out of the station, Royal was there. He stepped to the side and frowned at the firefighter. Wesley didn't even look twice at him.

Avalon bolted through the door and met Royal on the station's steps.

"That man looked like the grim reaper." Royal peered after Wesley. "Never a good look."

"The cops have Beau in custody."

"That would be why I got the Code Avalon." He extended his hand to her. "We need to get the hell out this place."

"Uh, no. We need to get the hell back *in* there." She jerked her thumb over her shoulder to indicate the station. "And we need to help Beau!"

High heels clicked on the steps. "That's why I'm here!" Ophelia waved as she hurried toward them.

Lane shadowed her steps.

"They won't stop me from seeing Beau." Ophelia's voice

was slightly breathless. "I can do this scene in my sleep. I'll have him out of here in no time. Provided he doesn't say some asshole comment, piss off the cops even more, and screw us all to hell and back before I can get in there to shut him up."

"It's a mistake." They all needed to understand this. "They're charging him with assault. Saying that he attacked an arson investigator."

"Did he?" Lane asked. He stood just behind Ophelia.

"A mistake," she repeated. How many times would she have to say that? Mistake. Misunderstanding. Dammit. "We didn't know who the guy was. As soon as Colton—"

"Colton Ross?" Ophelia practically jumped at her.

"Yes, Colton Ross. As soon as he identified himself as an arson investigator, Beau lowered his knife."

Royal squeezed his eyes shut. "Of course, he'd have a knife. He always has one."

"They're interrogating him now, aren't they?" Ophelia's gaze snapped toward the station's doors. "Lane, come on! We need to be in there."

"Uh, *I* need to be in there, too." Avalon needed to be at Beau's side.

Royal's eyes opened. "A Code Avalon means I am supposed to get you to someplace safe. I'm supposed to stay as your guard until Beau can come to your side. I'll go out on a limb and say, I don't think he believes just hanging out at the police station is the place you should be right now."

Sympathy darkened Ophelia's gaze as she studied Avalon. "You will not be able to help him here, but I can. I'll get him free as fast as possible, and then he will come to you." Her lips thinned. "Colton Ross once served on the New Orleans FD. Lane and I haven't been able to dig much, but pulling up his background was easy enough. The guy was in New Orleans, and now he's just succeeded in getting Beau locked up here in Savannah. Beau is locked up, and as far as Colton knows, *you* are on your own, Avalon."

"She's not," Royal said at once. "Consider me her human shield." His hand was still up. Waiting for Avalon.

"I will get Beau out of here," Ophelia promised. "*Trust me*."

Avalon nodded. "He said to trust you." Her gaze darted to Lane. Then to Royal. "All of you."

"If you trust him," Royal did not lower his hand, "then trust us."

No part of her wanted to leave that station. But she wasn't the one who could help Beau. Not then. "Get him out," she told Ophelia.

A grim nod. "I will. But in order to do that, *he* will need to know you're safe. If he's crazy with worry for you, the man is going to be even more difficult to handle than normal. And that's saying a lot."

"Code Avalon," Royal murmured.

Avalon finally took his offered hand. "By the way, when this mess is over, we are having a serious talk about your extracurriculars."

His brows flew up. "I have no idea what you're talking about."

"Whatever. Consider yourself warned. The party is over."

Sighing, he curled his fingers around hers. "Beau never mentioned you were such a buzzkill."

Chapter Twenty

"Save us all time and effort and, for once in your life, do the right thing." Campbell glared down at Beau with disgust on his face. "Confess to your crimes. Admit the truth about what you've been doing."

Oh, sure, he could confess to some things. "I admit—"

The door flew open. Ophelia filled the doorway. Lane stood just behind her.

I admit that you're an asshole. Aw, he hadn't gotten the chance to share those heartfelt words with the detective. Too bad. Maybe next time.

There would always be a next time.

"*What* is happening here?" Ophelia demanded, voice dramatically accusing. "Surely it is *not* two detectives, interrogating a suspect, without the suspect's lawyer present?"

"The man never asked for a lawyer," Campbell snapped back. "And you should not be here. Why the hell is everyone always busting in like this is some free-for-all? It's a closed interrogation room."

Beau cleared his throat. "I actually did ask for a lawyer. An important point, I believe, to note."

Campbell blinked at him. "What?"

"It was the first thing I did when the uniforms pulled me over. Told them that I really wanted to chat with my friend Ophelia." He shrugged. His cuffed hands scraped over the top of the table. "I believe I even told them that I didn't want to chat without my very 'good buddy' with me. Yet here we are. Chatting away."

"I'm his *good buddy* Ophelia Raine," she clarified sweetly. "His lawyer."

"You're the PI." Campbell's face had scrunched up. An even worse look than normal for him.

"I'm a PI and a lawyer." A little smirk came and went on her face. "Go ask some of your detective buddies. They know exactly who I am. A woman who adores wearing many hats because they all make me look stylish." She waved a hand behind her. "And this is my partner, Lane."

Lane wasn't a lawyer. He was a PI. So, yes, technically her partner. But she'd worded things ambiguously with the cops. Beau had learned that trick from her and now used it to his advantage at every opportunity.

"If you had my client talking after he specifically *asked* to speak with his lawyer..." A sad shake of her head. She even made a tut-tut click with her tongue. "That is going to prove highly problematic for you."

"He was *just about to admit his crimes!*" Campbell's breath heaved in and out as a vein bulged near his forehead.

"Really? Why would an innocent man confess anything?" She hauled a chair away from the wall and put it right next to Beau. "By the way." Her nails tapped across his arm as she settled into her chair. "Colton Ross used to be a firefighter in New Orleans."

Beau lunged up.

But Lane had sidled behind him, and Lane's hard grip on his shoulders pushed him right back down.

"Thought you'd like to know that," Ophelia murmured as both Lynn and Campbell frowned at her. "And also know that Avalon has left the station. She's in good hands. But she really, really wants you to hurry home to her." Her fingers came together in a little steeple in front of her as she faced off with the detectives. "Now, how about we speed this situation along? I've got an innocent client. You've got a misunderstanding with a man who may or may not be tied to this whole twisted mess that stretches back for years...and I want to know what needs to happen so that Beau walks out of here. Preferably in the next thirty minutes."

"How does it go back for years with Colton?" Lynn asked as her head cocked. She craned forward a bit.

"*Beau isn't walking out of here. Over my dead body does this killer walk,*" Campbell snarled.

"That could be arranged," Beau offered.

Lane's grip tightened on his shoulders. "My friend, you are not helping things."

No, he probably wasn't. His bad. But playing nicely with Detective *Cuntingham*? So hard.

* * *

"You should get some sleep," Royal advised Avalon. "It's nearing midnight."

And Beau still wasn't home. She'd been pacing for hours. Glancing out of the front windows far too many times.

They were in Beau's house. With Beau's security system firmly in place. But Beau was nowhere to be found.

"Ophelia texted me an update not too long ago. She isn't giving up. Colton came to the station. Went over his statement again and left. When the cops tried to ask him about his time in New Orleans, he clammed up and got the hell out of there."

Like that wasn't a big, flashing, warning sign?

"Ophelia thinks the cops are suspicious of him now, but you still have the word of an arson investigator going against Beau. And, well, Beau did confess to pulling the knife." He rubbed a hand over the back of his neck. "The man is confessing to far too damn much these days."

She let the curtain fall. Beau wasn't close. She should stop looking into the dark. "You're referring to the extracurriculars?"

"I have no idea what you mean."

Avalon turned toward him. "I mean the habit you and Beau seem to have where you track down killers, knock them out, and leave them cuffed for the cops to find. Oh, and you put red bows on them. Because that's just a touch that can't be forgotten, am I right?"

He folded his arms over his chest. "Why the hell would I do something like that?"

"Because you don't like the idea of killers getting away with their crimes?" That was her suspicion. "But it's one very deadly habit."

Royal grunted. "You're one to talk. Though I guess, technically, yours isn't a habit so much as it is a deadly career path."

It had certainly taken a deadly turn recently. "You're playing with fire."

Laughter. "No, I think that would be the guy after you. He's the one starting fires left and right." Now he rose from the couch. "Come on, Avalon, would you really be pissed if

Beau and I caught the man who has been after you for so long? If we cuffed him and had him waiting for the cops like a way early Christmas present?"

"Is that the plan? Cuffing him? Or is it killing him?"

Royal closed in on her. "I think if Beau had his way, the guy would just wind up in the ground."

"And is that what *was* supposed to happen? Beau started an investigation on the arsonist, he pulled in his team, and when the perp was located, you and Beau were just going to step in?" She held her breath as she waited for the answer.

His head cocked. "If I say yes, will that make you hate Beau? Will you go running from him because you think he's some kind of monster?"

Her lips pressed together.

"He's loved you for years." Blunt. "I get that he's not exactly Prince Charming, and I told him that he should just freaking talk to you and not hang in the shadows, but he's never felt like he's good enough for you. When you're thrown away by the people who are supposed to protect you, it's hard to ever feel good."

He's speaking about himself. Him and Beau. "Beau is plenty good."

"Good enough for you to ever love? Can you look past what he is—what he's done—to ever love him? Or when he takes care of the dirty work and clears up the ashes so that you're finally safe—truly safe—will you walk away and never look back?"

They needed to be very clear on this. "I have no intention of walking away from Beau."

His eyes widened.

"But I also have no intention of letting the father of my future children sneak out and hunt killers every night. Far too dangerous of a pastime, don't you think? I'd prefer that he take up golfing. Much less stressful."

"He can't golf for shit." A dazed shake of Royal's head. "Did you just call him the father of your kids?"

"Future children. Don't have any yet. Can't have any until he gets his butt out of the police station." Once more, she headed back for the window. She peered out.

Darkness.

"You're in love with him."

"And I have been since he nearly died saving my life. I've got one hell of a hero fixation, and the only hero I ever see? It's him. So don't talk to me about Beau not being good enough." Her grip tightened on the curtain. "He is everything I want."

"You want a man with a dark side?"

"You have no idea how much darkness I have inside myself. Beau fits me, perfectly." In every way.

Now come home, Beau. Come home to me.

* * *

"THIS IS ABSURD!" Impatience spiked Ophelia's words. "We've been here for hours. My client should be home in bed, sleeping! Not answering the same questions over and over again in an endless loop!"

Lynn exhaled. "I think we're done here."

The voice of reason. About time. Beau knew it was after midnight. The freaking clock had been tick-tick-ticking all night. At least the detectives had relented and removed his cuffs a while back.

"He's not leaving," Campbell denied quickly. "We've got a cell waiting for him. He'll be arraigned tomorrow."

"Oh, the hell—" Beau began angrily.

The door opened. "He's free to go."

All eyes whipped toward that open door.

Douglas Baptiste stood in the doorway. A bandage was on the side of his head.

"But—but DA Baptiste," Campbell sputtered.

"I already talked to your boss. The charges aren't sticking. The case has been dropped. I spoke with Colton Ross on the phone, too. All a misunderstanding." His head inclined toward Beau. "You're free to go."

"No!" An immediate denial from Campbell.

"Yes," Douglas responded with a sigh. "And if you have a problem with that, take it up with your captain."

"I will," the detective vowed. "I am not done with you, Beau LeBlanc!" He stormed from the interrogation room.

"I worry he has a crush." Ophelia slumped back in her chair. "Some people just don't let go easily."

Lane took her hand and pulled her from the chair. "You're exhausted. And I'm taking you to bed."

"Perfect." Her other hand fluttered toward Beau. "I'll send you a bill."

"Of course, you will." He stood. Stretched his back. How the hell long had he been in that seat?

"We'll also talk very soon about...other things," she promised.

He was sure they would. But Detective Baker was still watching them, and the DA was in the room, so they'd definitely save that chat until later. Right then, all he wanted to do was get to Avalon. "I owe you."

"Absolutely. You owe me so much."

Lane tugged her toward the door. "Stay out of trouble for the rest of the night, would you, buddy?"

He would make no promises.

Beau moved to follow them out.

Douglas stepped into his path. "You saved my life."

"Nah. I just picked you up when you'd fallen." Or when a prisoner had knocked his ass out.

Without looking away from Beau, Douglas said, "Detective Baker, mind giving us a moment of privacy?"

"Take as many moments as you want. I'm going home." She shuffled past them. "Listen to your friend," she urged Beau. "Stay out of trouble. I don't like having you in my interrogation room."

Not like he loved being there. *I want to be with Avalon.* With a soft click, the door shut behind the detective.

"That inmate who bashed my head in? His name is Shamus Quarrel. I sent him to prison on a life sentence."

"So he doesn't love you, check."

"When his punishment was read in court, it took three guards to haul him away. And as they did, he kept screaming about how he would rip me apart." A pause. "If you had left me in that corridor, I would be dead right now. Make no mistake about it. So..." A cough. "You said I could thank you later. Consider this moment my thanks."

Interesting. "You always pay your debts so fast, counselor?"

"No. Sometimes it takes me a while to catch up and understand things. But I do catch up. Always."

"Good to know."

"I'm assuming you already *know* the body found in Slater Wade's home was that of a prison guard from McKinley?"

"I believe Campbell mentioned that fact once or twice. He's a chatty one, that detective."

"That particular guard was in the room when Avalon and I were talking to Everett Thomas the first time."

Beau nodded.

"He had phone records that tied to Slater Wade. He was the connection between Slater and Everett. So it does look like Everett might have given the order for Slater to attack Avalon at her home."

He could buy that. But pieces were still missing. "Who the hell killed the guard? And torched Slater's rental house?"

"Thought maybe you would know. Or at least have a few ideas that you wanted to share with the class."

"If I knew, he'd be dead."

Douglas winced. "Take a tip from a new, semi-friend. Don't tell shit like that to the DA."

"Colton Ross is on my list."

Douglas's forehead wrinkled. "Because he had you arrested?"

"Because he used to work for the New Orleans Fire Department around the time Avalon was caught in a Garden District blaze. Because I found him poking around in her bedroom hours ago. And because he had my ass arrested, yes."

"Any other names you want me to run? People I should be checking out?"

"Since your detectives seem busy focusing on me and not on other possible killers...yeah, here's something to explore." Like he was going to turn away help from the DA? Not happening. Then again, he'd never thought the DA would offer to help. "Your guy Campbell knows one hell of a lot about fire."

His eyes widened. "You're suggesting a detective is involved."

Beau shrugged. He figured the DA could connect the dots. He'd said what he'd said, after all.

"Fantastic." Douglas sounded like it was anything but fantastic.

"My team found a few other potential victims of the arsonist."

"You have a team now?" A nod. "Sure. Why not?"

"I'll send the intel to your office. We can make progress faster together."

"Damn straight, we can." Douglas extended his hand to Beau. "Sorry about the time I tried to get you locked away for murder."

"I was innocent." He stared at the hand. "Don't do it again."

"How about I only promise to lock you away for murder if you're guilty?"

"Sure. But don't forget, self-defense isn't murder." He took the hand. "Am I right, counselor?"

Silence. Then, "You are one hard-to-figure-out sonofabitch."

"I have been told that before."

Douglas let him go. "Got your Jag out of impound. Consider it part of my thanks." He rattled off directions to find the Jag. "Should be a quick walk for you. Keys will be waiting inside so you can drive off and go find Avalon. I know she's your priority. I saw the way you watched her at McKinley."

"Don't need to find her. I know exactly where she is." *Home. And I'm coming home to you, sweetheart.* "Thanks for the assist, DA."

Douglas stepped out of his path. "Thanks for the ass-saving, LeBlanc."

Beau headed for the door. "Did anyone mention that I carried you out? Ever-so-carefully?"

"Sonofabitch."

Smiling, Beau left interrogation. On his way out of the station, he flashed a one-fingered wave to a glowering Detective Campbell Cunningham.

Ophelia and Lane were waiting near the station's front door.

"Need a lift?" Lane asked.

"Thanks, but apparently, my ride is waiting." Courtesy of the DA.

* * *

WHEN HER PHONE RANG, Avalon jumped an inch. The sudden cry shocked her. Not that she'd been sleeping. She hadn't even been in bed. She'd been pacing near the piano and waiting for word on Beau.

She grabbed the phone and whipped it up to her ear. "Beau?"

"I'm coming home."

Her breath shuddered out. "You're clear? They dropped the charges?"

"Your buddy Douglas Baptiste got the charges dropped."

"Sorry. We must have a terrible connection. I could have sworn you said the DA just had your charges dropped."

"He did." A whistle. "Maybe he's not a complete jackass."

"He's not," she whispered. Royal sidled in front of her. She mouthed, *Beau is coming home.*

Royal's breath expelled in a rush.

"Getting my car and coming back to you." A pause. "Royal is close, isn't he?"

"Standing right in front of me like an insanely fierce bodyguard."

"And you two are playing nicely?"

Not exactly playing. "Don't worry about us. Just get here."

"But I do worry about you." Soft. "All the time. I want you safe, Avalon. You matter. You get that, don't you?"

Her hold on the phone tightened. "You matter, too, Beau."

"You don't have to tell me what you think I want to hear."

"I-I'm not." *You matter*.

"I can see the Jag. It's near the curb." He said something else, and this time, she did lose the connection.

"Beau? I can't hear you."

"Coming...home..."

"Wherever you are, the connection is crap." She didn't want to let him go, and Avalon was afraid their connection would completely die at any moment. "Be careful? Hurry home. I'll be waiting for you."

"Avalon..." Soft. A little sad. "I've been waiting...my whole life for..."

"Beau? I couldn't quite make out—"

But the call had ended.

* * *

I'VE BEEN WAITING *my whole life for you*.

She hadn't heard him. He'd lost the call right at the end. But that was okay. Soon enough, he'd be with Avalon, and he could tell her again just how much she mattered. He never, ever wanted her to doubt that she meant everything to him.

261

His Jag waited to the right. The cops had impounded the vehicle. They'd cuffed him at the scene, put him in the back of the patrol car, and then Avalon had launched in after him.

Avalon.

She'd ridden in the back of the patrol car to the station. Once at the station, she'd kept telling anyone who would listen that there had been a mistake. A misunderstanding.

She'd kept defending him. She knew his secrets. All of them. But she kept *defending* him.

Mistake, my ass.

He opened the unlocked door. Who left an unlocked Jag with the keys inside it? Were they *trying* to get his ride stolen? Even near a police station, a Jag wasn't going to be completely safe. Damn.

Beau slid inside. He still gripped the phone and—

Something jabbed into his neck. Hard. Like a bee stinging him. His hand flew up, still gripping the phone, and he smashed...

What the hell? A needle?

Soft laughter teased his ears. "Didn't you learn anything from Owen Bell? Because I did."

Some bastard was in the backseat of his Jag. Beau swung out with his fist and clipped the freak in the jaw. But it was a sloppy hit. Weak. Wild. Because—

I don't feel right.

"Owen always used horse tranquilizers on his vics. The tranq knocks them out so easily. I pumped the syringe so full, my friend." More laughter. "Nighty-night, asshole."

No. No. He still had the phone. Clutched in his hand. The hand he'd fisted and swung, and his fingers fumbled over it as he tried to make a call.

His contacts...

Contact one...

"When you wake up, you're going to be in hell. I promise you that."

Beau felt the last of his consciousness flow into a sea of black.

***

ROYAL'S PHONE RANG. Frowning, he pulled it from his pocket and frowned at the screen. "Didn't he just talk to you like...two seconds ago?" he asked Avalon as he brought the phone to his ear. "Bro, you need to have better service if you're wanting to talk to—"

"*When you wake up, you're going to be in hell.*"

His blood iced. "Beau?"

"*I promise you that.*"

Not Beau's voice. Not his freaking brother's voice. "Beau!" Royal roared. And Avalon lunged toward him.

But the line had gone dead.

Chapter Twenty-One

Beau's lashes fluttered open.

"You broke the syringe before I could pump enough tranquilizer in you."

Darkness. All around him.

"I was thinking you wouldn't open those eyes again until the flames had started, but I guess, this way, you can take it all in and know why you have to die. I can also have the pleasure of carrying out a friend's very special last request."

His arms...were behind his back. Something cold and hard was around his wrists. He jerked. Handcuffs, again? *It is so not my night.*

"Yeah, those would be handcuffs. You can't break them. Owen Bell couldn't break out of his when you slapped them on him. Neither could Everett."

A light flared in front of Beau. A match striking. And that match lit up the face of the man speaking. A smile curved his lips. "Surprised?" He blew out a hard breath.

The match died.

Darkness came back.

"Mostly..." Beau growled, "just pissed."

Laughter chased him in the dark.

* * *

"THE APP TO locate his phone still has Beau showing near the police station, but Douglas swears that the Jag is gone. That Beau is *gone*." Fear was about to rip Avalon apart as she spoke on her phone to Ophelia.

"Lane and I are here now. We came back to the station as soon as Royal called us." Worry filled Ophelia's voice. "Beau's not here. I don't see—*oh, no*."

"What?" She nearly broke the phone. "What is it?"

Royal crowded behind her.

"Beau's phone. Or at least, I think it is. Smashed to hell near a curb."

Royal swore. Avalon had the phone on speaker, and she held the device gripped in her right hand.

"Someone took him."

Avalon heard that statement clearly. It had come from Lane.

"She can hear you." A quick retort from Ophelia. "I am trying not to freak her out."

"Too late," Avalon shot back. "I'm freaked. Someone *took* him?" The arsonist. And if he had Beau...

What had Royal told me that he overheard? Something about Beau waking up...in hell.

Hell was fire. Flames that surrounded you. Trapped you. Killed you. "No." Low. Hard. "*No*." Louder. Harder. "*No!*"

Royal swore again.

"We're going to find him," Ophelia promised quickly.

"You stay where you are, understand? We're going in the station to get help. *We will find him.*" She hung up.

Avalon stared down at her phone. But she didn't see the device. She saw flames. "He's going to put Beau in the fire."

"The fuck he is."

Her head whipped up so that she could meet Royal's glare. "We both know what hell is." Hell was flames that consumed you.

Royal swallowed.

"We have to find Beau," she said. "Now."

"We don't know where to look—"

A ring broke through his words. Not her phone. His.

Hope rushed through her. The last time a call had come through on his line, it had been Beau.

No, not really Beau. Beau's phone, but someone else speaking. Royal had said the voice was male. Hushed.

The phone rang again.

"Answer it!" Avalon practically yelled.

He shook his head as if waking from a stupor, and he answered the phone.

"Speaker, speaker!" Avalon had to hear everything.

His finger swiped on the screen to put the call on speaker.

"Royal? Hey, man, it's Kai."

Royal's breath expelled in a disappointed rush. "Not the fuck now, Kai."

"I know it's late, but I can't get Beau on the phone."

A tear slid down her cheek. *I need Beau. I need him.*

"He wanted me to call him if an arson investigator showed up at the bar."

"*Not. Now,*" Royal snarled.

"Jeez, what the hell is wrong with you? Look, I swear I saw someone *go in the bar*. The place has that yellow police tape up everywhere, but someone just went in. At this hour, I doubt if it's the arson investigator. Probably just some punk-ass kids thinking they are gonna find liquor inside. But I wanted to report to Beau. I'm going around the back of the building now and—*oh*."

That was it. Kai just stopped.

"What is it?" Royal demanded.

"Beau's Jag. Guess it's him inside. Sorry for the false alarm. Didn't see him pull up. I was, uh, on a nature call. Forget I—"

"No!" A sharp cry from Royal.

"*No!*" An equally wild cry from Avalon.

"Uh...there a problem?"

"Get eyes on Beau," Royal ordered him. "But be careful. *Very, very careful.*"

Avalon was already running for the door. Beau was at LeBlanc's, so that meant she was about to be at LeBlanc's, too.

"What's happening?" Kai's worried voice.

Avalon heard the question from right behind her. She looked back.

Royal was on her heels.

"We think Beau's in danger," Royal said.

Think? Oh, there was no *thinking* about it. Beau was in danger.

And they were going to save him.

* * *

"Everett Thomas and I grew up together. Did you know that? No? You've certainly been a busy bastard. Digging up the past left and right. Figured you'd either hit on that point or were damn close to the discovery." A flash of another match lit his face. He bent the match and lit a candle. The light sputtered around him. A thick, white candle that sat on the charred remains of a table inside of LeBlanc's.

Not in the main part of the bar. No, the main part had been destroyed. The fancy counter. All of the rows of expensive whiskey that he'd stocked for customers. Gone in an inferno that left ash and destruction in its wake. But the building had once been a huge warehouse. Full of twists and turns. Back rooms. Patches on the first floor had been spared in the fire.

Even in the faint light of that flickering candle, he recognized his place. He'd sweat blood to reshape LeBlanc's from what it had first been when he bought the building. How could he not know it?

Beau was in a chair. One of the few that had somehow survived the blaze. The chair wobbled beneath him. Not close to steady. When he inhaled, he smelled smoke and... *whiskey?* Yes, the scent of whiskey was everywhere. And his clothes...why where his clothes so wet?

But his clothes didn't matter at the moment. What mattered was the killer who waited in front of him. Right near that white candle.

"If you had stopped poking at the past, you wouldn't be here right now. But you were digging. Digging and digging. You'd left New Orleans. I'd left. Even Everett had left...but you would not stop, would you?"

Beau lifted his chin. "Fuck yourself."

"You moved here because she did, didn't you?"

Yes.

"Can you keep a secret? Oh, wait, you'll be dead soon. Of course, you can keep it." His hand waved over the flame of the candle. The light from the match had long since died. "We came here because of her, too."

Avalon.

"Everett got off on killing women who looked like her. Did you notice that? All the same build, height, and hair close in shade to hers. Even the eyes were the same. It was because she got away. Made her special. I tried that bit a few times, too, but...hell, I knew they weren't her. No substitute for the original, am I right?"

"You're...dead." His tongue felt thick in his mouth, and Beau swore he could taste ash.

"No, but you will be, soon enough. I'm going to carry out Everett's last wish. It's kind of the least I can do, considering I'm the one who ordered the hit on him."

"*Bastard!*"

He picked up something that had been on the table near the flickering candle. Sauntered forward. "Do you recognize this?"

Beau squinted.

"You should because it's your knife. It was in evidence at the station. I took the liberty of slipping it out of evidence. I waited for you to come out. I knew you'd go for your Jag." More laughter. "After all these years, you had to go for the Jag again, didn't you?"

"How..." His heart thudded. Almost painful. Heavy in his chest.

"That tranquilizer hits hard, doesn't it? I'm really not good with doses. And I have no idea how much actually got into your system before your burly ass broke the syringe. Drugs aren't my thing. And, honestly, knives aren't, either." He peered down at the knife in his hand. "Too much blood. I don't like blood. Everett, though? He did. When we were teens, we experimented."

The cuffs bit into Beau's wrists. The chair rocked as he strained. Rocked.

"I liked the fire. Started small. You know, burning the foster houses I was in. Burning clothes. Toys. Took a while to work up to people."

"Because you're...not supposed to burn people!"

"Royal is like your brother, isn't he? But not really? That's how Everett and I were, too." He still held the knife. "He came into the group home where I was one day. Sometimes, you just connect with someone, you know? Everett liked to use his knife. I tried to tell him it was too messy. Since I was fire, I thought it would be cool if he was my opposite. I burned. Why not let him drown? Fire and water. Kinda cool, huh?"

No, it wasn't.

"We tried water for him. Didn't work so well. Everett said you couldn't hear the screams under the water. He liked to hear the screams. For him, I think that was the best part."

"Because he was...a sick...fuck..." Beau could feel blood dripping from his wrists. He'd strained so hard against the cuffs that he was bleeding.

"He was. Agreed. Damn but I loved that about him." A sigh. "He got me to kill my mom. Like yours, my mom dumped me. I was seven. She just walked away. Told people I scared her. *Me.* A freaking kid. But I found her. Everett and I did. She had a whole other life. Another kid. I watched her and I waited and when she was alone, I trapped her in my fire."

The first victim. The forty-year-old wife and mother. "You killed your...own mother?"

"It was what she deserved. Mr. Carter was next. My old shop teacher. He was going to turn me in because he caught me messing around with some flames in his class. So I messed around with flames at his house." He took another step toward Beau. "You're so much like me, do you see it?"

"I see...a sick freak." *And I will be killing you.*

"Your mom abandoned you. You made your own family —a brother—with Royal. I've been watching you. *I know.* My mom abandoned me. I found my own brother, Everett."

"You just told me." His breath heaved out. The bastard was so close with that damn knife. "You just told me you... killed Everett."

"He was going to tell you about me. He didn't like being locked up. He couldn't handle it. I knew he'd break when Avalon went to see him. I told you already, his victims? They were *her*. It's because of the day at the pool. It's because—"

A door slammed.

The killer's head whipped around. His body went still.

Beau rocked forward in the chair. Kept straining against the cuffs. Rocked back. The unsteady chair swayed.

No other sounds followed the slamming of the door. The killer's shoulders relaxed. "This building is gonna come down. Well, it's going to burn again, then come down. Everyone will say it's a reflash. That happens. Fires can reignite in places like this." He looked back at Beau. "I first saw Avalon at her birthday party. A fancy country club gig. Everett had gotten a job as a lifeguard. That was why the drowning death would have been so brilliant! He had a girl, and he was holding her under the water while I watched. Avalon came rushing up, so we had to let the girl surface. *We thought for sure Avalon saw us.* We tried to act like we were helping the girl. But what if Avalon knew the truth? That was why I had to go to Avalon's house. Avalon couldn't talk to any cops. What if she remembered us? I set the fire to stop her." Fast, rushed words. Almost as if he talked more to himself than to Beau. "She should have died. But you—you came to save her."

"Will...always save her."

"No, you won't. You'll be dead. The dead can't save anyone." He glanced at his knife. "Everett told Avalon that he wanted you found, and he wanted your intestines cut out and tied in a bow. Don't you think that's the least I can do for him? Fulfill his dying wish? He was just like a brother to me. This part will be for my brother." He raised the knife and—

"*Get away from him!*" A voice blasted from the shadows.

Kai's voice.

Kai burst from the darkness. He ran forward.

The killer whirled toward him.

Even as Kai ran forward, Beau lifted his legs and slammed them into the killer. As hard as he could. He caught the killer in the back and upper thigh, and the man slammed into the ash-covered floor. The chair swayed beneath Beau and then it toppled straight back. It fell, and the wood broke apart. Beau twisted and heaved, and he managed to jerk free of the chair, but the cuffs were still behind his back. He jumped to his feet.

Just in time to see the knife plunge into Kai's chest.

* * *

"Kai's not answering his phone." Royal's voice was tight with fear and fury. "Dammit, I should be driving!"

"I've got this." What she had was the gas pedal all the way down to the floorboard. They'd taken Beau's backup ride, an SUV, and she was currently hurtling them toward LeBlanc's. "You texted Ophelia and Lane?"

"Yes, they're going to meet us at LeBlanc's." His hand slammed into the dashboard. "This can't be happening!"

It was happening. Beau was in danger. Every moment counted. The road was dark and empty ahead, and the car couldn't go any faster.

Why couldn't the car go faster?

Hold on, Beau. Hold on.

* * *

"Stay where you are, or I will slice his throat." The knife was at Kai's throat. "He's currently still breathing, but you take one more step toward me, and he'll be choking on his own blood."

Was Kai still breathing? Beau couldn't tell for sure. But he stopped advancing because this was Kai's life.

"Another hero." Disgust. "What are you doing now, recruiting them?"

"You don't want to kill him."

"Well, I didn't want to kill you, either, but you wouldn't stay away from Avalon. I wanted to kill her years ago. I tried. Everett tried. But she always had guards. *Because of you.* It was fucking unfinished business, don't you get that? *She saw us at the country club.*"

"What happened to the girl at the country club?" Beau knew he had to keep the prick talking. Talking and not slicing Kai's throat. Beau also knew exactly what had happened to the girl. *She's dead.*

"Avalon came close to the pool we were using. It was supposed to be a private area. Avalon's stupid party was on the damn other side of the country club! She shouldn't have been there. Damn Avalon."

Beau inched forward.

"We had to let the girl go. But only then. Only for a moment. Everett took care of her when everyone was gone. She was so drunk that she didn't even realize what we'd been doing to her. That was the trick for Everett back then. Get them drunk. Then they don't care, not until the pain starts." He lifted the knife away from Kai's throat. "He liked these so much. Loved them. Said there was nothing on earth like the slice into flesh. Don't worry, I made sure that he got to feel lots of cuts before he died. A tribute, wasn't it?"

Not exactly. Beau took a lunging step—

"*Stop!*" The knife was back at Kai's throat.

Beau stopped. *Keep him talking.* "How'd you get the inmates to attack Everett?"

"Like you are the only one with gang ties? How do you think I survived in New Orleans? The circles you and I ran in were so close back in those days. So very, very close. We could have been best friends in another life. A life without Avalon."

Beau weaved. No, his damn knees buckled. A sudden wave of dizziness had him crashing back to the floor.

"That would be the tranquilizer. Okay, I'm starting to see why Owen Bell enjoyed it so much. Note to self, it can be useful."

Beau blinked blearily. His eyes locked on the candle flame. It flickered over and over.

And then a booted foot kicked him in the face. Beau stopped tasting ash and instead tasted blood as he flew back. His head slammed into the floor, and the cuffs drove into his back as he fell on top of his bound hands.

Then the knife was at *his* throat. "I sent them after you in the hospital."

The gang members that had come to kill him when he'd been sixteen.

"You were supposed to steal a car that night. Not steal my prey. I told them you couldn't be trusted. That you were going to talk to the cops. Tell them everything about the car theft ring. You should have left my Avalon alone. Let her burn."

"Not..." He spat out blood. "Yours."

"She will be. You and that bastard over there? You're both about to burn. You'll be alive when it happens. That's the best part. I'll trap you in here, and you won't get out. But first...about that bow that Everett wanted..." And the knife dropped down Beau's body. It sliced open his shirt. And the bastard stabbed him in the gut.

Beau roared in pain. The knife stabbed him again.

And again.

His arms were behind him. He couldn't fight back with his fists. His body was too damn weak.

"I didn't want to kill Everett, but I had no choice. Then I had to take out the guard who'd helped us communicate because I can't leave witnesses behind. That's why I have to finish with Avalon. *No witnesses.*" He pulled the knife back. "I *hate the blood.* It gets everywhere. It's slimy and messy, and I don't know why Everett enjoyed it so—"

Beau headbutted him. As hard as he could, he just rammed his head right into the prick's. The knife flew from the guy's hand. Beau saw it hurl across the room. But in the next instant, the man's fist was swinging toward Beau's face. One punch. Another. Another.

Beau's head banged into the floor once more. Hard. He turned and he saw the flicker of that candle.

The fist hit him again.

He'd been stabbed over and over. He felt damn numb. From the tranquilizer? From the blood loss? Beau didn't know. Part of him just wanted to close his eyes. To rest for a moment.

But another part of him...wanted Avalon. And he wouldn't see Avalon again if he closed his damn eyes.

He rolled his body. A hard, awkward twist that got him away from that swinging fist. Then Beau heaved up on his knees. Freaking cuffs! His attacker came at him again, and Beau launched his shoulder into the man's chest. They both crashed onto the floor once more. The candle wobbled. The flame flickered and flickered and...

"Beau?"

Someone was calling him.

"Beau!"

Someone important. The call pierced through the numbness. *Avalon!*

And the bastard with him was laughing.

"Do you think..." A whisper in Beau's ear. "That she'll fight the fire for you? My money says she won't. I think she'll run as soon as she sees the flames." Then he shoved Beau. Leapt to his feet.

Beau tried to rise. His legs...dammit, he hated being so weak!

His gaze darted around the darkened room. He'd heard Avalon's voice. Where was she?

His eyes drifted past the candle. The candle that flickered and danced. Flickered and—

"Did you wonder why your clothes were so wet? I used all the good whiskey the last time I was here, but don't worry, I brought my own this time. A much cheaper version, but it will still get the job done." And he yanked up the candle. Put it...put it next to some kind of puddle in the middle of that darkness and—

Fire.

It leapt to life. It raced out, flashing as if following a perfect trail that had been created just for it.

Beau realized why he'd smelled so much whiskey when he first opened his eyes. Why his clothes were wet. *He doused me with whiskey. He doused the whole room.*

And the fire was coming for Beau.

The bastard lit more matches. Spread his fire. And it blazed toward Beau.

"Beau!" Avalon's scream.

"*Get away!*" Beau tried to yell back. "*Stay away!*"

The fire closed in.

Chapter Twenty-Two

"BEAU!" FEAR HAD AVALON'S HEART RACING IN A triple-time rhythm as she jumped from the vehicle. "*Beau!*"

Where was he? And, *dear God, please let him be okay.*

"Hardly anything is left in the front of the building," Royal snarled. "Has to be in the back!"

They raced for the back. Avalon's feet pounded over the earth as they headed around to the rear of the dark building. Kai had said that he'd seen the Jag in the back. And she—

"Smoke!" Avalon gasped out. "I smell smoke!"

Royal tore forward.

"Beau!" she screamed as she gave chase. "*Beau!*"

They reached the back door. Or was it a side door? The former warehouse was absolutely huge, but the door was ajar, and Royal was already rushing inside, and the scent of smoke just got stronger and, oh, no, she could hear the crackle of flames. She raced after him and entered darkness until—

"*Stay back!*"

Real words? Or was it just the crackle of the fire? Because fire was raging. She and Royal had burst into some kind of big storage room. And fire surged across the floor in a serpentine line. A snake striking everything in its path. Terror held her rooted to the spot for a moment as her past came back and slammed straight into her.

"There's a body on the floor!" A shout from Royal.

Her heart stopped. No, no. Not Beau. "No!"

She and Royal dodged the flames. They reached the body. Face-down. Royal rolled him over.

The flames surged.

Not Beau.

"Kai," Royal said.

There was a whole lot of blood on Kai's chest. Blood revealed by the twisting, churning flames that were getting bigger and bigger every second. She yanked up her shirt to cover her mouth even as her shaking fingers went to Kai's throat.

A pulse. Weak. But there. "Alive," she gasped. But he wouldn't be for long if they didn't get him out. "You...have to take him."

"Beau is in here." Royal crouched over Kai. "I'm not leaving Beau!"

Neither was she.

"Take...him!"

Both of their heads whipped toward the right. That had definitely been a voice. One that merged with the fire. A terrible shout.

Beyond the flames, trapped on the far side, she could see...Beau?

"Take...him!" Beau was up against the wall. That was how it looked. Up against the wall. Were his hands behind his back? Why? *"Get...out!"*

The fire separated them. Fire...

Fire everywhere.

"Fuck." Coughing from Royal. "You can't...lift Kai."

Kai was twice her size. She could drag him. Lift him? No.

"I'm coming back," Royal swore. "You hear me, Beau? *I'm coming back!*" He hauled Kai over his shoulder. Kai hung limply. Royal tried to go back the way they'd come.

Flames.

He had to dodge and weave as he turned and finally ran into the darkness. A different path than they'd originally taken. *Please, get out. Make it out.*

And she remained crouching as she tried to figure out how to get to Beau.

Her gaze took in the room. The fire that had formed a half-circle around him as he pressed back against the wall behind his body. The fire was between them. So many twisting flames.

"Love...you." Beau's words.

Had he dropped to his knees?

"Get...out." Rough. Breaking in the fire.

Her head turned to the left. Fire.

To the right. Fire.

"*Get...out!*" A plea from Beau.

She'd have to jump over the fire in order to get to him. Even if she made it past the flames, they'd both be trapped.

How much longer did he have? Smoke thickened the air. Heat lanced her skin. "I...love you." Could he hear her? Or was the fire crackling too loudly. "I. *Love. You!*" Then she turned around and ran from the fire.

* * *

He laughed when Avalon left.

He'd known she would run.

But Beau, had he known? Or had he thought that she would fight for him?

Beau was on his knees. He could see him. But not for much longer. The flames would be taking over.

Not for much longer.

Goodbye, Beau LeBlanc.

***

Avalon raced out of the building. She gulped in gasps of air as she looked frantically around the lot. Right... *there.*

"Avalon!" Royal's shout.

She ignored him. Ran for the Jag. She yanked open the door. The keys—they were inside. Just waiting. She jumped in.

"Avalon!" Royal banged his hand into the windshield.

"Get back!" she yelled.

But then someone was pulling him back. Hard arms grabbed him. She frowned and tried to see through the darkness. Was that—Detective Cunningham?

Royal spun and drove a fist into the detective's jaw.

She cranked the engine. She grabbed the wheel. And she hooked her seatbelt. Fuck it. She rammed the gas pedal down and raced toward the building. Smoke everywhere. But she remembered the spot. The spot where Beau had been. Trapped against the wall.

Don't let the car kill him. Don't let the smoke kill him. Don't let me kill him.

She didn't have a lot of room to pick up speed. This stupid idea might not work. Locking her teeth, praying, she gripped the wheel, and she hurtled the Jag right at LeBlanc's. Right at the spot where she *thought* Beau might have been trapped. *Come on, structural integrity. Be weak. Be weak enough.*

She drove right into the wall. And she bounced back. Or the car did. But there was damage. To the building. To the Jag. Weakness. She just had to hit harder.

She reversed. Flew forward.

Don't let me kill him. Don't let me kill me, either.

And she hit again. The crunch of metal. The scream of glass.

This time, the air bag deployed. Her face slammed into it. Everything went white around her.

She shoved against the air bag.

Everything was white except for the flames that were now shooting from the side of the building.

Behind her, she heard the wail of sirens.

*   *   *

AIR HIT HIM. Cleaner air. Air that didn't choke him and a fucking car had almost hit him, too. Beau blinked a few times as he tried to keep his heavy eyelids open, and he stared at the front of a Jag as it jutted into the building. Smashed to hell, but definitely a Jag. It had torn right through the wall.

"Beau!"

Avalon's voice. Avalon fighting and kicking her way out of the Jag and crawling through the opening she'd made in that wall. But the flames were bigger. Stretching. More oxygen in the air had them surging ever higher. She couldn't come closer. She needed to get the hell out. How many times would he need to tell her?

But Avalon was right there. She grabbed his arm. Smiled at him.

And then someone else grabbed him from behind.

Beau looked back.

A firefighter stood behind him. Mask in place. Breathing through the regulator. Full turnout gear covering his body so he'd be protected from the flames. Helmet on to protect his head.

The killer stood behind him. Wearing his disguise. But Beau knew exactly who he was.

The firefighter shook his head. He—

Avalon threw her whole body against the firefighter's. She slammed into him, and surprised, he staggered back. He slipped. Fell.

"*Let's...go!*" Avalon's cry.

At least, Beau thought that was her cry. She pushed against him, and he scrambled with her. They scraped past the Jag. Made it into the night that waited. A small opening had been created when the Jag had met the wall...and the wall mostly won the fight. They lurched outside and Beau choked in air. "Cuffed. Covered in...booze! If fire...touches me..."

"Oh, God." Avalon's terrified voice. She pushed him onward. "Get away from the building! Get away!"

He almost fell, but her steely grip held him up. They tumbled forward. *Get away. Get away.*

Detective Cunningham appeared in his path. Gun drawn. "What the hell is happening?"

"Handcuff keys!" Avalon cried out. She coughed. Choked. "They're...universal. Give them to us, now!"

His gun wavered. But then he hurried forward.

Beau spun around. Faced the fire. Faced the hell that was LeBlanc's. How many times could one place burn? Fuck.

He still didn't feel the pain from his injuries, and he

knew that wasn't good. How many times had he been stabbed?

"That's blood." Avalon's broken voice. "Beau...?"

He felt the cuffs give way. His hands were free. He stared into the fire. The hole on the side of the building that had been made courtesy of Avalon and the Jag. Fire and smoke poured from the hole.

More of the wall tumbled down as he watched. And then—a firefighter leapt out of the flames. But he wasn't running for Beau. His hands were extended toward Avalon. One hand gripped a knife.

No.

Beau's now free right hand grabbed the gun that Detective Cunningham had just holstered. He yanked it out of the holster. Aimed.

Fired.

One.

Two.

Three.

Four...

Four fast blasts. The firefighter went down.

There were yells. Shouts. Screams. No, not screams. Those were the wails of sirens.

Cunningham snatched the gun from Beau. The detective ran for the fallen firefighter. The man wasn't moving.

Beau was still on his knees, but even that felt like an effort. He wasn't so numb any longer. Despite the fire raging, cold crept through his veins. "That's...killer," Beau managed.

Cunningham ripped off the firefighter's helmet and mask.

"Lieutenant...Wesley Vaughn," Beau muttered.

Hero.

Killer.

Dead.

Beau had just made sure of it. One more thing he needed to make sure of? His head turned toward Avalon. Alive. Safe.

That was what mattered.

He smiled at her, then pitched forward into the darkness.

Chapter Twenty-Three

"I don't like it when heroes turn out to be the bad guys." Detective Lynn Baker glowered as she stood behind her desk. "Makes my job one major pain in the ass."

Beau grunted. His stitches pulled but he wasn't about to complain. He was finally out of the hospital. No charges were being filed against him. And Avalon was safe. One hundred percent safe. "What about when the bad guy turns out to be the hero? How do you feel about that situation?"

Avalon's soft fingers slid down his arm. "We have been over this. You are *not* the bad guy."

"Debatable," Detective Cunningham muttered as he perched on the edge of Lynn's desk. "Still not so sure you needed to fire four times."

Ah, such a suspicious man. "I was out of my mind because of the horse tranquilizer that Wesley Vaughn had given me when he *drugged and abducted me*. I saw him coming at Avalon with the knife, and I reacted. I was afraid he'd stab her or try to pull her back into the flames." *Or do both because he was a crazy, murdering bastard.* "I barely remember pulling the trigger." Oh, yes, he did remember firing. Again and again.

Had to make sure he was dead.

"You have plenty of evidence to tie Wesley Vaughn to the crimes," Avalon said. Voice crisp. "Frankly, you should be *thanking* Beau. It's because of him that a dangerous predator was finally stopped. I know the cops and Feds have been able to tie Wesley with dozens of arsons now."

Yeah, dozens. And they feared there were more. The man had been starting fires for years. Then he'd go in with the other firefighters and put out many of the fires he'd created. The guy had been a sick sonofabitch.

Just as sick as his buddy, Everett Thomas.

Wesley Vaughn. Not the man's real name. Turned out, his dental records and his fingerprints had traced back to a Daniel Alexander. Kid who'd aged out of the foster care system in New Orleans and seemingly vanished. Only he hadn't really vanished. He and Everett had just moved on.

Daniel Alexander had reinvented himself as Wesley Vaughn. He'd become a firefighter so he could get close to the flames that he loved so much. And he'd continued his killing ways.

What were the odds that two twisted killers had found each other when they were so young? The Feds seemed fascinated by their cases.

They'd grown up together, perfected their crimes together. Turned into monsters together. And now, they were both in hell together. Fitting. Or at least, Beau thought it was fitting.

"You really don't remember seeing Everett and Wesley together when you were a teen?" Lynn asked Avalon. Her question brought Beau's attention snapping back to her.

Avalon shook her head. "I had my birthday party at the country club that year. But no one...no one drowned."

"Because you interrupted before they could kill her," Beau growled.

"I don't remember." Her head turned toward him. Her gaze was stark. Sad. "And that's one of the things that guts me. We just go through our lives and don't even realize that there are victims out there—victims every single moment. They could be right in front of us, *and we don't see them.*" A shake of her head. "I didn't see her." A tear twisted down her cheek. She swiped it away. "I barely recall that birthday at all."

"We think we found her." From Cunningham. "Or at least, found out who she could have been. A sixteen-year-old girl named Cassidy Gorgas was reported as a runaway around the time of Avalon's house fire in New Orleans. She worked as a waitress at the country club. The Feds are going to talk to her family. Looks like she might have been an early victim of the Slasher."

Back when he'd been trying to figure out how he liked to kill.

Water muted their screams.

Beau saw Avalon swipe away another tear from her cheek. He ached, but not from the stitches this time. He hated her pain. "Sweetheart..."

Her head turned toward him. "I wish that I could remember Cassidy. But when I think about that time, all I remember is fire and fear and you." Her hand lifted to brush his cheek. "Always you. You saved me. No one saved her."

His head turned. His lips pressed to her palm. "You saved me, sweetheart." In ways she probably would never imagine.

"Yeah, she did." A murmur from Cunningham. "Drove

a damn Jag through a wall to save your ass. Almost hit me in the process."

Avalon pressed another kiss to Beau's palm. "You were clear, Detective Cunningham." Prim. "You were busy fighting with Royal."

"Thought he might be the bad guy. I rushed to the scene because Ophelia and Lane said it was an emergency situation. At the time, I didn't know that Royal was the one who'd texted them to come to LeBlanc's." A sigh. "I got there and saw him banging on your car's windshield like a maniac. I tried to *help*."

The cop had helped. So Beau wasn't using his nickname any longer. Or at least, not for the moment. The cop's handcuff key and gun had come in mighty handy.

"So, are we free to go?" Beau asked. There were no charges against him. Douglas had already been clear on that score. The DA was currently trying to sort through every fire case that Wesley Vaughn had ever worked in the area. The DA and the Feds were unraveling a spider web of lies and secrets tied to both Everett and Wesley.

Two serial killers. Together for far too long.

"You're free." Cunningham slid off the edge of the desk. "Try to stay on the straight and narrow, would you?"

"I make no promises." Especially not if trouble came looking for him.

Beau and Avalon left the station. As they walked down the steps, a limo slowed and pulled to the curb. Ah, their ride. Perfect timing.

Royal exited the vehicle. Sent him a big grin. "I'm assuming you're a free man now?"

"You know it."

Royal opened the side door. Avalon slid inside. Beau didn't, not yet.

"There is no one hunting your lady any longer?" Royal asked quietly. "Since there is a fairly fresh body in the ground, courtesy of you?"

"She's free."

"Great. Then no more bodyguard duty."

"You don't even have to be driving the limo," Beau muttered. "We could have driven ourselves."

Royal slapped a hand on his shoulder. "Did it for old time's sake. And because I wanted to make sure my friend was all right." His gaze held Beau's. "You *are* all right?"

For the moment, yeah. But he'd meant what he just said. Avalon was free. She didn't need the past holding her back any longer. *She doesn't need me.* No more watching from the shadows. No more secret protection duty. It was time to back away. "Sure." Beau flashed a wide, fake smile for Royal. "Why wouldn't I be?"

"Try lying to someone else. Though I wouldn't recommend you lie to her." Royal's voice had dropped even more. "I think she'll see right through you, too."

He wasn't going to lie to Avalon. He was about to give her the truth. And a choice. But first, "Kai is good?"

"Good as ever. Knife missed his heart by a whole half-inch. The two of you are both our walking, talking miracles. A little more recovery time, and I plan to throw you guys the biggest party you've ever seen. Because I am an awesome friend like that."

Beau studied him. "You are."

"Damn straight."

"You're also an awesome brother. Thanks for being there for me."

"Shit. Don't you dare get emotional on me. If you make me cry, I will never, ever forgive you." Royal backed away.

"Get in the freaking limo. Tell Avalon you love her. Go get your happy ending."

He wasn't so sure it would be happy. Not for him. For her? *Yes.* She deserved everything good in the world. And that *good* might just mean that she walked away from him.

He eased into the limo. The door slammed shut behind him.

Avalon waited.

He sat across from her. Tried to figure out what to say. Where to start. The last two weeks had been a whirlwind. At first, he'd been trapped in the hospital. Hooked to tubes and monitors. The stitches would come out soon. He'd get the all clear from his doctor. His life could go on. But would it go on with Avalon? Or without her?

He clearly remembered shooting Wesley Vaughn. What wasn't so clear? Sometimes, Beau thought he recalled Avalon saying...

I love you.

But maybe he'd imagined that part because he wanted it so badly. Wanted *her* so badly.

"You're not the bad guy." Her husky voice. "You've always been my hero."

She'd always been his everything. He looked down. "You're not in danger any longer."

"Doesn't seem that I am."

"You...you still have to be careful when you interview criminals." Like he'd ever be thrilled about that aspect of her life. "I can still get you protection. You can have—"

She touched him. Stopped his words. She'd leaned forward and put her hand on his knee. "We need new ground rules."

Ground rules? A distant memory rang. She'd wanted those before.

"Rule one. No more staying in the shadows for you. You don't get to be my creepy but hot protector."

Creepy. Wonderful. He winced.

"Instead, you get to be in my life. One hundred percent *in.* You get to be my hot and dangerous boyfriend or, maybe one day, my hot and dangerous husband."

He could not move.

"Am I jumping ahead? I'm probably jumping ahead." She snatched her hand back. That hand immediately fisted on her lap. "You said you loved me, and I love you, but I shouldn't jump ahead. You just got out of the hospital. Your bar is *gone.* And I'm rambling and telling you things you don't want to hear."

He wanted to hear everything that she had to say. "I told you not to do that." He reached over. Unfurled her fingers. Stroked lightly over the half-moon marks that she'd made in her palm. "I never want you hurt."

"I don't want you hurt, either." Tears filled her eyes, but Avalon blinked them away. "There was fire all around you. I didn't know how to get you out."

He smiled at her. "Sweetheart, you drove a Jag through the wall."

"I didn't know if that would work or not. It didn't the first time. I had to hit twice."

"You got me out."

"If you'd died..." Her gaze fell to their hands. "I would have been lost."

That's how I will be without you. "You should have a good life, Avalon. No, a great one. One without some messed-up guy like me dodging your steps."

Her head whipped up. "Did you miss the part where I said *I love you?*"

His back teeth clenched.

Her lips parted. "You're afraid to believe me."

He was. Because he wanted her so badly. If he thought he had her love and he lost it...lost her...

"Oh, Beau." She jumped to the seat beside him. Her body brushed against his. "I love you. I love every single part of you."

No, she couldn't. Some parts were dark and twisted. But he'd work on them. He'd tried before and he'd do it again.

"Every. Part." Both of her hands rose so that her fingers pressed against his cheeks. "My dark protector. My badass, bar-owning boyfriend. I love you. When I think of my future, it's *you*. You are what I want. What I need. You walked through fire for me."

"You drove through it for me."

Her lips curled. Those gorgeous dimples of hers winked.

He loved her smile. Loved *her*.

"Ground rule two." Avalon cleared her throat. "We fight for what we want. What I want? It's you. What do *you* want?"

"I'm staring at her."

Her dimples flashed again. "Then nothing else matters. We'll forget all the other rules. It's you and it's me. And we're going to be together. Nothing will break us. Nothing. We're stronger than fire."

He needed her mouth. Needed her. "We'll go slow," he promised because he was still afraid to hope too much. "If I scare you, then—"

Her laughter stopped him. "You can't scare me. We've been over this, remember? You're the one thing that doesn't scare me." But her laughter died away. "You didn't ask for help."

His brow furrowed.

"When the fire was around you, you didn't yell for help. Anyone else would have. You told Royal and I to get out. That is *not* what you do in a fire."

Beau shook his head. "If I'd called for help, you would have been hurt." He'd wanted her out and away from the flames.

"Beau, life without you would hurt. I know. I lived without you before. And I was empty and cold. I never want life without you again. I want life with you. Wild, exciting, passionate life *with you*."

"You have me." Simple. Did she get that? From the moment they'd met, he'd belonged to her.

"And you have me." Her lips came close. Barely an inch separated them. "My hero."

He shook his head.

"*My* hero." Her mouth pressed to his.

My everything. His arms wrapped around her. If she wanted him, if she was choosing him...then, hell, no, he would never, ever let her go.

My. Everything.

Epilogue

"The place looks incredible," Royal told Beau right before he let out an admiring whistle. "Seriously. I love this joint even more than I did the original." He lifted his flute of champagne and saluted. "Congratulations, bro. The new LeBlanc's is killer."

Smiling, Beau's gaze swept the crowd. The old building —what little remained—had been torn down. He could have just opened a different bar somewhere else. But Beau had decided to rebuild.

LeBlanc's was back. And, as a tribute to his now fiancée, he even had a bonus back room in the place for VIP's. One that had been designed to feature a Jag hurtling through the wall. A bit tricky to get the aesthetics just right, but in the end, a creative builder had taken care of things for him.

It was really just the front end of the Jag. There was a wall behind it. Clever tricks just made it *look* as if the Jag were barreling forward. When Avalon had seen the special room, her laughter had warmed his heart.

He caught sight of her as she walked through the crowd.

A gorgeous red dress hugged her curves. The people present for the big reopening were all at their glamorous best. Men in suits and tuxes. Women in evening gowns and cocktail dresses as jewels dripped from their necks and fingers.

This scene was a far, far cry from the rough streets Beau had once known. A lifetime away from them.

Avalon paused to talk with Ophelia and Lane. Ophelia hugged her tightly.

I even had some upgrades included when I made space upstairs for Ophelia and Lane's new PI office. They'd helped him out so much. They deserved all the fancy upgrades.

Avalon pulled from Ophelia. Her head turned. Her gaze met Beau's.

"She loves you," Royal said.

Avalon flashed her dimples at Beau.

"Don't screw this shit up," Royal warned him. "You wanted her for too long. Don't do anything to throw this chance away."

Like he had to be warned. "She wants me."

"Yeah, I got that."

"She *loves* me."

"Yeah, got that, too, you lucky bastard." Royal sipped his champagne. "You're on the straight and narrow now. Living that crime-free life. Living the picket-fence dream."

Beau slanted his friend—his brother—a glance. "We're *both* living that crime-free life. We gave up our extracurriculars, remember?" Especially since those extracurriculars had been part of the damn problem that led to an inferno.

Royal didn't sip his champagne this time. He drained it.

Then put it on a nearby table. "Absolutely. Living it and loving it."

Avalon was almost close enough to hear their conversation. Almost close enough to touch.

"Got to make sure the staff has everything under control. Congrats, again, on the engagement and on the reopening." Royal's eyes glinted. "Glad you have the life *you* want."

Then he was gone. Ducking through the crowd. He paused long enough to slap Kai on the back and shake his hand.

And Avalon was there. Right in front of Beau. Smiling for him. Staring at him with love clear to see in her gorgeous green eyes.

Yes, he had the life he wanted. He had the woman he wanted.

He pulled Avalon into his arms.

Sonofabitch, he actually had a happy ending.

How about that?

* * *

Lying had always come easily to Royal. Second nature. But he still hated lying to his brother.

Maybe he should duck out of Savannah for a while. He'd always gone in and out of Beau's life over the years. After the wedding, he'd take a trip. Give Beau and Avalon some time on their own.

And go some other place for my hunts.

Because his extracurricular activities? Nope. He had not stopped them. They were too important to stop.

Slowly, he crept through the darkness. He'd slipped out

of LeBlanc's and gone on the trail of new prey. Prey he believed would be alone and vulnerable that particular night. He was currently in the middle of nowhere. An old winery that had long since been abandoned. His prey's vehicle waited. A faded sedan that most people wouldn't look at twice.

Royal eased past the sedan. His eyes were on the ramshackle building up ahead. He—

Thud.

Royal tensed. His head turned back at the sound.

Thud.

He focused on the sedan.

Thud.

Was that his heart? Or was that thud seriously coming from the trunk of the sedan? Slowly, carefully, he approached the vehicle.

Thud.

Shit. That was from inside the trunk. He hurried to the driver's side. The window was half down. He shoved his hand inside. Opened the door. Found the little lever that would pop the trunk.

And even as that trunk was rising up, he ran back to the rear of the sedan. He pulled out his flashlight and shone it inside.

Holy shit.

A bound woman stared back at him. Duct tape over her mouth. Raised hands tied together. Her wide, desperate eyes stared into his.

Terrified, beautiful eyes. A terrified, beautiful woman.

A beautiful woman who was trapped in the trunk of a killer's car.

With his free hand, Royal carefully removed the tape from her mouth. But she winced. Shuddered.

"Are you...going to kill me?" A low whisper.

Royal shook his head. "No." He scooped her out of the trunk. Into his arms. Then said something he never, ever expected to say, "I'm going to save you."

Don't miss Royal's story in BRUTAL ICE.

In the mood for another cold case romance? Royal's story is coming in BRUTAL ICE. Get ready for a dark, hot ride...

Author's Note

Thank you so much for reading Avalon and Beau's story! I hope that you enjoyed it.

I love creating the "Ice Breaker Cold Case Romance" books. Blending suspense and romance? My favorite thing to do! These books have been such a joy to write, and I am incredibly grateful to my readers for giving me the opportunity to tell these stories.

Thank you, again. And more Ice Breakers will be coming!

If you have time, please consider leaving a review. Reviews help readers to discover new books—and authors certainly appreciate them!

If you'd like to stay updated on my releases and sales, please join <u>my newsletter list</u>.

I'm also active on social media. You can find me on <u>Instagram</u> and <u>Facebook</u>.

Best,

Cynthia Eden

cynthiaeden.com

More Books By Cynthia Eden

Ice Breaker Cold Case Romance
- Frozen In Ice (Book 1)
- Falling For The Ice Queen (Book 2)
- Ice Cold Saint (Book 3)
- Touched By Ice (Book 4)
- Trapped In Ice (Book 5)
- Forged From Ice (Book 6)
- Buried Under Ice (Book 7)
- Ice Cold Kiss (Book 8)
- Locked In Ice (Book 9)

Wilde Ways
- Protecting Piper (Book 1)
- Guarding Gwen (Book 2)
- Before Ben (Book 3)
- The Heart You Break (Book 4)
- Fighting For Her (Book 5)
- Ghost Of A Chance (Book 6)
- Crossing The Line (Book 7)
- Counting On Cole (Book 8)

- Chase After Me (Book 9)
- Say I Do (Book 10)
- Roman Will Fall (Book 11)
- The One Who Got Away (Book 12)
- Pretend You Want Me (Book 13)
- Cross My Heart (Book 14)
- The Bodyguard Next Door (Book 15)
- Ex Marks The Perfect Spot (Book 16)
- The Thief Who Loved Me (Book 17)

Wilde Ways: Gone Rogue
- How To Protect A Princess (Book 1)
- How To Heal A Heartbreak (Book 2)
- How To Con A Crime Boss (Book 3)

Night Watch Paranormal Romance
- Hunt Me Down (Book 1)
- Slay My Name (Book 2)
- Face Your Demon (Book 3)

Trouble For Hire
- No Escape From War (Book 1)
- Don't Play With Odin (Book 2)
- Jinx, You're It (Book 3)
- Remember Ramsey (Book 4)

Death and Moonlight Mystery
- Step Into My Web (Book 1)
- Save Me From The Dark (Book 2)

Phoenix Fury
- Hot Enough To Burn (Book 1)
- Slow Burn (Book 2)

- Burn It Down (Book 3)

Dark Sins
- Don't Trust A Killer (Book 1)
- Don't Love A Liar (Book 2)

Lazarus Rising
- Never Let Go (Book One)
- Keep Me Close (Book Two)
- Stay With Me (Book Three)
- Run To Me (Book Four)
- Lie Close To Me (Book Five)
- Hold On Tight (Book Six)

Bad Things
- The Devil In Disguise (Book 1)
- On The Prowl (Book 2)
- Undead Or Alive (Book 3)
- Broken Angel (Book 4)
- Heart Of Stone (Book 5)
- Tempted By Fate (Book 6)
- Wicked And Wild (Book 7)
- Saint Or Sinner (Book 8)

Bite Series
- Forbidden Bite (Bite Book 1)
- Mating Bite (Bite Book 2)

Blood and Moonlight Series
- Bite The Dust (Book 1)
- Better Off Undead (Book 2)
- Bitter Blood (Book 3)

Mine Series
- Mine To Take (Book 1)
- Mine To Keep (Book 2)
- Mine To Hold (Book 3)
- Mine To Crave (Book 4)
- Mine To Have (Book 5)
- Mine To Protect (Book 6)

Dark Obsession Series
- Watch Me (Book 1)
- Want Me (Book 2)
- Need Me (Book 3)
- Beware Of Me (Book 4)

Purgatory Series
- The Wolf Within (Book 1)
- Marked By The Vampire (Book 2)
- Charming The Beast (Book 3)
- Deal with the Devil (Book 4)

Bound Series
- Bound By Blood (Book 1)
- Bound In Darkness (Book 2)
- Bound In Sin (Book 3)
- Bound By The Night (Book 4)
- Bound in Death (Book 5)

Stand-Alone Romantic Suspense
- Waiting For Christmas
- Monster Without Mercy
- Kiss Me This Christmas
- It's A Wonderful Werewolf
- Never Cry Werewolf

- Immortal Danger
- Deck The Halls
- Come Back To Me
- Put A Spell On Me
- Never Gonna Happen
- One Hot Holiday
- Slay All Day
- Midnight Bite
- Secret Admirer
- Christmas With A Spy
- Femme Fatale
- Until Death
- Sinful Secrets
- First Taste of Darkness
- A Vampire's Christmas Carol

About the Author

Cynthia Eden loves romance books, chocolate, and going on semi-lazy adventures. She is a *New York Times*, *USA Today*, *Digital Book World*, and *IndieReader* best-seller. She writes romantic suspense, paranormal romance, and fun contemporary novels. You can find out more about her work at www.cynthiaeden.com.

If you want to stay updated on her new releases and books deals, be sure to join her newsletter group: cynthiaeden.com/newsletter.

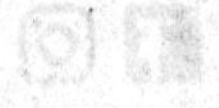

www.ingramcontent.com/pod-product-compliance
Lightning Source LLC
Chambersburg PA
CBHW011149310726
48973CB00010B/2836